PRAISE FOR

DARE TO RUN

"Dark, edgy . . . McLaughlin's well-crafted characters are relatable, sympathetic, and appealing."

—*Publishers Weekly*

"McLaughlin pairs the ultimate bad boy with a strong female counterpart to deliver an exciting novel where tension mounts on every page. The story provides excellent insight into life on the other side of the law . . . When love enters the equation, it upsets the carefully established balance."

—*RT Book Reviews* (4 ½ Stars, Top Pick)

MORE PRAISE FOR THE NOVELS OF JEN McLAUGHLIN

"Sexy, hot chemistry and heroes to die for!"

—Laura Kaye, *New York Times* bestselling author

"Jen McLaughlin's books are sexy and satisfying reads."

—Jennifer Probst, *New York Times* bestselling author

"I'm a huge Jen McLaughlin fan—she never disappoints."

—Monica Murphy, *New York Times* bestselling author

"I devour [Jen McLaughlin's] books no matter what genre she's writing in."   —Romance for Every World

"[A] really enjoyable read. No one does angst and romance quite like Jen McLaughlin does . . . I laughed, shook my head, and swooned."   —Once Upon a Book Blog

"As love blurs the line between privilege and misfortune, readers will root for this unlikely duo. The action is heart-stopping, and reformation occurs at a believable pace without diminishing the unpleasant truths of gang life."

Also by Jen McLaughlin

DARE
TO
LIE

THE SONS OF STEEL ROW

JEN McLAUGHLIN

BERKLEY SENSATION
New York

BERKLEY SENSATION
Published by Berkley
An imprint of Penguin Random House LLC
375 Hudson Street, New York, New York 10014

Copyright © 2017 by Jen McLaughlin
Penguin Random House supports copyright. Copyright fuels creativity, encourages
diverse voices, promotes free speech, and creates a vibrant culture. Thank you for buying
an authorized edition of this book and for complying with copyright laws by not
reproducing, scanning, or distributing any part of it in any form without permission.
You are supporting writers and allowing Penguin Random House to continue to
publish books for every reader.

BERKLEY and BERKLEY SENSATION are registered trademarks and the B colophon
is a trademark of Penguin Random House LLC.

ISBN: 9780451477613

First Edition: February 2017

Printed in the United States of America
1 3 5 7 9 10 8 6 4 2

Cover photos: Man © Claudio Marinesco/Ninestock
Backcover: Skyline © holbox/Shutterstock

This book is for Cynthia and Ashley.
May you live happily ever after, just like
they do in my books.

ACKNOWLEDGMENTS

As always, first thanks has to go out to my family. Thank you for always understanding when I'm stuck in edits or writing, and for always being patient. You guys know once I'm finished, I'll always return your call, or take you to the basketball court, or watch that show with you, and that's invaluable to an author like me. So Greg, Kaitlyn, Hunter, Gabe, Emmy, Mom, Dad, Cynthia, Ashley, Tina, Erick, Danny, Connor, Riley, Mom M, Dad M, and everyone else I'm lucky enough to call family, I love you.

To my friends, some of whom I'll name here, but none of whom I'd ever thank less because they're not named here because I suck and I forgot, thank you for being there for me. Whether it was for me to bounce ideas off of you, grab a few drinks or a meal with, or if you sit with me on the sidelines at basketball or cheerleading practice, or if you let me stay with you for a week because you just rock that much, you're frigging awesome. I love you Jay, Liz, Michelle, Joanne, Jill, Rebecca, Christia, Heidi, Erin, and so many more that I'm not typing out because I've got edits to do (story of my life), but even if you're not here . . . I love you.

To my agent, Louise, and Kristin, who I also work with, and all the people at the Bent Agency . . . thank you for standing by me and my work, and always believing in me. Thank you for picking me up while I'm down, but also for giving me that kick that knocked me down in the first place if I needed it. I feel better for having you by my side, fighting for me and with me, and I wouldn't have it any other way, Louise. Thanks for being my Mama Bear.

To Kristine, my editor here at Penguin, and the marketing, publicity, editing, art, and everything else I'm not thinking of here at Berkley . . . thank you for giving me your time and trust. I love this series, and all the characters in it, and I'm so happy I've been able to write these books with all of you as part of my team.

To all the readers out here, reading my books, and telling your friends about them . . . THANK YOU. I love writing, and it's something I've wanted to do since I was old enough to know people did this as a job. Because of you reading my books, and helping spread word of them to your friends, I am able to do this for a living, and quite honestly, I don't know what I'd do if that ever changed. Writing is my life. My passion. My love. And because of you, I get to live it. So thank you for hanging in there with me on this crazy ride I'm on as an author, and for trusting me to bring you on adventures that are worth your time and hard-earned money.

Without all of you listed above, I wouldn't be me.

And I'll never take that for granted.

I love you.

Jen

CHAPTER 1

SCOTTY

A bullet flew by my ear, with a soft *whizz*, sounding deceptively softer than its hollow-point reality. It would rip through flesh without mercy. I squeezed the trigger of my gun as sweat rolled down into my eyes, and watched a Bitter Hill asshole fall to the ground, clutching his chest, blood bubbling out of his mouth as he breathed his last gurgling breath due to my bullet.

Shit.

That was going to be a lot of paperwork.

The Bitter Hill men had come at us when no one had their pistols drawn, giving them an advantage against us—one that hadn't lasted long. Chris O'Brien moved to my side, squeezing off shots without even a sign of hesitation. "You okay, Scotty?"

I nodded once, wiping my forearm over my forehead, and scanned the alley for more of the opposing gang members. "Where the hell did these guys come from?"

Another one came around the corner, and Chris and I simultaneously fired. Mine hit him in the chest, directly over the heart. Chris's was dead center in the forehead. He liked head shots and was one of the only men I knew who could consistently nail them.

Blood sprayed behind the Bitter Hill man and he was dead before he hit the ground.

"I don't know," Chris shouted back, his eyes locked on the opening of the alley where they'd cornered us, just like mine. We'd come a long way, me and Chris. If someone had told me he would try to kill my brother, but then we'd become closer because he failed, I would've laughed in their faces—or shot them.

"They picked the wrong day to attack. Tate's pissed as hell."

I looked over my shoulder, eyeing the man in charge of the Sons of Steel Row. Tate looked to be seconds from pulling a grenade launcher out from behind his back and going all kamikaze on the Bitter Hill scum who dared to attack us when we were on our way to a funeral for one of our older members, Gus. May the fucker not rest in peace.

The Sons was the most influential gang in Southie, and up until recently, that title had gone undisputed. But then my "dead" brother, Lucas, started a war with Bitter Hill over a chick he was into and everything had gone to shit afterward.

Now we were waging a full-fledged war with Bitter Hill . . .

One we just might lose, if we didn't play our cards right.

A bullet hit the wall next to my head with a spray of brick dust, and Chris growled angrily, squeezing his trigger in rapid succession at the fucker who'd tried to take me out. I couldn't get a shot on him, since he was out of my line of fire. A groan sounded to the left of us as one of our men went down, taking a hit to the shoulder. Next went Roger, staggering back and clutching his arm. Cursing, I tried to find the shooter—and finally did. He was coming around the corner, aiming for Chris . . . who had just fired his last bullet.

Luckily, it had taken the other guy down.

Biting back a curse, I aimed and took the second shooter out before he could take out my friend, shooting directly over Chris's shoulder. For a second, Chris looked like he thought I was aiming for him. He was the only other man who knew I wasn't just another street thug, but was in reality in the DEA. Maybe he thought I was trying to kill the only man who could blow my cover? Not that I would do that, but I could understand the logic.

The man I shot fell to the ground, convulsing as he, too, died. My aim was true.

Great. Even *more* paperwork.

After glancing over his shoulder with wide eyes, Chris turned back to me, breathing heavily. "Thanks, man."

I nodded, not saying anything.

He had a scrape on his temple, and blood trickled down his face from the wound, but besides that, he looked okay enough. His girlfriend, Molly, would still be upset. I'd promised to return him unharmed. After all, we were only going to a funeral. But still, with tensions high between us and Bitter Hill, we'd suspected something like this might happen.

So we came prepared. Thank God.

Tommy, another lieutenant, called out, "Everyone alive?"

"Yeah," Brian growled, nodding at me from the brick doorway he'd taken cover in.

Frankie nodded, his blond hair in his eyes. "Yeah, man."

Me and Chris called out, too, and then we all came out of cover when Tate said, "We're good. Everyone, reload in case they come back."

I slowly lowered my Sig, eyeing the carnage in front of us as I pulled out my extra mag. I'd taken down three, and Chris had as well. Who knew who took down the rest? We all reloaded silently. It had been twelve Bitter Hill guys against nine Sons. Not a fair fight for them. None of us had been killed, a gift given only by the grace of God. They came at us when we were backed into a corner, a strategic move that didn't pay off well for them. They should have known never to back a Son into a corner.

We always came out swinging.

Tate tucked his pistol into his suit jacket, scowling at the dead bodies in front of him. His red hair was immaculately styled; the gun battle hadn't budged a strand. "Leave them for the Boys, or for Bitter Hill. I'm not cleaning up their damn mess for them this time."

We tucked our guns away, murmuring consent. I nodded at Chris, who did the same. It was time to go.

Before we could head for his Mustang, Tate came over to Chris, clapping him on the shoulder. "Nice shot, Chris."

Chris grinned and gestured to the last corpse we'd taken down together. "Thanks, sir. I was particularly proud of that one."

"Me too. Nice teamwork, guys." Tate raised his voice. "Roll out, boys."

We walked to our cars, watching for another ambush. I was halfway into the passenger seat of Chris's Mustang when Tate called out, "Donahue?"

I froze, my hand on the roof of Chris's car. "Yes, sir?"

"Ride with me." He gave me a hard look. "We need to talk. Now."

Well, *shit*. That couldn't be good. Not when I was living a lie, right under his nose. Most of the time, when Tate singled out a man like this, they didn't come back. "Sure thing, sir."

"Both of us?" Chris called out.

I appreciated the effort and all, but if I was going down, I wouldn't be dragging him down with me. Molly would kill me. "Just me," I said, my voice hard.

"Yep, just him," Tate said, frowning. "Ready, Donahue?"

I mussed up my hair, grinning like I didn't have a care in the world. "Yes, sir. Whatever you want."

Chris cleared his throat as I closed the door, latching gazes with me over the roof of his car. "Everything okay?"

"I hope so," I muttered, smoothing my suit jacket over my abs. The only way Tate could have been told about me was if someone knew, and the only other person who knew was staring at me with concern. I was pretty damn certain he hadn't ratted me out. "It should be."

Chris nodded once, flexing his jaw. "Be smart."

"Always," I murmured, heading toward my boss with long, carefree strides and shoving my hands in my trouser pockets. As I slid into his town car, which was driven by Tommy, I plastered an easy grin on my face, playing the part I'd been cast into years ago, of Lucas's charming younger brother. "What can I do for you, sir?"

Tate closed the door behind us, tapping on the window that separated Tommy from us. It pulled forward immediately. "You look young enough to be in college. How old are you?"

I blinked. "Sir?"

"Your age." He cocked a reddish-brown brow at me. "What is it?"

Out of all the things I expected him to ask me, this was not one of them. "Twenty-five, sir."

"Hmm." He rubbed his jaw, looking me up and down. "You look half decent in a suit."

I swallowed, having no clue where the hell he was going with this, but pretty damn certain I wouldn't like it. "Thanks . . . ?"

"How are your acting abilities?" he asked distractedly, staring out the window as we drove. "At playing a part that no one would expect you to play?"

Well, if that wasn't a trick question, considering my secret life, I didn't know what was. If I said yes, he'd wonder if I was playing a part right now—and I was. If I said no, I wouldn't be as valuable to the gang, and I'd lose any headway I'd gained over the years. So I chose silence instead. "What do you need from me, sir?"

"I'm getting there. What I tell you can't leave this car. If it does, I'll know it was you, and I'll act accordingly for the breach of trust." He squared his jaw, finally turning back to me. He looked seconds from pulling out a gun. "Understood?"

I nodded once. "Yes, sir."

"Good." He cleared his throat. "I have a sister."

I blinked at him, taken aback. I'd done my research on Tate long before I officially became a Son. Before I was formally a DEA agent, too. I never entered anything blindly. That was a fucking death sentence. And yet I'd never found even a damn hint about Tate having a sister. "You do?"

"Yeah. She's twenty-three and in med school." He leaned back in the seat, staring straight ahead at the tinted window. "She's not like us. She's good. Does charity work all the time, and has no clue what kind of life I lead."

So the apple fell far from the tree? I found that hard to believe. More likely than not, she put on a good front. "I see. And you're telling me this because . . . ?"

"She thinks I'm the CEO of an investment firm—which

I am, on all fronts—but that's all she knows. She doesn't know about my ties to the Sons of Steel Row, and she thinks I'm like any white-collar almost-thirty-year-old man. So she wants me to do a bachelor's auction for date for charity, to play nice with some spoiled rich socialite who would probably want more than dinner and a bottle of champagne from me." He turned to me, looking about as happy as he would if he'd been shot in the ass. "But I don't play nice with women. Not like *you* do."

I stiffened, knowing where this was going now. And I'd been right—I wasn't going to fucking like it. I'd rather be strapped to an electric chair and pumped with a thousand volts than do what he was about to ask me to do. And the worst part? I wouldn't have a choice. "Sir?"

"Since I now have to deal with the mess of this shoot-out, you're going to go in my place. Tell her you're a grad student, like her, and interning at my office. I'm regrettably held up with work—which I am now, with this shooting—so I sent you in my place. I promised her I wouldn't leave her a man short for tonight, since she had a hard time finding men who would volunteer. That's where you come in." He gestured to me. "You're already in a suit and everything. You didn't get shot, right?"

"Not this time, sir." I half laughed, half groaned. "But wouldn't I be more valuable in the office, with you, plotting our next move?"

He stared at me, his blue eyes cold. "No. I want you with her."

"Yes, sir," I said through my clenched teeth. "Anything you need, I'm your man."

"Good." Tate smoothed his tie over his chest. "When you're done paying your respects to Gus, you can go. The auction starts at six, at the Lower Boston Country Club."

I stared at him. "Seriously?"

"Dead." He shrugged. "We're members there. The best way to blend into society is to pretend to be one of them, right? I also have a condo nearby, in the gated complex on the golf course."

We all knew about *that* apartment. Tate said it was a front, that he used it to launder money out of the watchful eye of the feds. All the guys joked it was his bachelor pad, where he took chicks he scored for a night of fun, before ditching them to return to his place in Steel Row. But now, I couldn't help but wonder if it was more. Maybe his sister also lived in that community, and every time we assumed he was banging some chick in his fancy place, he was, in reality, going to see *her*. "Wow. I never pegged you as the country club type, sir."

"It's just for Skylar. I never go," he said, even though I knew for a fact that he played golf there every Saturday at eight A.M.

"Right." I grinned. "Of course not."

"Like I said. No one knows she exists. I'm telling you because I think I can trust you to keep my secret." He gave me a hard look, and I knew if I showed the slightest sign of proving him wrong, I'd be done for. No big shocker there. "You're good at that, aren't you? At keeping secrets?"

I forced a laugh. "Uh . . . yeah. I can be, when the situation warrants it."

"I figured," Tate said dryly. "This one does."

I nodded. "Yes, sir."

"Wear that suit, and be charming. Call yourself Scotty, instead of Scott. It sounds more innocent and college-student-like. Remember: You intern at my company and go to grad school at Boston . . . University," he said slowly, eyeing my outfit. "No leather coat."

"Not Boston College?"

"No." He shot me a look out of the corner of his eye. "She goes there, so it will invite too many questions."

"Okay." I lifted a shoulder. "What's my major?"

"Marketing."

Nodding, I tapped my fingers on my thigh. "Got it, sir."

The car stopped at the funeral home, and I reached for the knob. As I grasped it, he grabbed my arm hard, stopping me. "And Donahue?"

"Yeah?" I asked hesitantly.

"This goes without saying, but I'll say it anyway, just to be perfectly fucking clear on the matter. Touch Skylar . . ." He dug his fingers into my bicep. ". . . and I'll cut you into pieces and feed you to my saltwater fish for dinner. Understood?"

Touch Tate Daniels's *sister*?

I'd sooner eat uncooked liver.

"Completely."

CHAPTER 2

SKYLAR

I pushed past the matronly ladies whispering in the corner of the room, gossiping worse than any sorority girl would ever dare, while ignoring my aching feet, thanks to the bright red high heels I never should have worn. I was more of a flats kind of girl, but this was my first big charity event, and I'd wanted to look more mature. I'd wanted to look the part.

I should have stuck to flats.

Half the reason I decided to aim for med school was because I could wear scrubs and Crocs all day. The other half was because I wanted to help people. I'd never confess which half I considered more important, but, just a hint, I was tossing these heels the second I got home.

The men who were being auctioned off were all either getting drunk, or late—like my brother, Tate, who I was going to *kill*—and the matrons that would be bidding weren't much better. The dry martinis were flowing, the voices were getting louder, and this whole thing was going to be a gigantic disaster of the worst kind.

I should have stuck to books and Netflix.

But even though I was sure this would be an epic fail . . . I had to admit it looked pretty freaking nice for a disaster. I was at the country club my brother and I belonged to, and the whole dining hall had been transformed into a soft oasis of romantic lighting. Black tablecloths covered round tables, with pink cloth centerpieces topped with crystal candleholders and small tea light candles on top. A soft orchestra played in the background and the room was filled to the brim with people.

Not so bad for my first charity gala.

All I needed was for my brother to show up.

Then we could get this show on the road.

He hated these things, but in my opinion, it was a way of putting a bit of good energy back into the world—something he could use a little help with, if you asked me. I smoothed my short black Chanel dress over my stomach nervously, swallowing hard, and tucked my hair behind my ear. I'd curled it gently with a curling iron, and I'd gone for soft red lipstick to match my shoes. It had been a bold choice, but I was going out of my comfort zone already with the heels, so what the heck.

Go big or go home, right?

That's what I kept telling myself, anyway.

My phone buzzed and I glanced down. It was a text from my friend Marco. He was supposed to be here tonight, too, but he'd backed out at the last minute. He was a few years younger than me, and only a sophomore, but we'd hit it off immediately upon meeting in a study group when he'd been a freshman. We had a lot in common.

Sorry again. Got held up in lab.

Yeah, sure you did.

A pause, and then:

Buy you a coffee tomorrow to make up for it?

Or two. Lots of tests this week.

Deal.

Smiling, I glanced up as I rounded the corner. I turned at the last second because I spotted Mallory, a fellow med student and my co-chair of this event. "Find a manager and ask for more waiters. We're dying out here, and it would be best to keep the guests distracted with drinks or appetizers. We need to get things moving," I said.

Mallory flipped her brown hair over her shoulder, and gave a thumbs-up, grinning. Maybe I should have told Marco she would be here. Then he would have shown up. He had a thing for her. "I'm on it!"

Shaking my head, I barreled around the corner—and right into someone. The man—I assumed it was a man from his height and the fact he was made of pure muscle—sent me off balance, and I flew back with a soft *oof.* I braced myself, sure I was going to hit the ground hard, but at the last second, he pulled me into his arms. I ended up securely nestled against a muscular chest, and that was somehow strangely comforting.

I sucked in a deep breath because even though I hadn't looked at him yet . . .

Something about him brought me to *life.*

I didn't know how to explain it, but it was like the second he touched me, he brought out this long-dormant part of myself I hadn't known was asleep. Slowly, almost *hesitantly*, I lifted my face to his. "I'm so . . ." I trailed off. The second our gazes met, that feeling—that instinctive reaction to a man I didn't know—wormed its way further into my body. ". . . sorry."

He gazed down at me, stealing my breath. His eyes were a soft moss green, and he had red hair. His jawline was hard, and he had a slight dimple in his cheek, but not an actual dimple—which made no sense, but somehow did. My heart picked up speed, and I gripped his suit jacket, hanging on for dear life, because, God, I had to.

His lips were parted as he stared down at me in surprise, as if he hadn't meant to catch me, but now that he had, he wasn't sure what to do with me.

He was, hands down, the most handsome man I'd ever met.

I immediately wanted—no, *needed*—to know more about him.

His gaze dipped down to my mouth then shot back up, and his brow furrowed. His grip at the small of my back shifted, and he bunched my dress in between his fingers. He held me in his arms like we'd been dancing and he was preparing to dip me. I ached for him to pull me more firmly into his arms, which was crazy, because I *didn't even know the guy.*

I've always been good at reading people. My older brother, Tate, always teased me that I should join the CIA and be an undercover agent, because within minutes of meeting someone, I generally knew their whole life story, without them saying a word. And this man had lonely, lost soul written all over his face. Like he'd seen too much and was trying to make the world a better place. Like his only desire was to leave a mark on the world, a good one, to make up for all the bad out there. In fact . . .

He reminded me of *myself.*

"Are you okay?" he asked softly, his harsh Southie accent as clear as day.

Funny, he didn't look like your typical Southie guy.

"Y-Yes," I answered, forcing a smile even though this guy had thrown me more off balance than I'd been in my whole life. "Thank you, Mister . . . ?"

"Donahue. Scotty Donahue." He pulled me back to my feet, only letting me go once I was steady. His hands lingered on my waist, as if he didn't want to stop touching me—or was that my imagination? He shot me a slow, seductive grin that did something to me. "And you are?"

"Skylar Daniels," I said quickly. "I'm in charge of this event."

Something crossed his expression, and he stepped back, his nostrils flaring. The grin faded immediately, and I saw him retreat, both physically and mentally, the second he heard my name. "*You're* Skylar?"

"Yes . . ." I bit down on my lip, because the way he said those two words, the *hardness* behind them, made me feel like my identity didn't come as welcome information. Was he one of *those* guys, who thought the Danielses were beneath him? "Do I know you?"

"No," he said, pressing his lips into a thin line. "But I know your brother, Tate."

Oh. *Oh.* Of course.

Tate was always waving all these snobby, stuffy, bland Wall Street men in front of me, men who talked about nothing but stocks and money, in the hopes I'd pick one and marry a guy exactly like him. Problem was . . . I didn't *like* any of them. I was far too busy studying to waste time on a guy who would, more likely than not, end up being a complete bore, in bed *and* out of it. Chances were, this man would be exactly like the rest.

What a disappointment.

"Whatever he told you about me is a lie," I said, glancing at him through my lashes, trying to lighten him up a bit. He looked as if he'd swallowed a box of nails. Even with me in heels, he was a good six inches taller than me. "I'm not nearly as much of a spoiled brat as he made me out to be."

"Actually, he hasn't said much about you at all," he said slowly, glancing down my body before slamming his gaze back into mine. My legs trembled, my pulse raced, and the breath left my chest. I'd been checked out in a lot of ways, by a lot of guys, but none of them had ever made me feel all shaky and uneven inside like *he* did . . . or as uncertain. "I guess I can see why, now that I've met you."

My cheeks heated at the—*maybe?*—compliment. Something told me he could charm any woman he wanted, but with me, it seemed like he was holding himself back. "Are you here to watch him be sold to one of the vultures behind me?"

"Not exactly." He tugged at his tie, offering me a sheepish smile, glancing at the women I referred to. "I'm here to be sold off in his place, all in the name of charity."

My stomach twisted in knots. He was going to be on that stage . . . looking hot as hell . . . and go on a date with the lucky winner? Something slammed into me, something I didn't recognize, but the thought of him going out with one of them?

Yeah, it sat about as badly in my stomach as expired sushi.

"Oh."

"He sends his regrets," he added, seeming to think my short reply was due to my brother's absence. While I was upset Tate had blown me off and sent someone else in his place, that wasn't what had me all worked up. It was *him*. Scotty Donahue. "I'll do my best to fill his shoes, being tonight's man-candy."

"I'm sure," I said, smiling tightly, because Scotty more than fit the part. That was the problem. "How do you know him?"

"I'm an intern at his office." He rocked back on his heels and shot me a sexy grin while looking at me like I was the only woman on the Earth. God, did he even know how hot he was when he looked at a girl like that? Who was I kidding? Of course he knew. "But he asked me to take his place, and to let you know that he was sorry for missing tonight. To ease the sting of his absence, I'm here to offer any services you might need."

Any services. I couldn't tell if he was flirting with me or not, which was weird. It was almost as if he wanted to, but was holding back, and as a result, he was sending mixed signals I couldn't decipher. And, God help me, I could think of a few services I wouldn't mind him giving me. "Well, thank you for coming. I appreciate it."

"Of course." He bowed slightly, keeping his gaze locked with mine. "Anything to help a beautiful woman in distress."

A nervous laugh escaped me, and I pressed a hand to my stomach. He followed the motion, his brow furrowing. "Are you actually flirting with me?"

He cocked a brow at my question, looking way too handsome for his own good. "And if I am?"

"Then it's fine. It's just . . . Tate's always throwing all these fancy suit guys at me," I said, waving a hand toward his suit, which made him frown. "Guys like you. He's always trying to get me to date one of you, so I can never tell if—"

He held a hand up, the charming smile slipping away like it never existed in the first place. "I'm here because my boss asked me to come." He pointed at the older women in the corner, his south Boston accent thickening with each angry word. "And to raise some money for whatever charity you've got going here. That's it. No matter what he's done in the past, I'm not some boy toy sent to you for your pleasure. I don't play that way."

My cheeks got even hotter, embarrassment scorching through my blood. "I didn't mean to insinuate—"

"Ah, but you kind of did, sugar."

Anger warred with embarrassment, and I stiffened. Where did he get off lecturing me like I was some errant child and he was my father? *Screw him.* He'd been flirting with me, so if I'd gotten the wrong message, then it was as much his fault as it was mine. "*Sugar?* Did you seriously just call me *sugar*?"

"Yeah. *Sugar.*" He looked me up and down, his nostrils flaring slightly. "The way I see it, something as sweet as you has gotta be made of pure sugar. But there's only one way to find out for sure." He stared at my lips, his meaning all too clear. "Too bad I've got no intentions of doing so."

Sucking in a deep breath, I stared at him.

He stared right back.

There was no way Tate sent this man to me hoping I'd hook up with him. He was too real. Too raw. Too cocky. Too . . . *dangerous.* Yes, that's what was humming under the surface of this animalistic attraction I felt for him. *Danger.*

And while that should scare me away, it did the opposite.

It made me want to know even more.

I saw through his transparent asshole act, right down to his core. He was more than he put out there, no matter how many times he called me *sugar*. My sixth sense had kicked in, and I saw him for what he was. And I was never wrong. I got the feeling that he'd hidden behind a lie for so long, he'd lost track of himself, and that he was trying to fix that, one small step at a time. What had he done that was so wrong, it haunted his eyes like a lost memory? I was dying to know. "You're staring," he pointed out.

"So are you," I replied quickly.

"Only 'cause I don't like to lose." He smirked. "And we're clearly having some sort of competition."

He thought he could scare me off with a staring contest? Please.

I had an older brother. I knew how to handle men like Scotty Donahue.

"Good to know," I said softly, forcing a smile. "I don't like to lose either."

Out of the corner of my eye I saw Mallory flagging me down.

Apparently, so did he.

"Unfortunately, it looks like duty calls," he said, his tone flat, that indifferent asshole act slipping into place like a well-worn mask. "Run along, sugar. It was nice meeting you."

Digging my nails into my palms, I continued the battle we were waging, knowing if I backed down I would lose more than a staring contest. I cocked a brow at him, mimicking his own stance. "I'll run along when I'm good and ready, thank you very much. The bachelors are supposed to line up at the bar."

A soft laugh escaped him before he cut it off with a shake of his head and broke eye contact. Looked like I'd won. Satisfaction hit me, and it was exhilarating. "Maybe you take after your brother after all."

"You have no idea." I gave him what I hoped was a smirk matching his, because no matter how much he tried to act like he was an asshole, it wouldn't work. His act only made me want to learn what he hid behind that cocky smirk, and I knew the perfect way to do so. "It was nice meeting you, Scotty. We'll be talking again, real soon, I'm sure."

With that, I flounced off, my heart racing, and my blood pumping, and every single nerve within me focused on him. The man I shouldn't want . . .

But *did*.

CHAPTER 3

SCOTTY

Settling in on a bar stool, I lifted my old-fashioned to my lips and watched Skylar. For some reason, I couldn't stop. There was something about her, about the way she held herself, that threw me. I was good at figuring out people's motives. It was my thing. It kept me alive out there when it came to deciding to calmly talk to someone, or if pulling the trigger would keep me breathing instead. But with Skylar . . .

I couldn't get a read on her.

Part of me thought the whole sweet-sorority-girl thing was all an act, and the other half almost believed it was the truth. But then she stared at me from across the room, basically daring me to take on the enigma that was Skylar Daniels, and I was sure there was no way in hell she was for real. Not when she looked at me like she wanted to strip my clothes off, which made me want to do things I shouldn't be thinking about. Not when it came to Tate's baby sister.

Damn her.

And damn the soft curves that had pressed against me so perfectly.

I didn't normally get this kind of reaction from girls like her, but then again, I wasn't dressed like the guy I really was. Tonight I played a different kind of game and wore a suit instead of a leather jacket. I was used to playing a part, pretending to be someone I wasn't. Right now, I was a DEA agent, pretending to be a loyal gang member, pretending to be an intern, pretending to be a good guy who hadn't just been in a deadly shoot-out.

It was almost too much, even for me.

My phone dinged, and I pulled it out of my pocket. It was a text from Chris.

Everything okay?

I quickly typed: Yes. I'm at a country club, wearing a suit, and trying to deal with Tate's baby sister, but besides that, I'm fine. I'd told him about her existence before I left the funeral.

Is she hot?

I took a sip of my drink. I could feel her watching me, but I didn't look. Yes.

Dammmmn.

Setting my empty drink down, I typed: What?

Don't do it.

I glanced her way, and sure enough, she was watching me. Instead of turning away when I caught her, she crossed her arms and gave me a tight smile. She was begging me to engage with her. She was in over her head, and had no clue. I gave her my back and typed: I won't. I'm not that stupid. I'll text you when I'm out of here safely.

Stay smart.

I thought of Skylar, and those long, long legs of hers . . . that I wouldn't be touching. Forcing my mind off her, I quickly typed: Always.

As I tucked my phone away, the music stopped playing and Skylar's voice echoed over the room. "Hello. First off, before I hand the mic off to our auctioneer and we start with the fun we have planned for the night, I wanted a chance to thank each and every one of you for coming here tonight to support our charity. Without you, we wouldn't be able to make sure the underprivileged children in the poorer parts of our city have access to the medical care they so desperately need. Because of you, they won't suffer in silence anymore."

Jesus. These preppies thought they could save the kids of Southie with free checkups and vaccinations? Hell, I'd been trying to make Southie better for five years now, and all I'd accomplished so far was a few bullet holes in my body. I held my empty old-fashioned up to the bartender, who nodded and immediately started making me a new one.

I'd need it to get through tonight.

Another man in a suit sidled up next to me. "Too bad they're not auctioning her off tonight, huh? I'd pay for the chance to spend a few hours with her. I love redheads."

"Yeah. Too damn bad." I grabbed my drink, tossed down a twenty, and turned back to Skylar, watching her as she smiled down at the crowd like a goddamn princess. I didn't point out that her hair was more strawberry blonde than red. "What's her deal, anyway? Is she as squeaky clean as she seems?"

"More so." The man leaned on the bar, sighing. "She's untouchable."

"Oh, I doubt that." She'd seemed pretty damn touchable earlier. Maybe that was why I couldn't shake the attraction I felt to her. Before I'd known who she was, I'd held her in my arms and discovered just how perfectly she fit against me. "You ever meet her brother?"

"Yeah, he's some big-shot CEO. Came up from nothing and thinks he's a king now." He tugged on his tie, still watching Skylar. I didn't like the look in his eye. He stared at her as if he'd like to climb up on that stage, throw her over his shoulder, and stalk off with her. That shouldn't bother me . . . but it did. "Does a lot of charity work, too, like her. I heard he anonymously backed a community center for underprivileged kids recently."

I choked on my drink, because Chris had secretly started up that community center—and he'd received a big chunk of money from an anonymous party. *Tate*. What kind of Alice in Wonderland world did I fall into when I walked through these doors? "If it was a secret, how do you know about it?"

"A buddy of mine told me." The man rubbed his hands together. "He works at the bank Daniels uses."

I didn't say anything else.

Skylar continued. "As we welcome the men on stage, I ask that you check them out and decide who you'd like to bid on. Be warned, though," she said, smiling angelically. Locking eyes with me, she lifted her glass of champagne and said, "A few of us girls intend to bid tonight, too. So you'll have competition."

The college girls chuckled in the corner as the older women smiled and nodded in approval. I stiffened. Why the hell was she staring at me? I was the last guy she should be picking to go on a date with tonight. *"Shit."*

The man next to me whistled through his teeth, and looked at me. As she continued moving into the crowd, he asked, "What did you say your name was again?"

"I didn't," I growled, tossing back the rest of my drink.

If she bid on me, and I had to go on a date with her . . .

Tate would literally *kill* me.

"Can the bachelors please come up?" another woman asked, stepping up to the mic nervously. "Once they're all in place, we'll begin the bidding."

We all filed up there like soldiers falling in line behind their commanding officer, me behind the dickwad from earlier. As we stood there, looking out at the crowd of women, I glanced at Skylar—and she smirked at me.

Motherfucking *smirked*.

Gritting my teeth, I offered the rest of the audience a charming smile. I knew how to work a crowd—I'd been doing it since I was old enough to understand what manipulation was, before I even knew how to spell the word. Lucas always said I could charm the panties off a nun, if I put my mind to it, and I'd lived up to those expectations my whole damn life.

Today would be no different.

I searched the crowd until I found my perfect mark, settling on a woman with dark brown hair, strands of gray peppered throughout. She smiled at me, fingering her pearls, and I winked back. She laughed and sipped her champagne, glancing away flirtatiously. Judging from the Gucci dress and Louis Vuitton bag hanging off her arm, she would be bidding a lot to bring me home. If Skylar thought she was going to win a date with me easily, she was in for a rude awakening.

I couldn't afford to be tempted . . .

And she wouldn't be able to afford me by the time this was over.

The woman glanced at me again, and I smoothed my jacket over my abs, shooting her a sexy smirk. She flushed like a schoolgirl, just as I expected. She wanted a younger man to pay attention to her, to make her feel desirable, and I could absolutely give that to her.

She was much safer than Skylar. I didn't mess with people I couldn't read, and Skylar was like a foreign language to me.

One by one, men were auctioned off like cattle, and I found myself cursing Tate Daniels for sending me here. Out of all the shitty things he'd done to me, and *around* me, this was pretty much the worst. I'd rather be shot and gutted than wait to be bought. Dickwad went for a few hundred dollars to one of Skylar's blushing friends, and he walked down the stairs to join her.

Which left . . . *me*.

Smiling at me as if she heard my thoughts, Skylar crossed her arms as the woman running the show walked to the mic. "And now, for our last auction, we have Scotty Donahue. He's an intern at a big firm in the city, and he's also a grad student. We'll start the bidding at fifty dollars."

The college girl auctioning me off paused, and I gritted my teeth, watching the thinned-out crowd. The lady I'd winked at came through. She lifted a hand regally. I smiled at her.

"Do I have seventy-five?" the girl asked.

Another woman to the left raised her hand. She was brunette, and only a few years older than me. Pretty, too. I perked up, smiling at her, too, and tugged on my jacket.

"One hundred? I see here that Mr. Donahue enjoys long

walks on the beach and fine dining. If you win a date with him, he's also a good dancer."

Skylar grandly raised a hand.

I stiffened, forcing my attention from the brunette in the corner. I frowned at Skylar, shaking my head slightly in a silent warning. She didn't want to play this game. Not when she had no idea what she was getting—a killer who would eat her up in one swallow if she wasn't careful. If she persisted on pursuing me, I'd give her exactly what she asked for.

Trouble.

"Mr. Donahue also enjoys opera music and Broadway musicals in his spare time. Do I have one twenty-five?"

The older woman lifted her hand, and so did the pretty brunette.

I smiled at both of them.

Skylar smiled icily and called out, "I bid one seventy-five."

I didn't smile at *her.*

It went on like this a few times, the bidding climbing higher and higher, and Skylar not backing down. Luckily, neither did the other two women. The rest of the crowd watched as the numbers climbed with rapid succession, and I laughed uneasily, rubbing the back of my neck. I lifted an arm and flexed a bicep playfully for the brunette, and the crowd cheered with excitement as the brunette's eyes heated with desire. This date was in the bag.

Skylar gave me the side-eye, watching me as I flirted. Lifting her chin, she smiled, raised her hand, and called out, "I bid one thousand dollars for Scotty."

The crowd gasped. That was a jump of a few hundred dollars, and no one else had done that for any of the other men.

"Is that allowed?" the older woman asked, frowning. "Aren't you in charge of this event?"

"I am, but I don't think anyone will argue over money going to a charity for a good cause, will they?" the girl at the mic asked sweetly, smiling. "I mean, that's why we're all here, right?"

"I . . ." The older woman scowled. "No, of course not."

The auctioneer smiled, then said, "Does anyone else object?"

No one spoke.

"All right, then, the bid stands. One thousand dollars."

The old lady huffed, and turned away, clearly giving up. *Damn it.*

"*Fuck me*," I muttered, turning to the brunette hopefully, shrugging my jacket off to give her another glimpse of the goods.

She opened her mouth, closed it, and shook her head once.

"Shit," I growled under my breath.

Skylar's eyes sparkled with excitement, and victory.

The girl at the mic called out, "One thousand going once . . . twice . . . sold, to Skylar Daniels."

I fisted my hands. Tate Daniels's blood money had just bought his little sister a date with me. Forcing a calm smile, I went over to the stairs, walked right up to Skylar, and shoved my hands into my pockets as I approached. The second I was in front of her, I leaned down and whispered, "You have no idea who you're messing with, sugar."

She cast a quick glance at me, her breath quickening. "Oh, I beg to differ. I know exactly who I'm messing with. The question is, can you say the same about me?"

No. And that's what I didn't like. "Yeah. I know what you are."

"Good. Then there's no confusion or miscommunications." With a flutter of her lashes, she turned, plastering a sweet smile on for everyone else as she went up onstage again. Stopping in front of the mic, she said, "Thank you for participating, and for your generosity, all for a good cause. The children and their parents thank you."

Applause broke out, and her grin widened as she came back down the stairs. I watched, my heart pounding, as she turned to me, holding her hand out. "Let's go pay, and then we're going out somewhere a little more . . . private. Maybe to one of those fancy restaurants you like so much."

Greeeeaaaat. I didn't move. Just frowned at her outstretched hand, gritting my teeth until my jaw ached. "Why did you bid on me?"

"You intrigue me." She shrugged. "I want to know more about you."

"I work for your brother, and he'll kill me if he finds out I went out with you, so I know everything I need to know about you already." I gave her a smirk, instinctively knowing it would piss her off. "You're a spoiled rich girl who's used to getting what she wants, and who is in for a rude awakening because I'm not the type of guy to give girls like you what they want."

Her nostrils flared. "That only makes me more interested in you."

I tensed. *"Why?"*

"Because Tate's always throwing his coworkers at me, and they're as dreadfully dull as he is." She stepped closer, resting her hand over my heart. Reaching up on tiptoe, she whispered into my ear, "Knowing you're off-limits just makes you sexier, because I'm *that kind of girl*. So keep telling me how bad for me you are. I'll eat it up, *sugar.*"

She thought she liked bad boys. She had no idea what a bad boy really was. "You're so naïve to think that you can take on a guy like me and walk away unscathed."

"And you're naïve if you think I'm so easily scared off," she said, laughing and giving me a once-over. "Guess that makes us a good match."

Skylar and I were not in any way, shape, or form . . .

A good fucking match.

I'd become a DEA agent to try to make the world a better place, to try to make Steel Row clean again, to atone for being the reason behind Lucas's actions. Everything my brother had done was to support me after Ma died. His descent into hell had been all my fault—and as such, it was my job to fix it. In doing so, I couldn't afford to get tangled up with a gang boss's sister.

That was simple fact.

I snorted. "You have no idea what I do—"

"Sure I do. You're a college student interning at my brother's company." She flipped her long strawberry blonde hair over her shoulder. "Ooooh. Wow. *So dangerous.*"

I bit my tongue. Damn Tate and his stupid cover. If I'd been able to make my own, then I would have made it something a little more edgy than marketing. Like . . . shit, I don't know. An MMA fighter or something. "My job isn't my whole life. I don't live at the office. Besides, how could you possibly recognize true danger, being locked up in your ivory tower all the time?"

She stiffened. "My brother, for all his faults, is hands down the most overprotective brother to ever walk the earth. He won't even leave me alone with people I've known my whole life, let alone someone I just met. Therefore, if you are *soooo* bad that you would ruin me with a simple touch . . ."

She leaned in, her cheeks flushing prettily. "Why are you here, alone with me, right now?"

Damn it, I had no answer for her, because *I* didn't know why, or even why Tate trusted me. If he was always throwing clean, wholesome men at Skylar, why didn't he send one of them to this black tie event, instead of a gang member? Some of us were on the books at the firm, to look legit for the IRS and feds, but there were real employees there, too, who had no idea what their boss did when he wasn't in his office. There had to be a reason he'd chosen me, instead of one of those clean employees, to be at his sister's side.

And I had a feeling, whatever it was, it wasn't *good*.

CHAPTER 4

SKYLAR

Two hours after I won Scotty for the night, we left the country club. I'd had to finish up at the gala before we could slip away. While I was making sure every winner paid before leaving with their bachelors, Scotty had stood in the corner of the room, frowning and occasionally taking a sip of his drink.

Now that we were alone at my favorite restaurant, I was no closer to discovering who and what Scotty Donahue really was, and quite frankly? I no longer cared.

Apparently my sixth sense had failed me this time, because Scotty Donahue was as empty as a bag of air. He was closemouthed, borderline *rude*, and he refused to give me any information on himself, no matter how creatively I asked.

He had successfully bored me to death.

Lifting my wine, I took a big swallow of the Shiraz I'd ordered for us before setting the glass down, internally rolling my eyes. We were at L'Espalier, a French restaurant in Boston. There were white tablecloths on every table, and beige fabric covered the lights overhead, creating a romantic ambience with candlelight, good wine, better food. It was the perfect atmosphere for easy conversations, which were happening all around us.

At every table but *ours*.

"So, how many months have you been at my brother's company?" I asked hesitantly, knowing it was useless.

"Ten."

I pressed my lips together. "Sounds nice. Would you like to know what I'm going to school for?"

He cocked a brow at me. "No."

"I'm in medical school."

He nodded. "Cool."

"I'll probably specialize in pediatrics. I'm good at reading people, so I think that'll come in handy with uncooperative teenagers, or babies who can't speak yet."

He didn't say anything. Just stared at me.

I continued, even though this was easily the most awkward conversation I'd ever had in my life . . . if you could even call it a conversation. "If I do my job right, maybe I could actually leave a mark on the world. A good one. I think we need a little bit more kindness, so I'm going to try my best to help."

He blinked at me.

Scotty's iPhone buzzed twice, and he picked it up off the table, frowned even more—which I didn't think was possible—and set it down without answering. I waved a hand toward it. "Please. Text whoever it was back. You should talk to *someone* tonight."

And that someone clearly wouldn't be me. He was determined to be an asshole, and he was succeeding. Such a pity, since my hopes had originally been high. He initially seemed like a down-to-earth guy, and there had been that undeniable desire I felt for him, too. I'd hoped . . .

It didn't matter what I'd hoped.

All night long, he'd treated me like an obligation, and nothing more. He'd barely looked at me. He shrugged his broad shoulders. "It can wait."

"Wow. Three whole words in one sentence." I widened my eyes. "Are you sure you meant to say that much? You can take it back if you'd like."

He stared at me, a muscle in his jaw ticking, and remained silent.

Of freaking course.

Sighing, I picked my wine up, finishing it. "You know what? You can go now. I free you from your charitable duty."

He cocked a brow, shifting in his seat. "Seriously?"

"Yep. Dead serious." I set my empty wineglass down. "You've been a complete and utter ass to me this whole night, and you're clearly determined to not like me, for whatever reason you've secretly decided upon. Maybe I'm not good enough for you, or maybe you don't like my brother or the way he treats his employees. Whatever the reason, the second you heard my name, you decided not to like me, which is fine. I've been dealing with people not liking me because of who I am, and who I'm related to, for more years than I'd like to admit."

He blinked. "Why would people not like you?"

"Not everyone likes my brother, or the fact that he came up in the world from nothing through ruthlessness and a little bit of manipulation. They often paint me with the same brush, but with you, I thought it would be different. It's sad, because when we met, I thought . . ."

He leaned in. "What did you think?"

"Does it really matter?" I asked, holding a hand up in question. "You clearly want to go, so go."

Instead of leaving, he reclined in his seat, eyeing me with more interest than he'd shown all night. "What did you think?" he asked softly.

"I thought you were like me," I said honestly, letting out a frustrated breath. "When I looked up at you, I saw a man who was alone in the world, but who was trying to make it better somehow. I saw a guy who acted like he was expected to, but who was different underneath. I thought you were kind, and brave, and interesting, and I wanted to know more about you." I gave him a quick glance, shrugging. "But instead, you treated me as if I was an annoying nuisance. I thought you were a man who would give me a chance, instead of brushing me off as a social-climbing bimbo with rocks for brains, but I guess I was wrong about that."

He sat up straight, clearing his throat. "You got all that after talking to me for a minute?" he asked, his Southie accent more pronounced.

"Like I said before." I shrugged. "I'm good at reading people . . . usually."

He winced, and rubbed the back of his neck. "You weren't completely wrong. And I'm not a snob."

"Yeah. Sure you're not."

We locked eyes, and my heart pounded hard against my ribs. For the first time since he found out who I was, he was actually looking at me. "I'm not from your world, and I'm not rich. I'm an intern who practically lives off ramen noodles. I have absolutely nothing to be stuck up about, sugar."

". . . Oh."

"And I had no idea you got hate for having a brother like Tate," he said, his voice low. "I know how that feels. My brother used to be a lot like him."

Something told me his brother wasn't half as disliked as mine was. And that he wasn't nearly so bad. "You didn't ask me anything about myself, so why would you know?"

"Look, I'm s—"

"You can stop right there." I held a hand up. "I didn't say all that to make you feel bad for me, or for you to stay out of some misplaced sense of guilt. I prefer spending time with people because they're interesting, not because they pity me. I was just being honest, because that's who I am, and you asked me. But please. Go. I'll eat my meal on my own, and I assure you I'm perfectly fine with that. In fact, most of the time I prefer it. I like being alone."

Maybe I could get some studying done while I waited for my food.

That brow rose again. "Yet you bid on a date with me?"

I shrugged. "I thought maybe we might get along. But you weren't interested in finding out if that was the case, and I'm done trying, so you can go."

"I'm sorry." He reached across the table and closed a hand over mine. I stiffened. His palm was calloused and warm. It dwarfed mine. "You're right. I'm being an asshole on purpose, but it's for a good reason, not because I think you aren't good enough for me."

His skin on mine was electrifying. I pulled away, putting my hand safely in my lap. "Then why are you doing it?"

"You've been straightforward with me, so I'll give you the same honesty. I'm not a respectable guy, and I'm not going to leave a good mark on this world like you. Normally, I'd eat you up like chocolate mousse pie, and leave you naked and trembling in your bed for hours, but you're my boss's sister, so I really don't want to mess with you and piss him off, because I'll lose my job. The risk isn't worth the reward. No matter how beautiful you are, I won't touch you, because it'll end badly for me. I'm selfish like that."

My mouth opened, closed, and opened again. "But if Tate wasn't . . . ?"

"I'd bring you back to my place, fuck you any way you wanted me to, as many times as you wanted me to. I'd make you mine in every way, lick every inch of your body, whisper hot, sweet words in your ear . . ." He dropped his hand, which had still been resting on the table, in his lap. "And then I'd walk away. I'd forget your name, and everything we talked about, and move on to the next girl, the next night, without a hint of guilt. I never sleep with the same woman twice. That's who I am."

I held my breath, images of him "using" me until I trembled sending a surge of lust rolling through my body. Which was stupid, because he was literally telling me he had no interest in me besides sex. And yet . . . I didn't really *care*. I'd never felt a hunger like this for a man before, and there was no point denying it. I generally didn't bother with relationships, or the drama they brought, so I was consistently single.

Wait, scratch that.

My boyfriend was my *studies*, and getting straight As, and being the best in my class—that was my *relationship*. And I was good at it. At doing my best. It was the least I could do for my brother, who had done so much for me. He might not be a good man by most standards, but he was the best brother a girl could ask for.

Acing medical school was demanding and didn't leave much free time, so maybe Scotty offered me the perfect opportunity. I could have my fun with a man who was clearly accustomed to one-night stands, and then move on, knowing he wouldn't want more from me than I was willing to give.

No broken hearts. No hurt feelings. Just pleasure.

"What if I promise not to tell him?" I asked softly, knowing I was putting myself out there, but really, what did I have to lose? "What if you show me the real you, the one I thought I saw, and I don't tell anyone? Because I have a feeling you're exhausted from always pretending to be something you're not. And I bet you never let your guard down. With me, you can."

He snorted, shifting on his seat. "You think you've got me all figured out, don't you?"

I pushed my hair off my shoulder, and he followed the motion, staring at me with heated eyes. But underneath that I saw a haunting emptiness, which explained the whole sleeping-around thing. In that moment, I was never more confident that I was dead-on with my reading of him. "I do, but feel free to prove me wrong. Actually talk to me, give me a *real* date with the *real* Scotty Donahue, without games or pretenses between us, and I promise not to tell my brother you were nice to me for one night."

He hesitated, rubbing his chin, staring at me. "I don't know . . ."

"What have you got to lose?"

Sardonic amusement crossed his face, but he shrugged. "Fine. Whatever. Let's start over, then." He held a hand out, shooting me a small grin. "I'm Scotty Donahue."

Smiling, I slid my hand into his. "I'm Skylar Daniels. Nice to meet you."

"Likewise," he mumbled, pulling free. "Want to know a secret?"

I leaned in, nodding, my heart picking up speed, because he was looking at me as if he saw all my secrets. "Of course."

"I don't actually enjoy fancy restaurants, which is why I didn't order anything to eat yet." He glanced over his shoulder, then back to me. "I prefer red meat. Like . . . rare steak. Burgers. Fries. Mashed potatoes. *Motherfucking beer.*"

The way he left the r off the end of beer . . .

God, it was so hot.

"They have steak here," I managed to say.

"With snails on it." He shuddered. "I prefer my snails smooshed under my shoe."

A laugh escaped, but I tried to hold it back, so it ended up sounding like a snort-slash-choke. "Okay, then. Do you want to go somewhere else? Since we haven't ordered yet."

"Also, I'm not big on fancy appetizers. I like my meal fast. No waiting. Sitting around a restaurant all damn night only makes it more likely you'll be there when it gets robbed or shot up at closing."

I blinked. *Robbed?* "Where are you from that that's what you worry about?"

"Steel Row. *South* South Boston."

Suddenly, his statement made perfect sense.

Steel Row was overrun by gangs. No wonder Tate warned him off. When my parents had divorced, my mother had gotten me, and my father had gotten Tate. They just split us up like we were possessions instead of family. Mom and I had been so poor, I couldn't afford basic school supplies, let alone fancy dinners like this . . . while Tate had lived in a mansion.

He'd spent the rest of his life trying to make up for that.

Even though *he* wasn't the one to blame.

"Do you have an apartment there?" I asked slowly.

"A house, actually." He tugged on his tie and shifted on his chair. "It's my old childhood home. I bought it back a year or so ago, after my brother . . ."

I cocked my head. "After he what?"

"Died," he said simply. "He died."

"I'm so sorry." I covered his hand, like he had done to mine earlier. His knuckles were hard, but the skin was smoother than his palms. "How did he . . . ?"

"He got shot." He locked eyes with me. "In Steel Row. Him and his girlfriend, Heidi. They were in their apartment, and there was a home invasion."

My heart twisted. "I can't even imagine."

"I can." He paused, swallowing hard enough for his Adam's apple to bob. When he looked at me, the pain in his eyes was raw. Real. It hurt. "I miss him every day."

Scotty blinked, almost as if he was surprised he'd offered that information.

"I'm so sorry. I can't imagine my life without Tate, no matter how annoying he is."

"Hopefully you won't have to." He leaned back in the chair again, lounging sexily. He stared at me from under his lowered lids, and the way he watched me—like it was only a matter of time until he saw me naked, no matter who my brother was—sent chills running up my spine. He picked up his wine and finished it. "Lucas lived a dangerous life, and in the end? It caught up to him, like it always does. Guys in Steel Row? We don't live long."

"But you're majoring in marketing. The most dangerous thing there is, what, a paper cut?"

He stared at me for a second, then shrugged. "True. But even so. Life's too short to mess around, so I'm sorry I was a prick to you. It's not my style to play dirty."

I had a feeling that hadn't come easy to him—that he wasn't the type of man to say he was sorry lightly—so it meant even more than an apology from someone else would have. And something he said, about men in his town not living long, made it sound as if, despite his relatively safe career, he expected to be one of those men. I scanned my mind for something—anything—to say in response to that, and came up empty. So I settled for: "Do you actually enjoy long walks on the beach, or was that a lie, too?"

He cocked his head. "I don't know. Never really tried it."

"I see." I stood, smoothing my dress over my thighs, and smiled at him brightly, even though my mind was still on his brother and the awful things that had happened to him. And I didn't like that Scotty seemed to think he shared his brother's fate. "Let's go get some burgers and beer."

He laughed, grabbing my hand and trying to tug me back down to my seat. "It's fine. I'll find something on the menu."

"Life's too short to settle, and I love burgers, too." I pulled my wallet out of my purse. "Let's pay for our drinks and ditch this joint."

He shook his head, pulling his own wallet out. "I've got this. You bought my company, which is a pretty shitty deal considering all you got was me, so the least I can do is cover the meal and our drinks. But are you sure?"

I held out a hand for him, watching as he tossed down three twenties, which was more than enough for our wine and the tip. I felt bad that he was paying, but I sensed he wouldn't appreciate me pointing out that I should pay, since I had more money than he did. "Absolutely. Let's go get drunk at this lovely little pub I know. They have handcrafted Irish beer on draft."

He gave me a look, before laughing. "You're gonna regret this. I can drink an alcoholic under the table . . . and have, several times."

"I'm tougher than I look." I pulled my purse onto my shoulder. "I get that from my brother. He told me there would be plenty of people trying to knock me down, so I had to learn to stand tall, despite the blows. I took that advice very seriously."

He cocked a brow. "With drinking, too?"

"Everything. I can take a good pounding, and walk away without limping."

A laugh escaped him, and he shook his head, rubbing his jaw as he tucked his wallet away into his pocket. His moves were always fast, and unpredictable, but somehow fluid and graceful. That didn't seem to make sense, and yet it totally did. "Don't say that ever again, please."

Wait. Why? I replayed the words in my head, then suddenly I knew why he'd laughed. God, I was such an idiot. My cheeks heated. "Deal."

He offered me his hand, still laughing. "Ready, sugar?"

Fire flushed through my veins, making my blood boil and my pulse race and every nerve come alive—and all he'd done was smile at me and call me *sugar.* Scotty probably called all the girls *sugar,* but whatever. It was hot. His power over me was ridiculous, and scary, and thrilling . . . all at once. "Ready."

His hand closed over mine, and I sucked in a deep breath at the sensation of his skin on mine. Out of the corner of my eye, I saw him staring down at our hands, brow furrowed, as he tightened his grip on me. Did he feel the weird charge between us, too? Or was I just hoping it wasn't one-sided? Yeah, given what he'd told me about his past and his inclinations, it was the latter. Right then, I had a feeling he was right. Someway, somehow, someday . . .

I was going to regret this.

But I was going to do it anyway.

CHAPTER 5

SCOTTY

A few hours later, we stumbled down the street, both laughing hard at something Skylar had said. All night long had been like this. Ever since she called me on my shit, and I stopped acting like a dick, we'd been having a fantastic fucking time. I'd never felt so damn free before, which was stupid as hell, because I was with Tate Daniels's baby sister, and if he knew I had my arm around her, holding her against my body like this, he would flip his shit.

But I was having too much damn fun to care.

I'd worry about Tate tomorrow.

"And then he walked in, soaking wet, wearing his Gucci suit and leather shoes, hair dripping down his forehead, and calmly goes, 'Did you happen to change the times on the sprinkler system without telling me?'" She burst into laughter again, pressing a hand to her stomach. "And I lost it. Just *lost* it. He looked so ridiculous, standing there, dripping all over the hardwood floors, in his work clothes."

I smiled, supporting her as she held on to me. The urge to pull her closer and hug her was strong, even though I never, *ever* hugged women just for the hell of it. Her amusement was contagious. But under all the smiles and the urges, there was an uneasiness settling in my gut that I tried my best to ignore. The stories she told me about Tate had shown me a whole other side to the man who was in control of the gang. In that world, he was hard. Uncaring. Cold. A killer. But with Skylar, he was a brother, first and foremost.

There was no other way to put it . . .

He reminded me of Lucas, and how he'd been with me.

And that didn't sit well.

Lucas spent his entire life trying to take care of me. He became a criminal to ensure there was food on the table, and a roof over my head, and heat in winter. Every day, he went out into Steel Row, risking his life and compromising his honor, so *I* would be safe, simply because he was the one who was born first. He never complained. Never made me feel as if he blamed me for the way his life had turned out.

And yet, *I* did.

I blamed myself.

And I'd spend the rest of my life trying to make sure his sacrifices hadn't been in vain. If not for me, and his duty to me, what would his life had been? Would he have focused on his studies? Gotten a scholarship to some fancy college, with some fancy degree? Would he have been the type of guy who wouldn't have to run away from his home, from me, to be happy . . . and *alive*?

Those were questions that would never be answered, but I'd do my damned best to make this city a safer place, taking out one gang at a time. The problem was that at some point, maybe soon, the DEA would want me to rat on the Sons. They didn't typically go after the gangs that dealt with guns—that was ATF territory, and I'd purposely avoided that division so I'd never be forced to go after the man who had taken my brother in—but there was no guarantee that the Sons wouldn't get caught in the crossfire, or that the DEA wouldn't team up with the ATF, since they already had a man deep undercover.

Every time the Sons discussed possibly taking on drugs, and dipping into that world, I'd voted against it emphatically, knowing if we went down that road, I'd have to betray them all. Taking down the man who survived in a world of violence so his little sister would have a better life wasn't something I wanted to do. After all, Lucas had done it for me.

Who the hell was *I* to judge?

"Thanks for letting me stay at your place," she said, hugging my arm against her side. Her soft breast pressed up against me, and I gritted my teeth, because hot damn, she had some amazing tits. "I can't believe I lost my keys."

Yeah. Me either. "It's not a problem. But whatever you do, don't leave my place without me. This isn't your country club anymore, sugar."

"I know." She glanced around, tightening her grip on my arm. The streets were quiet for a Tuesday night. No one was out, no voices raised in anger or amusement, like there would be on a Friday night. All was still . . . except for us. "I grew up here. I know what it's like."

I glanced at her. Tate had been raised in a mansion, so that had to be a lie. By the time Tate and Skylar had been born, their father was extremely wealthy off the profits of the gang he'd founded. As far as I knew, Tate had lived in the Daniels mansion for the past fifteen years. and I assumed that Skylar had grown up there, too, in secrecy. "You did?"

"Yeah. Up until high school."

I frowned. What game was she playing? "I thought you grew up in West Boston."

"Tate did." She pressed her lips together, not meeting my eyes. "I wasn't always in an ivory tower. When our parents split up, I went with my mom, and Tate stayed with our father. He grew up in West Boston, and I was here, a few streets over, with my mom."

So *that's* why no one knew about her. She'd been raised separately. This was the kind of intel I never would have gotten if not for this date. The kind of stuff we would have only been able to guess about, under other circumstances. "And your dad didn't support you?"

"No," she said, her voice short.

I said nothing, since she was clearly uncomfortable talking about her dad. I pulled her to a stop gently. "This one's mine."

She glanced up, her brow furrowed. My home was an end row house, and the brownish-red brick exterior was cleaner than any other on this block. I made sure to take care of the house I grew up in, where Ma had lived and died. I'd installed new windows last summer, and the porch had been rebuilt, too. It had taken a hell of a lot of sweat, but I'd done it.

All by my damn self.

I took pride in that.

She glanced around the whole street of brick homes and broken streetlights, taking it in. Run-down homes. Even more run-down cars lining the streets. And if she could see the people living inside those homes, she'd probably race off in the opposite direction, miraculously "finding" her keys, no matter that she'd once lived here. Steel Row had a way of sucking the life out of you until you were an automaton with a broken soul.

Trust me.

I would know.

"Yours is the nicest on the block," she finally said, staring at it again. "You did all this work yourself?"

"Yeah," I said, staring down at her, brow furrowed. "How'd you know?"

"I told you, I'm good at reading people. You look proud. Your chest puffed out with pride as you looked up at your home." She lifted a shoulder, glancing up at me through her lashes, a seductive glint to her expression that I couldn't ignore no matter how hard I tried. "You're clearly good with your hands."

Normally, I'd make some sexual innuendo that would have her naked in less than three minutes, but this was Skylar Daniels. I fisted my hands at my sides so I wouldn't touch her—because *Christ*, I wanted to touch her—and simply said: "Yeah."

"Well?" She smiled and pulled at my arm tipsily. I grinned back, swaying slightly, pretending to be as messed up as her, when in all reality, I was completely sober. She steadied me even though I was easily twice her size, concern crossing her expression. She was so damn free with her emotions, and there was no guesswork involved. If she was happy, you knew it. I had a feeling she made her anger just as clear. I'd gotten a small taste of it earlier. "Let's go in. I can't wait to see the inside."

I heard her words, felt her tugging on me, but I didn't move. The moon shone down on her hair, and the streetlight reflecting off her bright blue eyes made them twinkle with life. She shone, almost like she was from another world, and I couldn't look away. She was so clean, so damn pretty—far too shiny for a guy like me—and she had no place being in Steel Row, but still, I was glad she was here with me. Which was strange, considering the fact that I never brought chicks home. This was my sanctuary. My home. The one place I could truly be myself, and it wasn't for anyone else but *me*.

And yet, here we were.

Standing outside.

About to go in.

"Scotty?" she asked, staring at me with her nose crinkled up adorably. How she could be related to a ruthless guy like Tate Daniels was beyond me. She rested her hand on my chest, and my heart sped up at the innocent touch. "Everything okay?"

It took all my control not to reach out and push her strawberry blonde hair behind her ear with a gentle touch. What the hell was wrong with me? Where were all these soft, tender feelings toward a woman coming from? I wasn't an asshole, but I wasn't *this* guy either.

And yet here I was.

Wanting to do it.

Like a dumbass.

"Yeah," I said, clearing my throat, and leaving her hair untouched. "Come on."

We went up the stairs to my porch, Skylar watching me while I pretended not to notice. It was a game we all played on dates, and I usually played it well. But with her, my game plan was off. And I wasn't sure why. After I removed my key from the latch, I hit the light switch and motioned her inside, scanning the streets to make sure no danger lurked outside before shutting us in my home together.

I locked us in and turned to her.

She was taking it all in, spinning in a slow circle, and I looked, too, trying to see what she saw: hardwood floors I'd sanded and stained myself, and the spot in the corner where a jagged edge had sliced my palm open. I pressed my finger to the scar and eyed the beige carpet I'd stapled in place on Memorial Day weekend last year. It led into a kitchen with white cabinets, and a blue tile countertop I was dying to rip up. Pale yellow walls continued throughout the downstairs level, the same color Ma had painted them years ago, but with a fresh coat. There was a white banister on the carpeted stairs, leading to three bedrooms and a bathroom upstairs.

A few family pictures, mostly older ones, and not much else.

It wasn't much, but it was *home*.

And for some reason, it was important to me that she like it. "Does it live up to expectations?" I asked, keeping my voice dry.

She turned to me, an angelic smile lifting her perfect pink lips at the corners. She had dimples in her cheeks when she smiled. As if she wasn't already pretty enough. "Yes. You have a beautiful home, Scotty. It's so . . . so . . . warm. It reminds me of my old house, with my mom. And it's totally not what I expected."

My brow rose. "What did you expect?

"I don't know." She shrugged her coat off, tossing it on the chair by the door I used when I needed to sit to pull my boots on. "I guess . . . more of a bachelor pad. Black furniture. Tan walls. Artistic renderings of the naked female body. Empty beer bottles lying on their sides all over the furniture. Stereo system that starts with a snap of your fingers."

A small laugh escaped me before I could choke it back. "Wow. Turns out, you read me wrong after all."

"Guess so," she said softly, stepping closer to me, hips swaying as she approached. When she was mere inches from me, she trailed a finger from my shoulder down to my abs. "It's a pleasant surprise, though. Being wrong."

"I bet it is," I said, my voice coming out in a croak as I caught her hand and stopped her an inch shy of reaching the promised land. She'd been flirty all night long, that flirtiness growing with each glass of wine she drank, but she hadn't been so bold as to literally grab my cock. If I hadn't stopped her in time . . . well, there would have been no stopping me. *"Skylar."*

Grinning, she held her hands up in surrender. "Sorry. Sorry."

Yeah. Sure she was. And I was Martha Stewart. "It's late, and we both had a lot to drink. I'll show you to your room for the night, so that no one makes any mistakes they regret in the morning," I said, stepping back, out of reach, and gesturing to the stairs. "After you."

She wobbled where she stood. "But—"

"Bed. *Now.*"

That was part of the reason why I'd let her get away with her little lost-keys act. I wanted to keep an eye on her until she sobered up. I felt a responsibility to her, since I'd allowed her to try to match me drink for drink.

She stared at me for a second, looking as if she might argue about getting sent to bed like a child, but then she spun on her heel and headed for the stairs. I followed behind her, immediately regretting my choice. Her ass swung with each step, haunting me, *taunting* me, and looking as if it would fit in the palms of my hands perfectly. She wore a dress that hadn't seemed all that tight, and yet somehow, right now, it was. It barely hid a damn thing.

For the few things it did hide, my mind filled in the blanks very enthusiastically.

She reached the top of the stairs and paused, glancing over her shoulder. I sensed her attention turning back to me and I quickly looked away from her ass, but I was too slow.

At least, the smirk she gave me said I was, anyway. She gripped the banister hard and pressed her thighs together, shifting ever so slightly. "Which way?" she asked throatily.

"Left." It was the guest room farthest from mine—also, coincidentally, my childhood bedroom. "Last door at the end of the hall."

She turned left, reaching the door without catching me staring again—though that didn't mean I wasn't. I was a dude, and she had a fine fucking ass. As she pushed the door open, she turned on the light and drew in a breath, smiling. "Wow."

I glanced inside. There was a queen bed with a striped comforter in the middle of the left wall, three windows on the other two walls, and a chair beside a dresser. Understated, but elegant. I might be a killer and a DEA agent, but I knew a good room layout, and I had no shame about it. "Okay. Well. Bathroom is at the other end of the hall, and there's a Keurig downstairs in the kitchen if you wake up before me."

She stared at me, fidgeting. Her waist was so tiny I could probably encompass it with both hands. Her hips flared out gently, giving her a curvy appeal, and her slender legs were longer than you'd think on such a short woman. "That's it? You're going to bed already?"

I backed away a step, my hand on the knob, escape so close I could taste it on the tip of my tongue. "That's it. Good night, sugar."

"Wait!" she called out, lifting a hand.

My grip on the knob tightened. "Yeah?"

"I need help undressing." She shoved the piece of hair I'd wanted to touch earlier behind her ear, ducking her head and shooting me a shy look. "Can you unzip me?"

I swallowed a groan, knowing if I had to bare that skin

inch by inch, she might not leave here untouched, consequences be damned. "Can't you just do it yourself?"

"No, there's a latch, and it's too hard. I usually get my neighbor to help me."

Stiffening, I took a step toward her, feeling like I was walking toward a freshly sharpened guillotine instead of a drop-dead gorgeous woman. She was just as dangerous to my well-being. "Male or female neighbor?"

She lifted her brows, spinning and giving me her back. "Does it matter?"

"No." I rested my hands on her shoulders, breathing in her soft, floral perfume. "Yes. Answer the damn question, Sky."

"It's a girl," she answered softly, watching me over her shoulder. The way she looked at me—half seductress, half innocent smile—made my pulse soar and my gut clench tight. "The zipper?"

"Yeah. I got it."

I took a deep breath, running my hands over her shoulders, allowing myself one lingering touch, before I focused on the job at hand. Frowning, I wiggled the top of the dress until the latch came free. I could have stopped there. I *should* have stopped there.

But I, like a dumbass, unzipped the dress, slow inch by slow inch, baring smooth, creamy flesh that made my pants grow tighter by the second. I'd seen a lot of women's backs. Hell, it was hardly an erogenous zone, for fuck's sake. But on Skylar, that tiny patch of tempting skin was enough to make my breath catch in my throat and my pulse quicken.

The tips of my fingers brushed her, and she tensed beneath my touch, swaying closer. When the zipper was completely undone, I stood behind her, staring down at the present I'd unwrapped. I took a step closer, breathing in her scent, letting my chest brush against her back. I made sure not to let my cock touch her ass—I wasn't that much of a masochist. But damned if I wasn't tempted anyway. "Done."

Slowly, she turned to face me, holding the dress to her chest. I swallowed hard, my mouth dry yet somehow watering, too. Which made no sense at all. That was fitting, though, since she made me feel all tied up in knots. She bit down on her plump lip, her cheeks flushed, and her breath escaped her on a *whoosh*. Something about the way she looked at me, at the excitement building in her eyes, warned me she was about to do something stupid.

A perp usually got that look right before he went on a suicide mission and pulled a gun with ten DEA agents surrounding him. He knew once he reached for it, he'd have more holes in him than a damn pincushion, but he did it anyway. It was a last attempt at defiance, or a Hail Mary, if you wanted to call it that.

Skylar had Hail Mary written all over her beautiful face. And I had no one to blame but myself.

CHAPTER 6

SKYLAR

Scotty was watching me like he was torn between running away, pulling me closer, or tossing me out onto the curb in nothing but what I wore. I wasn't sure which of those things he was actually thinking about, although I was nearly positive I wouldn't be showing Steel Row the color of my underwear. Either way, it was all-or-nothing time. I'd come up with a lame excuse to get him to bring me back to his place, and I'd gotten him in a room with a bed. Now it was time to play my ace, and see if it got me a winning hand.

Sucking in a deep breath, I counted to two . . .

And dropped my dress to the floor around my feet.

His jaw dropped, and he stood dead still, not running, but not pulling me closer either. At least he didn't toss me over his shoulder and head for the front door. I guess I had that going for me.

Maybe.

His warm green gaze dipped down my body, taking its

time. He lingered over my chest and slowly focused on my hips before climbing back up to my face. By the time we locked gazes again, it felt like an hour had passed, though in all reality it hadn't been more than a couple of seconds. My limbs were trembling, and weak, and I swayed toward him even though he didn't move an inch toward me.

Scotty curled his hands into fists, slowly releasing his fingers one by one. I watched his hands breathlessly, like it was some kind of sexy countdown and once he reached the last finger he would . . .

What?

I didn't have a clue. But I was dying to find out. I had a feeling he wasn't the type of guy to rush into . . . well . . . anything. He thought out every single action with the possible outcomes, weighed the pros and cons, weighed them *again*, and then finally made a decision. I could literally *see* him deciding whether or not I was worth the risk of getting in trouble with my brother.

The second he released his pinky, I tensed, breath held. Decision time.

He lifted his foot like he was going to take a step toward me, but then he didn't. I could feel the magnetic pull between us—the same one I'd felt the moment he first touched me—and it was stronger than ever. It was like the universe was trying to tell me something, like this man was supposed to be mine, and I could see it. Feel it. Sense it.

He was *mine*.

But either he didn't feel it, or he was ignoring it, because he stood in the same freaking spot he'd stood when I first dropped my dress. And I was starting to feel like an idiot.

A mostly naked one.

"You shouldn't have done that," he finally said, his voice gravelly, sending shivers down my spine. "I don't know what kind of game you're playing, but I'm not kidding around when I tell you if I touch you, your brother will, quite literally, *kill me*."

I licked my lips, feeling a little bit ridiculous standing there in my bra and panties, getting lectured about my brother, when all I wanted was Scotty. "He's not that scary."

Scotty stared at me.

Just *stared*.

It was unnerving, to say the least. His ability to say so much without a word was a talent I wished I had. He effectively shut me down without even opening his mouth.

So much for letting my whimsical side take control for once.

Look where it had gotten me. Exposed and in a bedroom with a man who clearly didn't want me, because of who I was. Or, more accurately, who my brother was. I'd hoped a little bit of naked skin would change his stance on that subject, but clearly I'd overestimated my sexual appeal. My cheeks heated, and I wished—God, I *wished*—I was anywhere but here.

Laughing nervously, I raised my arms to my chest, crossing them over my breasts. "I get it. No more words needed. Sorry for . . . well . . ." I glanced down at my body. ". . . *this*. Thanks for taking my dress off for me, and for letting me stay here. I'll be gone first thing in the morning, and I promise I won't tell my brother I spent the night here."

Scotty's nostrils flared, but he didn't move. "You shouldn't cover yourself in shame, and you shouldn't avoid my eyes. You're goddamned beautiful, sugar. You're . . . you . . . *shit*. I shouldn't still be in this room with you, but damned if I can stop myself from standing here, staring at you . . ."

My cheeks got even hotter, but for an entirely different reason. "Do you feel it, too?"

"Feel what?" he asked immediately.

"The pull." I lifted my chin, feeling stupid, but I wasn't the type of girl to beat around the bush. Life was too short, too uncertain, to waste time with hesitancy. Either he felt it or he didn't, and I *needed* to know. "When you first touched me, it was like something was screaming at me that you were the one who could give me everything I needed, and even things I didn't know I needed. Like . . . like . . ."

He took a step closer. "Like you knew me somehow, on some level you don't fully understand?"

"Yes." I stepped closer to him. *"Do you feel it?"*

He stared at me, pressed his lips together, then released them. "It doesn't matter if I do or not. It won't change a damn thing. I'm not the man for you, sugar. You're gonna have to trust me on this."

"Because of my brother." I took another step toward him. Now there were only about six inches between us. I could smell his musky cologne, and hear his breaths. "Or, let me guess, because you're not a good guy."

"I'm not," he agreed.

"Liar."

He dragged his hand through his hair, laughing a little. "Not everyone is what they seem, Sky. Not everyone is so easily figured out." He shrugged out of his coat, tossing it on the floor. "Just because you *think* you're good at reading people doesn't mean you are."

I licked my lips, watching as he undid the top button of his shirt. "What are you doing?"

"Showing you how wrong you are about me." His fingers moved over the buttons deftly, his green gaze locked on me the whole time. He undid the last button and shrugged his shirt off.

Slowly, I lowered my head, and sucked in a deep breath, not releasing it.

Under his suit, he'd been hiding a torso of tattoos. He had more ink than skin showing from his shoulders down to the waistband of his trousers. There were dragons, and geometric shapes, a Sacred Heart, and a portrait of a woman. They covered his upper chest, shoulders, and arms . . . all done in black ink. There wasn't a hint of color to be seen on his skin. There was so much to look at, and not enough time to do so. I'd never seen so much ink on one person before.

And the muscles . . . holy freaking crap.

He stared me down. "See the one on my inner arm?"

I forced my attention where he told me to look. I'd been too busy admiring his six-pack, because hot damn, the man had one. They actually existed in real life. I'd always thought they were like unicorns, something people talked about wistfully, but that didn't really exist.

But they did. God, they did.

"Skylar. Focus."

I snapped myself back to attention. "Huh?"

"The tattoo right here." He lifted a hard, veined arm and pointed at the ink, in case I wasn't smart enough to figure it out, even though it stood out with clarity. It was a picture of two guns crossed over each other, with cursive black ink that said *Sons of Steel Row*.

The connotations of that tattoo, and what it meant, hit me hard.

That meant . . .

God. I was going to kill him.

Forcing a bland expression, I blinked. "Yeah . . . and? I already knew you were from Steel Row. Am I supposed to be shocked you got it inked on you? I happen to find tattoos sexy."

Or, at least, I did now.

Because *hot damn*.

He made a frustrated sound. "Do you recognize the name?"

"No." I blinked again, heart racing. "Should I?"

"It's a gang."

I frowned. "Why do you have the name of a gang on your . . . ?"

"You know why."

Uneasily, I looked at it again. The guns stood out with heartbreaking clarity. "You're . . . in a . . . gang?"

"Do you really think Tate would hire an active gang member?"

"Oh." My head was spinning, and I had no idea if he was telling me the truth or not. "I . . . see."

The idea of him being the type of guy who pulled a trigger on another person was horrifying. Even worse, if he was still in a gang, people would be pulling the trigger on *him*.

There was no denying that ink, or what it meant.

"I've done things. Bad things. I'm still the same man who joined the gang, the one who did that stuff. People don't change, Sky. When they're bad, they're bad."

My heart pounded against my ribs. I had no idea what to say, or how I felt about this, but suddenly his certainty that Tate would kill him if he touched me made perfect sense. Tate expected me to end up with a man who was as clean as he pretended to be—not a gang member, former or otherwise. He would never accept Scotty, with his dark past. "I know."

"I don't think you do. Just because a man is wearing a

suit doesn't mean he's a good guy, sugar." He shrugged his shirt back on, leaving it unbuttoned, offering glimpses of untouched skin and dark ink. He looked even sexier like that, so if he was attempting to ward me off, he failed. Big-time. Picking up his jacket, he draped it over my shoulders gently, covering my body, tugging it closed at the neck. "You need to remember that, before you misjudge another man. One who won't hesitate to take what you have to offer, even though you deserve so much more."

He was so close, too close, and despite all his warnings and my common sense that screamed at me to listen to him, to keep my stupid hands to myself, I reached up, touching his jaw with the backs of my knuckles. He stiffened, nostrils flaring, and drew in a ragged breath.

And there it was again.

That attraction that told me no matter how bad he was for me, he was *mine*.

"Do I?" I asked quietly, slipping my hand under his shirt, over his racing heart. I was right. He was harder than a rock, or a brick wall, or cold hard logic. And no matter what he said, or how much he pushed me away, the truth was there, in his heart, and in the way he stared down at my mouth like he was a dying man and I was his only chance at survival. He wanted me just as badly as I wanted him, and he felt it, too. That undeniable pull. "But, you see, I want you. Not someone else, not a guy who is a gentleman, or 'suitable,' or without a dark past. I want you. And I'm not too scared to admit it."

He stared at me, looking half a second from . . . *something*. I had no idea what.

"You're right. You're way too much like your brother. You refuse to back down from a challenge, even when it's clear you're going to lose," he said, his voice raspy.

"I don't see you as a challenge." I skimmed my fingers over his skin, marveling at the way his chest hair felt against my fingers. I thought it would be coarse, but it wasn't. It was soft, and inviting. "I see you as a reward."

Call it stupidity, call it destiny, call it whatever you wanted, all I knew was this man needed me—and I needed him. I'd never been much of a believer in kismet, or soul mates, or even love at first sight. I wasn't even sure if love really existed—not the kind they showed in the movies, anyway. Not that life-shattering, soul-changing, *I must have you or die* way. So it wasn't like I thought I loved him or anything.

I just *needed* him.

His grip tightened, and he lowered his face to mine. I rose on tiptoe, breath coming fast and hard, body straining toward his. As his lips came closer, I felt his breath on my mouth, and he slid his hand upward, creeping up my ribs toward my breast and leaving a trail of fire in his wake.

I let out a tiny, nearly nonexistent moan.

Apparently, it was enough to snap him out of it.

He froze, fisting his jacket, and splayed his hand across my torso, one finger resting under the edge of my bra. *"Shit."*

"Scotty . . ." I started.

He let me go and ran his hands down his face. I missed the feel of them on my skin immediately, but I could still feel the heat where his touch had been. He'd made up his mind—it was written all over his face. I'd lost the fight. "We both drank too much. All of this, everything we said, is bullshit. In the morning, you'll come to your senses, and you'll thank me."

I shook my head, hugging his jacket closed over me. "If you say so."

"Good night, Sky."

Without looking back, or even a hint of hesitation, he walked out of the room, leaving me standing there alone, half naked, filled with longing . . .

And with so much sexual frustration I could explode.

CHAPTER 7

SCOTTY

There was not enough coffee in the world to make me feel ready to face this day. No matter how hard I tried to drink her away, all night long I could feel Skylar's hands on my body, tempting me, teasing me, *killing* me. I don't know what she did to me, but I'd never lusted after a woman so damn hard, or lost sleep over one before. Then again, I'd never denied myself one before.

If I wanted a woman, I pursued her.

No games. No hesitation.

Hell, why would I hesitate? Sex was sex. If both parties consented, there was no reason not to engage. But then I met Skylar, and all that changed. Even though I resisted her mainly because of Tate, I did have other reasons that went a hell of a lot deeper than who her brother was.

I glanced down at the text my boss had sent me yesterday. Not Tate. Agent Torres. When I told him about Skylar, and that Tate had asked me take his place in the auction, Torres was very clear in his instructions. Instructions that didn't sit well with me at all.

Use this to get closer to her. She might have intel we can use.

And that right there?

That was why I really refused to touch her.

I'd played lots of parts in this life, and told lots of lies, but seducing a woman for information was not one of them . . . and it never would be.

There were lines drawn in the sand—unbreakable, uncrossable lines that weren't meant to be breached—and this was one of them. The second Agent Torres assigned her to me, she became a case, not a woman I'd like to get to know better. She'd already given me information that I could pass on to my boss, leverage on Tate Daniels. Leverage the agency would use. I'd told her that I'd been in a gang because my ink told the story for me. And if I was going to gain her trust, be her "friend," I needed to let her think she was right about me.

Not fucking her last night had been the first step.

Continuing not to fuck her would be the next.

I might not want to use her against her brother, but I'd do it anyway. Just not in the bedroom. My thumb hovered over the screen, my temples ached, and my heart twisted as I typed: What kind of intel are you looking for, sir?

Whatever you can get.

My gut clenched, and I ground my teeth together. Yes, sir.

Footsteps approached, and I tucked my personal phone into my pocket, running my hands through my hair to make it stand up a bit. I'd perfected the part of charming rascal over the last five years, and I played it well. It was all about appearance. A little bit of scruff. Hair that had recently had fingers running through it. A carefree, sardonic smile.

Sometimes, I forgot how to be *me*.

I wasn't sure I even knew who I really was anymore.

She came around the corner, holding the unzipped top of her dress against her chest, her soft hair wavy and messy around her beautiful face, her cheeks flushed pink naturally with sleep. I'd never seen a woman look so damn sexy fresh outta bed before. She looked so innocently seductive, like she wasn't even trying to look as tempting as she did, and I was pretty sure it wasn't an act.

She was just fresh, pretty, and naïve.

And I was supposed to use that against her.

When she saw me standing in my kitchen, she stopped walking, and tightened her grip on her dress. "Hi."

"Good morning," I said in return, coming around the island. I wore a pair of jeans, and a versatile button-up shirt today, rolled up at the elbows. After I dropped her off at her home, I would meet up with Chris at the warehouse, do some business, head over to the Sons' clubhouse for a meeting after that, go see Torres, and then write up a few reports. "Need help with that?"

She nodded once, giving me her back. "Please," she said, her voice carefully cordial.

"Of course," I said back, equally cordially. I gripped the bottom of the zipper, slowly pulling it up, letting my fingers trail over her bare skin as I went. She shivered, swaying closer to me unconsciously before she stiffened and stood straight. Every reaction she had to me was so obvious. So clear-cut. I had a feeling she didn't have a duplicitous bone in her body. "Did you sleep well?"

She nodded once. "Thank you for letting me crash here. I appreciate it."

"No problem," I said, latching the little hook on the top of her dress. "Do we need to call someone to bring you your keys?"

She spun and faced me, her cheeks even pinker. "Uh . . . no. Turns out I drank more than I thought last night. They were in the bottom of my purse the whole time."

I forced a bland expression to my face, even though she was a horrible liar. We both knew they'd been there all along. "Oh, good. Coffee?"

"Sure." She sat down on the stool at my island, tugging on her dress. "Thanks for the toothbrush, by the way."

I'd put a spare on the pillow next to her head. She'd looked so angelic, sleeping with her hands folded under her cheeks. I didn't say anything, since she'd thanked me enough damn times already, and I didn't deserve her thanks. Not with what I was planning to do to her. I'd always thought I was a good man, despite the horrible things I did, because it was for the greater good. It was all part of the grand scheme of making my city safer—kind of like Batman, but without the cool toys. But using a woman for information that would be used against her brother in the future . . . it wasn't something *good guys* did.

At what point did my actions stop being excusable?

When I didn't speak, she added, "I'll call Tate to come get me in a few minutes."

"What—?"

She let out a small laugh, holding her hands up. "Kidding, kidding. That was my poor attempt at cracking the ice in the room a little bit."

"It worked," I mumbled, sliding the coffee toward her. She caught it easily. As she wrapped her hands around it, I put a fresh croissant on a plate and placed it in front of her, too. I'd run out this morning to grab breakfast. "Hungry?"

"Starving," she admitted, setting the coffee aside and pinching a piece of the croissant off with two dainty fingers. "And a little hungover, too."

"I bet," I said dryly. "Told you that you couldn't keep up with me."

"Clearly," she agreed, her cheeks pinkening.

"I can drive you home, if you'd like."

"No, thanks. I'll cab it." She glanced out the window. The sun was shining and a car revved outside, followed by shouts. "You've done enough already."

A woman screamed obscenities as the car sped away, tires squealing. Skylar stared toward the noise, eyes wide as every curse known to man was screeched toward a guy who was long gone from the sound of it. Her cheeks flushed, and she lowered her head. She looked as out of place in my kitchen, in her designer dress, as I did at her country club.

I picked up my coffee and took a sip, ignoring the furious woman outside. "Do you have a headache?"

"A little one. I think a hot shower will fix that, though," Skylar admitted, wincing and touching her temple. There was the sound of breaking glass and more screaming from outside. Sounded like the woman had found another way to take her anger out on my neighbor. He was always screwing around on his wife, so chances were he picked the wrong girl to bring home last night. Wouldn't be the first time.

"What's going on out there?" she asked hesitantly.

"Sounds like a woman is busting into my neighbor's house."

She laughed uneasily. "Shouldn't we . . . uh . . . call the cops?"

"The Boys don't come here."

"Oh. Right." She tore off another piece of croissant. "I forgot."

I came around the side of the island, leaning on it directly next to her. More glass broke outside. "Regret coming here last night yet?"

She finished the bite of croissant she'd been chewing. "No. Why would I?"

"Fights. Hangover. Me."

"Nah." She gave me a sad smile. "I'm happy to have met you, Scotty Donahue."

My fingers ached to bury themselves in her hair, tug until she stood, and pull her close. I didn't move. "So I was right?"

"About what?" she asked softly.

"About you being drunk, and us being smart not to fuck last night."

"I was pretty drunk. You were right about that much," Skylar said slowly.

I should leave it at that. If I had any common sense, I *would* leave it at that. Nothing had changed since last night. I was still under orders to get intel from her, so she was still off-limits. "And the rest?"

"Well." Her parted lips exhaled a soft breath, and her focus locked on my mouth. Warning bells went off in my head as my cock hardened. "Should I say what you want to hear, or the truth?"

I'll take the lies. Definitely the lies. "The truth."

Damn it.

"I barely got any sleep. I was restless. Achy. Empty. And every time I closed my eyes, I saw you." She bit down on her lip sexily. *Christ, kill me now.* "You?"

Well, shit.

"I slept great," I practically croaked out, cursing myself for instigating this, yet unable to resist, because that damn pull between us that she mentioned last night was strangling me to death. Carefully, clearly, I stepped back from her, putting a safe distance between us.

If such a thing as *safe distance* existed with her.

"Good," she said, her voice cool. She stood. "Well, then, I'll just call—"

"I want to be your friend, Skylar."

She blinked. "What?"

"I know I said that we couldn't be together, that I was bad for you, and all of that's true." He forced a smile. "But I like you, and I'd like to get to know you on a platonic level, if you'll let me."

"As friends," she said slowly.

"Yes."

"What about my brother?" she asked.

"What about him?" I lifted a shoulder. "I don't see why he would mind us being friends."

She licked her lips, the tip of her pink tongue leaving behind a trail of wetness that tempted me more than anything else ever had. "That sounds nice. I don't have many of those, to be honest."

"Why not?"

"I don't know," she said. "I mean, I'm in a sorority, so I have girls who care about me and all that. But we don't really, you know . . . do things." She held her hands out palm up, then awkwardly dropped them back to her sides. "We're always studying, and when we're not, they throw crazy parties that aren't really my style. I'd rather . . . I don't know. Go to the movies, and then a twenty-four-hour diner for coffee and discussion. Maybe go dancing, and then drive home in the middle of the night with the windows down, no matter how cold it is. Get stupid, but not be stupid. You know?"

No. Not really. Everything she mentioned sounded fairly tame to me, not stupid. But she seemed so intense, so very vulnerable, and I didn't have the heart to burst her damn bubble. "Absolutely. You want me to get stupid with you," I said slowly.

"Yes. No. I don't know." She let out a small laugh. "Maybe?"

"Well, I can do that." I cocked my head. "I like to dance."

"You do?" she asked, seeming surprised, rubbing her temple.

"Yeah. Sure." I frowned. "Does it hurt a lot?"

"Yeah." She gave me a weak smile and tugged on her dress. "And, to be honest, this dress is squeezing me, and making breathing difficult on top of it all. I'd kill for a pair of sweats and a regular T-shirt."

"No killing necessary." I spun my finger in a circle. "Let's get you out of those clothes."

"What?" she said, blinking at me. "Why?"

I grinned. "For a shower. It'll make your head feel better, and you'll be out of that dress, which'll help, too. While you're in there, I'll grab you some Motrin. When I get headaches a hot shower and a few painkillers usually do the trick. And you can borrow a shirt if you want. I might even have a pair of sweatpants for you—I accidentally bought a size too small the other day, and didn't return them yet. They'll be big, but with a drawstring, it'll work."

"Oh." She tucked her hair behind her ear. "Are you sure? I can just shower at my place once I'm home. It's not that bad."

"I refuse to let you be in pain when I can help. Especially when it's my fault that you're suffering. I never should have bought you that last drink." I spun her around gently, efficiently undoing the latch on her dress. I was a pro at it now.

As I unzipped her, I made sure to keep my fingers off her skin. I could only resist so much temptation in one day. I walked a fine line here. I had to flirt with her enough to keep her around, but not so much that we ended up in bed naked. Considering my immense attraction to her . . . I was pretty much fucked. "There. Off you go. I'll grab those clothes while you wash up."

She glanced at me over her shoulder, her blue eyes blazing with a hunger my body recognized all too damn well. My cock strained against my pants, demanding I take what she offered. "Thank you."

"Yep. Upstairs. Last door on the right."

Skylar nodded, walking away, clutching the dress to her chest, letting it fall down a bit as she walked. I got a glimpse of bare skin and sheer satin panties, and as hard as I tried, I couldn't look away. I watched her head toward the stairs and gave a long groan once she rounded the corner. When the shower turned on, I let out a string of curses and glowered at my rebelliously hard cock. I reached down and adjusted my pants, trying to ease the pressure, but it didn't help.

Only one thing would . . .

But I wasn't gonna do it.

I pictured her taking her dress off, unstrapping her black bra, her breasts bouncing free once she let it hit the floor . . . and groaned again, my cock throbbing even more than before.

"Son of a bitch."

Knowing the desire wasn't going to get any better unless I did something about it, I undid my pants, went into the half bath, and left the door cracked so I could listen for any hint of trouble. Right now, above me, Skylar was naked and letting the water wash over her as she closed her eyes, pink lips parted. My breath quickened, and I slid my pants down enough to get a good grip on my erection. I needed to take away the harsh edges of the lust killing me.

Needed some damn relief.

Lowering my lids, I pictured her standing under the hot water, beads of liquid rolling down her hard nipples and in between her legs as she slipped her hand into her folds, touching herself like I touched myself right now. Groaning, I squeezed my cock, and tugged harder, rolling my fist over the head as my breath came faster and I—

A gasp sounded outside the bathroom, and I froze, knowing my luck couldn't be that bad, and yet somehow also knowing it *was*. With my cock still in my hand, I slowly lifted my head, and I met the horrified gaze of Skylar Daniels through the small opening of the door I'd stupidly left open so I could keep an ear out for trouble.

Motherfucker.

CHAPTER 8

SKYLAR

"Oh my God," I breathed, clutching my dress to my chest, staring at the vision that was Scotty Donahue, jerking off. He held his erection in one hand, and the other palm rested on the wall in front of him. I rotated my fist on the dress I held to my breasts to protect my modesty. I felt naked without my bra and panties on, but I'd been about to step in the shower when I realized I didn't have a towel. Hence returning downstairs.

To find *this*.

He had his pants unzipped. His hand was wrapped around his penis, but that didn't stop me from seeing how hard it was . . . or how *huge*. I was so caught up in staring at him that when he moved, I jumped, forgetting to hold my dress in place. "Oh my . . ." I bent down, cheeks burning, and yanked my dress up. "Sorry. So sorry."

His gaze slowly lifted from my body, which I'd covered up again, but it didn't *feel* like I'd pulled my dress back up.

The heat in his eyes, and the muscle ticking by his jaw, made me feel more naked than before. Breathing heavily, he came through the door angrily. "Why did you come down?"

"I needed . . ." I started, cutting off when he curled his hand around the base of my neck, threading his fingers through my hair. *"Scotty."*

He hauled me against his chest hard. "You shouldn't have come back down here, Sky."

I barely had a chance to register his words before everything changed. He—*oh God*—he lowered his face to mine, and he kissed me. But it wasn't just a kiss. The second his mouth closed over mine, claiming me with nothing more than flesh touching flesh, it was like a lightning bolt shot through the sky, pierced the roof of the house, and struck me dead.

Electricity pulsed through my veins, and I clasped his arms as he backed me down the hallway, into the kitchen, and against the cabinet. I forgot about my dress for the second time. It hit the floor between us, and his hands were on my skin, skimming over my shoulders gently as he traced my skin. Down my arms, back up, over my ribs, until he closed his hands over my hips, grabbing my butt with a firm grip, his fingers digging into my skin.

He growled low in his throat, a primitive sound escaping him that claimed me just as much as his lips did. Effortlessly, he lifted me to the cool countertop, perching me on the edge as he slipped between my legs. I tensed, knowing where this was leading, and wanting it so freaking badly it hurt—but it didn't stop the little niggling fear in the back of my mind. With Scotty, I was out of my league, as he was clearly more experienced than I was.

What was I doing?

Despite the way I came on to him last night, I wasn't

usually the one who instigated flirtation, let alone *this*. He pressed his erection against me, rubbing up against a spot that sent a surge of pleasure racing through my veins. I dug my nails into his arms, holding on for dear life as he slid his hands over my breasts, cupping them roughly as he dragged the side of his thumbnail over my nipples.

Pleasure—*pure pleasure*—puddled in my stomach, quickening my breath.

He thrust against my core, all the while squeezing the hard buds of my nipples between his fingers, making my world spin. I'd never felt so much, so fast, and to be honest, it was a bit overwhelming. I tore free, gasping in a deep breath, turning my head to the side. Without a word, Scotty dropped to his knees, putting his mouth to another use . . . one I'd only ever dreamt about at night.

Alone.

In my bed.

The second his tongue touched me, I screamed, burying my fingers in his hair and holding on tight. When he closed his mouth over me, rolling his tongue in a slow circle, I gasped and jerked away slightly, because the pleasure that he sent racing through my body was so intense, I lost control over myself. And I didn't *like* losing control.

When I jerked away from him instinctively, he pulled back, frowning up at me. "Do you not like it when guys go down on you?"

I shook my head, then nodded, then shook my head again, knowing I wasn't making any sense but past the point of caring. "I like. I like a lot."

"Good. Because you taste like heaven," he growled, spreading my legs apart even more as he buried his face in between my legs, his tongue touching places no tongue had touched before. And, oh my God, it was even better than I'd imagined.

He might think I *tasted* like heaven, but he *brought* me to heaven . . .

And that was so much better.

His fingers pressed my inner thighs, and I glanced down, breath quickening when I saw him there, kneeling between my legs, making me feel things I'd never felt before. And the fear I'd been feeling faded away to nothing, because if I was going to do this with someone—be uncharacteristically reckless like this—it had to be with Scotty.

It just felt *right*.

A raspy moan filled the room, and it took me a second to realize that it came from me. I arched my back, rocking my hips against him experimentally. Another moan escaped when I found out how freaking amazing that felt, and I did it again. Harder. Something inside me gathered really tightly in my stomach, radiating outward. He kept kissing me down there, making that pleasure tighten even more, until finally . . . *bam*.

It snapped.

I collapsed against the wall, breathing heavily, unable to put two thoughts together. But I was pretty sure this feeling rolling through my veins was the aftereffects of an orgasm— my very first one. And it was freaking incredible.

Breathing unevenly, I dragged a hand through my hair, laughing throatily. *"Scotty."* A wrapper crinkled, and I lifted my lids in time to see him rolling a condom that came from who knows where over his erection. His pants were gone, and so were his boxers. A little bit of fear trickled back in. I shoved my hair out of my face, sucked in a deep breath, and figured if I was going to talk, it was now or never. "I don't—"

"You're so damn sexy, waiting for me to fuck you." He wrapped his hand around the back of my neck again, pulling me close and resting his forehead on mine. "There are so many reasons I should stop right now, but I can't. Not unless you tell me to. Do you want me to stop, Sky?"

Resting my hands on his shoulders, I breathed him in. His arms were strong around me, reassuring, and the way he cradled me, as if he was protecting me—even from himself—made any doubt I had shut up and slink away to the back of the room where it belonged. I lifted his head so his mouth was a breath away from mine, and whispered, "No, I don't want you to stop. Kiss me."

A strangled sound escaped him, and he closed the distance between us, his mouth claiming mine again. His tongue slipped between my parted lips, and I was pretty sure I tasted myself on him as he stepped between my legs again, hauling me so I almost hung off the counter edge. The tip of his erection touched me intimately, and I sucked in a deep breath.

"Sky . . ." He whispered that nickname against my lips, kissing me again, nipping at my lower lip just enough to hurt a little bit. "Hold on tight, sugar."

I buried my hands in his hair, and nodded once.

Then he tilted me up, and slammed inside of me without another warning. A little bit of pleasure mixed with a lot of pain, and I cried out into his mouth. It felt like he'd ripped me in half, right in his kitchen, and with the size of him, some small part of me wondered if he *had*.

Scotty froze, his lips still pressed against mine, going hard. Slowly, he pulled back, his eyes narrow on me. "What the fuck was that?"

I forced a smile, and blinked back tears. Now that the

initial pain was over, he didn't feel so bad buried inside me. "Um . . . my hymen, I think?"

Murderous anger came over his expression, anger bringing color to his cheeks. "And you didn't think that was something you should have told me?"

"No?" I lifted my chin. "Yes? Maybe?"

"*Sky—*"

"This changes nothing," I said in a rush. "I wanted you, so I took you. End of story. It doesn't matter how many, or how few, men I had before you, just like I don't care how many women you had before me. It's *nothing*."

That muscle ticked again. "Bullshit. It damn well matters. Your first time should be special. It should be with someone you love. Not with . . . with . . ."

"You?"

He nodded once, not lifting his head. "Yeah. Not someone like me. I can't offer you anything, Sky. Just this." He tightened his grip on my legs. "This is all I have for you, and you deserve more, especially for your first time."

"But I wanted you, just this once." I cupped his cheeks, and he looked at me, his lips hard. "You're sexy, and covered in tattoos, and you make me want things no other man has made me want before. It's not some deeper meaning, or some way of telling you I want to be with you forever. I felt an attraction to you, and I acted on it. No one has to know, and nothing has to change, but please don't stop now. I'm dying to know what comes next."

He pushed into me a bit, sweat coating his forehead. "Are you sure?"

"I'm sure," I said, kissing him.

At first he stood there, not kissing me back, but then he let out a tortured groan, and he took control. His mouth tilted over mine, and he pulled out of me, stopping just shy of leaving me completely. Then, with a pump of his hips, he drove inside again, sending an even more intense bolt of pleasure through me. There was still a little bit of discomfort, but the pleasure far outweighed the pain at this point.

I gasped, digging my nails into his shoulders, and strained to get closer.

He broke the kiss off, asking breathlessly, "Is that okay? Does it hurt?"

"No, it doesn't hurt." I shook him slightly, torn between being happy he was concerned for me and pissed that he kept stopping when all I wanted was for him to make me come again. I'd gotten a small taste of the pleasure he could give me, and I needed *more*. "Do it again. Harder."

He nodded, swallowing, and moved inside me. "You're so damn tight, Sky. So—*shit*."

Something seemed to snap, and he growled as he pulled out, thrusting without mercy. He did that repeatedly, each time somehow managing to go deeper and harder. As I gasped for air and grasped for that peak of pleasure only he could give, he moved inside me, his hands roaming as he slammed into me, time and time again, driving me higher and higher until I wasn't sure if he'd ever bring me back down—and that was freaking fine.

I strained against him, my whole body getting tenser with each stroke of his erection. He groaned and reached between us, resting his fingers over my sensitive flesh and exerting pressure there. As he thrust again, I screamed, because the combination of both pleasures sent me shooting into the sky like a firework. And then I exploded into a million lights.

I thought that would be the end of it, but he kept going, moving faster as he sought his own pleasure. Watching him, *feeling* him get closer, amazingly sent me over the edge again, and this time, he was right there with me. He stiffened and collapsed until his forehead was on mine, breathing heavily. *"Sky."*

The way he said my name—all breathlessly low and sexy—made me shiver, and I nodded, even though he hadn't asked me anything. I clung to him, because if I didn't, I'd fall over, and he seemed to get that, because he pulled me against his chest, and didn't let go.

I closed my eyes, held in a breath, and then slowly released it. He pulled back, watching me cautiously. Almost like he expected me to self-combust or something now that we were done. He was probably worried I'd make this weird, since he was my first and everything.

"So . . . ?" he started.

I knew he was about to dive way too deeply into this, and the last thing I wanted to do was dissect what had been, for me, a beautiful thing. So I cut him off with a smile. "About that shower . . . I need a towel."

He frowned. "What?"

"That's why I came down. I needed a towel."

"Oh. Right." He glanced out the window, his profile hard and unyielding. "Sky . . ."

"Don't." I laughed, but it came out shrilly. "Nothing's changed from last night, when I told you I wanted you, and now. I was a virgin then, and I'm one now." My cheeks heated when I realized what I'd just said, with him *literally* still buried inside me. "Uh, I mean—"

"No, you're not." He caught my chin, watching me closely. "Not anymore."

I licked my lips. They still tingled from his kisses, and I swore I could still feel his mouth pressed to mine. As my tongue moved, he focused on it, his nostrils flaring.

"I know I'm not. Just like I know you don't do attachments." I pushed my hair off my face. "Luckily for you, I don't do them either."

He hesitated. "Why not?"

"Reasons that I prefer to keep my own." Things like my overprotective brother, and what would happen if my lover found out his secrets. "But, like I said, this changes nothing. It was just . . . fun."

He nodded slowly, staring at me like I'd grown an extra head or something. "You just wanted a one-night stand?"

"Yes." I shifted on the edge of the counter. It wasn't quite so comfortable now that we were no longer . . . you know. "We can still be friends, right?"

"But you were a virgin," he pointed out oh-so-helpfully.

"I *was*. Mostly to avoid a confrontation like this afterward," I said dryly. "At least that's done now."

He frowned even deeper. "So what comes next?"

"A shower," I said, smiling. "So . . . about that towel . . . where might I find one?"

He looked at me like he wanted to say something, like I'd angered him somehow, but ultimately he ended up shaking his head slightly and saying, "They're in the closet outside the bathroom. I'll show you, and I'll get the Motrin."

Hands on my hips, he pulled out of me slowly, his jaw flexing as he did so. It was the oddest sensation, having a man pull out of you after . . . *that*. It was sticky, sore, and somehow a little bit sad, because I knew this was the only time I'd get to feel him like this. He stepped back, shoving a hand through his hair, and headed for the trash can.

I couldn't stop staring at his naked butt.

As he removed the condom, he glanced over his shoulder at me, his gaze dipping over my body one last time, much like mine was doing to him. I slid off the edge of the counter, feeling incredibly vulnerable. Tucking my hair behind my ear, I rested an arm over my breasts.

There. Better.

Kind of.

He still stared at me, not moving, so I bit my lip, shifting my weight to my left leg. "What's wrong?"

He blinked, almost like he hadn't realized he'd been staring, then unbuttoned his shirt. I hadn't realized until now that he'd kept it on, while I'd been completely naked. He tossed it at me, and I caught it reflexively. "Nothing. It's just—you're beautiful, sugar. I hope you know it."

My cheeks heated, and my heart picked up speed, because he was looking at me like he wanted another round . . . or two. I pulled his shirt over my head, tugging it down to cover myself. It smelled like him, and I wrapped my arms around myself, breathing in his cologne. "Thank you. You're pretty good-looking yourself."

"Yeah." He gave me a lopsided grin. "And don't worry, I know it. I use it to my advantage every damn day."

I couldn't help but think that was a reminder to me not to get any ideas. I didn't know what to say, so I said nothing. He motioned for me to follow him and walked toward the stairs completely naked, and completely okay with that. I walked barefoot across the cool wood floor, watching his hard muscles flex with every step he took. It was crazy to think of it, but that man, that *body*, had been pressed up against mine, inside mine, just a few moments ago.

And that's when it hit me.

I'd done it. I'd actually *done* it.

I wasn't a virgin anymore, and I'd done something that was spontaneous, and fun, and kinda sorta crazy. And it felt . . . *weird*. But in a good way. In an *alive* way.

He opened the closet by the bathroom, and handed me a black towel. "Here you go."

I took it, my fingers touching his. "Thanks."

"You're welcome." Hesitantly, he reached out, brushing his knuckles against my cheek. "I think you're crazy to waste your first time on a guy like me, but I'm honored you did. I'll never forget you, Sky."

My chest ached as I remembered his words from last night. *I'd fuck you any way you wanted, and then I'd forget about you in the morning.* "I'll never forget you either."

Scotty nodded once, dropped his hand, and walked away.

His bathroom was a light blue and it had all-white utilities in it. The floors were laminate, and not so much as a stray comb lay on the pristine countertop of the sink. A container of cotton blossom soap stood by the hot water knob, and a hand towel hung on the wall beside it. Everything was so . . . *neat.* I touched the towel, and then turned on the water.

After I showered, I called a cab, and took the painkillers that he'd set on the counter for me. He'd also left the shirt of his I'd been wearing, along with a pair of sweats. I slipped into both, secretly happy that he'd left me this shirt, since it smelled like him. When I came out of the bathroom barefoot, I headed down the stairs. He was nowhere to be seen, and that was okay. I had a feeling he'd already said his last words, and if he followed through with his desire to be friends, then he'd contact me when he was ready. I sensed he wasn't the type of guy to say good-bye after a one-night stand. So the fact he'd given me one in his hallway was something special. Something real.

And honestly?

It was pretty much perfect.

Not wanting to ruin what we'd shared with another round

of why-did-you-pick-me, I scribbled a quick note for him on the notepad he'd left sitting on the nightstand in the guest bedroom, set it on the bed, and gathered my belongings. Then I walked out the door. As I walked toward the cab, I swore I could feel his gaze burning into me, leaving a permanent mark whether he meant to or not.

One only I could feel, but one that I'd never forget.

CHAPTER 9

SCOTTY

I stood behind Chris, hand on my gun, watching as he handed off the last of the AR-15s we were selling to the Moss Stones—another gang in Southie. They dealt mostly in stolen cars, chopping them or reselling, but they occasionally dabbled in drugs, too, which Bitter Hill wasn't very happy about. Chris's shoulders were stiff, and he looked seconds from jumping the guy who was handing him a wad of cash, but I wasn't sure why. So far the sale had been uneventful, and there were no signs of danger, cops, or duplicity.

Stepping closer, I watched him carefully, in case he did something stupid. But Chris didn't do stupid. It wasn't his style. Thank God for that . . . if He even existed.

I wasn't so sure anymore.

Once the money exchanged hands, I scanned the perimeter, in case feds came swooping in. Luckily, it was a routine sale, so I wouldn't have to deal with interagency cooperation today. After Skylar, and my role in taking her virginity, I wasn't exactly one hundred percent. She was on my mind, and I couldn't shake her.

And even worse?

I'd *fucked* her.

Chris slapped the cash against his palm, then tucked it into his brown leather jacket. As the Moss boys rolled off, he relaxed a bit, spitting on the ground. "Assholes."

I rubbed the back of my neck, forcing my mind off what I'd done to Skylar and back to the game. "Since when do you hate them so much?"

"One of them killed Molly's dad." Chris turned to me, his upper lip curled. "If I knew who, I'd take him down, but I don't, so I hate them all on principle, for her."

Molly was Chris's girlfriend, who was pretty much as opposite from Chris as you could get. She had no ties to this life, besides Chris, and taught kindergarten. Why she'd fallen in love with such a crazy asshole, I didn't have a damn clue. But I didn't understand love in the first place, so what the fuck ever.

"I can look into it, if you want. See if I can narrow down the playing field." I headed for Chris's Mustang, sliding my shades into place. "But would Molly want you to kill him, or would she want you to forgive him?"

Chris snorted. "I don't do forgiveness. I play better with bullets."

Yeah. Me too. Which was why what I'd done with Skylar this morning was screwing me up so much. The second I found out Agent Torres wanted me to use her for intel, I should have been strictly hands-off. But then . . . I'd gone and been her first lover.

Why? Why had she chosen *me*?

Chris settled in behind the wheel and stepped on the gas,

heading toward Tate's office for a meeting about the shooting yesterday. I had to face the brother of the girl I'd devirginized this morning. Then Agent Torres, to update him on my status with not only Bitter Hill, but with Skylar Daniels.

I was good at lying and keeping everything straight.

Right now, though, it all felt like way too damn much.

Skylar had mentioned last night that she sensed I was a man who played a part and never got to be himself. And, damn it, she'd been right. I wasn't sure how I felt about that.

"How'd the auction go last night?" Chris asked, glancing in the rearview as we stopped at a red light, his brown brows drawn tight. "Did you have to share a meal with a sixty-year-old woman groping your cock the whole time?"

I cleared my throat, only saying: "Not . . . exactly . . ."

He gave me the side-eye and stepped on the gas, turning left on Wescott. "Who was the lucky winner?"

"Tate's sister," I muttered. "She bid on me, and won. Don't tell him, though. She promised it would be between us, and I intend to keep it that way."

Chris's eyes widened. "You didn't . . ."

"Light's green," I pointed out dryly, avoiding his question that wasn't really a question.

"Did you fuck her?"

"Did you have sex with Molly last night?" I shot back.

Chris frowned. "That's none of your damn business."

"Just like who I fuck isn't yours." I rubbed the back of my neck.

"The hell it isn't." Chris stepped on the gas harder than necessary. "If Tate finds out—"

"He won't." I rested my fist on my knee, holding on tight. "There's nothing to find out."

"Are you sure about that?" he asked.

"Yes. There's nothing he needs to, or will, know about."
I tapped my fingers on the car door, unsure how much I
wanted to tell Chris, if anything at all. "We went to dinner
and had a few drinks, then it was done."

That much was true. He hadn't asked about this morning.

"And then you went home alone?" Chris asked, honing
right in on the omission like a damn hawk.

We pulled into the parking lot of the Sons' clubhouse. I
straightened, and dragged my hand through my hair to mess
it up more. ". . . I went to bed alone. Now relax, Father."

He pulled into a parking spot and shut off the ignition. I
could feel him watching me. "You forget I know you better
than them, Scotty. I know when you're lying."

"Well, in all fairness, you didn't know I was lying about
my profession until a few months ago." I opened my door
and slid out, shutting it behind me. I didn't wait for him to
catch up to me, just headed for the entrance. After I did the
Sons knock to announce our arrival, I reached for the doorknob, but Chris slammed a hand on the door, stopping me.
"Dude. What the hell is your problem?"

"You." He leaned in, hissing, "Your head isn't in the
game right now, man. Whatever's screwing you up, you
better fix it, before it screws *us*."

"My head is exactly where I need it to be. Now let go."

Chris shrugged. "Whatever. Just don't get us killed."

I ignored him, because it didn't matter that I was the DEA
agent and he was my informant; he would always think of me
as his best friend's little kid brother who needed his help to
keep his shit together. Nothing I said or did would change that.
The second his hand was off the door, I opened it and strode
inside, putting the same cocky swagger to my steps that had
secured me the part of the shitty brother all those years ago.

As I passed Brian, I clapped him on the shoulder. "Hey, man."

He gave me a nod. He was thirty, had dark blond hair and brown eyes, and was Tate's right-hand man. I liked him. He told it like he saw it, and there was no guesswork involved with him. He wasn't much of a ladies' man, despite his good looks. As far as I could tell from my background check on him, when he'd been twenty, he'd fallen in love and she'd left him. Since then, he'd kept to himself. Brian didn't seem like the type of guy to wallow over a woman his whole life, but then again, as stated, love didn't exactly make sense. "What's up, Little Donahue?"

I winced. I hated it when he called me that. "Lucas has been dead for months now. Think we could just switch to Donahue, or even Scott?"

"You mean Scotty?"

I gritted my teeth. "Just Scott."

"Nah." He rubbed his chin, considering me, picking up a glass of whiskey and taking a contemplative sip. "You're too young, too much of a baby, to be a Scott. It's Scotty, or Little Donahue."

Never mind that I was just a few years younger than him. "Suit yourself, man. Call me Pretty Woman, for all I care, as long as you share that whiskey with me."

He chuckled. "Yours is in the room, waiting at your spot."

"Excellent. How's life? Fuck any hot girls lately?"

Brian frowned, looking every inch the stick in the mud. He held a hand out. "Phone. Hand it over."

"Yes, sir." I reached into my back pocket and pulled my cell phone out. I'd left my personal phone at home. "Did you talk to your date like that last night? Did she like it?"

"Just because I like you doesn't mean I'm above kicking

your ass." He tossed my phone on top of Frankie's. "Arms up."

I grinned, letting Brian feel me up for wires. They wouldn't find any. DEA was smarter than that. Our technology had far surpassed wires years ago, no matter what you saw on the TV shows and movies. "Oooh. That felt good." I paused. "Did she say that, too? If not, you're doing it all wrong, man."

"Fuck off, Little Donahue." He pointed over his shoulder at Tate's office. "Go in. We've been waiting for you and Chris to finally show up so we can start."

Chris came up behind me, as if on cue. "I heard that."

I scanned the room, looking for what held him up, but it didn't take an agent to figure it out. His asshole father stood in the corner of the room, glowering. Mr. O'Brien had wanted Chris to kill me and Lucas, and claim Lucas's spot as a leader at the round table.

Instead, Chris chose to share it with me.

I waved at the asshole, forcing a carefree grin, and headed for the meeting room. As I approached, I took a deep breath, rolled my shoulders, and walked in. Tate stood at his spot, talking to Frankie, their heads together as they whispered. Tommy sat at his seat, a glass of whiskey in his hand, frowning. A newer lieutenant, Jamie, sat beside him, tapping his fingers on the table as he surveyed the occupants.

I nodded at Jamie as I passed, and took my spot next to him. The seat next to me would be Chris's. Tate saw me and stared, his gaze skeptical. I couldn't tell if he was about to kill me, thank me, or ignore me. He was as unpredictable as his sister. I nodded at him once, and he turned away, speaking to Frankie again. Frankie glanced at me, and nodded.

Shit.

I picked up my whiskey, lifting it to my lips. They were talking about me. The question was . . . why? Frankie looked back at Tate, said one more thing to him, and then came over to his seat on the other side of Chris's chair, thumping my shoulder as he passed. "Sup, Scotty boy?"

"Not much."

He sat down, leaning back and stretching, letting out a long groan as he did so. "Have a good night last night? You cut out of the funeral early."

"I had somewhere to be," I said carefully, glancing at Tate. He watched me too closely for comfort. I didn't need this kind of scrutiny from a jealous brother right now—which was all the more reason I should have kept my damn hands to myself. "Why? Did I miss something important?"

"Nah." He rolled his shoulders. "Just the typical funeral stuff. Crying. Silence. Dead dude in a coffin, going into the ground, and getting a bunch of dirt thrown over him."

It might sound cavalier, his attitude toward one of our fallen men, but when you were surrounded by death, and caused it more often than not, you had to look at it in whatever way helped you sleep at night. I didn't begrudge him that. "I figured."

"You chasing a hot piece of ass last night, like usual?"

I shrugged, avoiding Tate's eyes. "Something like that."

"Of course."

Chris came into the room, beelining right for me. He nodded at Frankie as he sat. "Hey, man. How's the Charger?"

"Getting there." Frankie's eyes lit up, and a piece of blond hair fell on his forehead at the mention of his baby—his '67 burnt orange Charger. The car was older than its owner by twenty years, but was in impeccable shape. "I just got my new exhaust in. Want to lend me a hand slapping that baby on?"

"That was more Luc's thing than mine," Chris said, crossing his ankle over his knee. "But I can try, man."

Only I saw the pain flash across his expression as he lowered his head and remembered his best friend—my brother—and only I knew the full reason for that sadness. However, Lucas was now happily living out his life with Heidi Green in hiding. Instead of wallowing in guilt, he should try being happy for Lucas instead. As far as the gang knew, Lucas was dead.

I'd made sure of it.

He was free, in a way none of *us* would ever be.

"Thanks." Frankie tipped his head toward Tate, who sat down beside Brian and tugged on his tie. Tate was the only one who wasn't wearing the dark brown leather Sons of Steel Row coat. "Looks like we're about to start."

Tate sat, resting his hands on the table. He was twenty-nine, only a few years older than me, but he commanded a presence that made him seem older. He wore his authority as well as I wore my charming-younger-brother role. "Bitter Hill came at us when we were down, and I won't let this go unanswered. We claimed this part of the city as our own, and didn't see the snakes creeping into our midst until it was too late. We gave them guns, and helped them grow, and now they're attacking us on *our* ground. It started with Lucas Donahue, and it will end with the attack on Gus's funeral. It's time to take down Bitter Hill, for good."

Everyone around the table nodded, including me. I wanted them taken down as much as Tate did, though for different reasons. I had a dream, a ridiculous one, of making Steel Row clean again. My mother had tried to give us a life full of promise and happiness and goddamn unicorns, despite the fact that our father didn't give a damn about us. I wanted to turn this town back into a place where people could dream, without nightmares chasing them.

Tate pointed at the table once the nods and voices of agreement calmed down. "We need to go back to the plan Chris came up with, from before we thought everything had cooled on both sides. We need to attack them on their home turf, like they dared to do to us. And we need to hit them harder than they hit us."

He was right.

We needed to reestablish our power over Bitter Hill, and destroy them.

Once Agent Torres heard that we were planning to attack, the DEA would start to plan their own operation. When it was all over, there would be nothing left of Bitter Hill. Their days of drug running and ruining innocent lives would be over.

For all Steel Row's crimes, we kept to ourselves, and we didn't hurt those who didn't deserve it. It was our code. Yet if the DEA could take down two gangs in one swoop . . .

They certainly wouldn't say *no*.

Which is what had me so damn uneasy about this whole mess.

Logically, I knew these men were criminals. They would pull a trigger without hesitation, and they'd kill me if they found out the truth. Yet I still felt a loyalty to the Sons that I couldn't shake, no matter how hard I tried. They'd given Lucas a home, a job, and it had allowed him to provide for me, which was extremely important to him after Ma died.

They'd saved us.

And I didn't want to take them down.

Chris pulled out the map he'd made and we studied the

layout of the Bitter Hill clubhouse. By the time the sun started to set, we had a plan—block off the back door, set a fire, and cut down the survivors as they ran out the front door. I could just picture the paperwork now, and I made my own plans to get clearance from Agent Torres to pull the trigger if need be. I was encouraged not to take men down if I didn't have to, but if I had to choose between one of my brothers dying and one of those assholes—

There was no choice.

I might be DEA, but I was a Son, too.

If it came time to choose between the two parts of my life, I knew what I'd choose—but it wouldn't be easy. It would tear me the hell apart.

I'd never be put back together again.

"I've got a guy," Chris said, rubbing the back of his neck. "I'll make sure they're still doing their mandatory meetings on the second Fridays of the month. If they are, then it'll be a full house."

"Perfect," Tate agreed, cracking a rare smile. "So . . . we wait two weeks."

"Patience will pay off in the end," Frankie agreed. "If anyone—*anyone*—comes out of there, we shoot. No questions asked," Frankie said, staring at each of us in turn.

Brian shifted, and ran his hands through his blond hair. "Even women?"

"If they're there, then they deserve it." Frankie looked harder than I'd ever seen him. Colder, too. This war had brought out a side of him I'd never known. "After all, they had no qualms taking out Lucas's side piece when they—"

Tate shook his head, cutting Frankie off without a word. "I appreciate the sentiment, but I can't agree with that. We're not monsters, and we won't take down innocent people."

I eyed Tate with new respect. He might be the head of a

gang, but the man had morals. And that was more than you could say for half the agents I knew. "Seconded."

"Third," Chris said.

Brian nodded. "Fourth."

"Fifth." Tommy winced. "Sorry, man, but I'm not shooting a chick."

"And that's enough to be vetoed." Frankie stood. "Looks like I'm outnumbered, then."

"Good thing you're such an understanding guy." Tate clapped him on the back. "All right. It's settled. Chris, check with your guy in Bitter Hill, make sure they're all going to be at that meeting in two weeks. If the intel is good . . . we attack at 8:03, just because that's a weird time no one will suspect."

There was a general sound of assent, and slowly the men cleared out, one by one. I nodded at Chris, and then we made our way to the door together.

I only made it two steps before:

"Donahue?" Tate called out.

I stiffened in response. "Yeah, boss?"

"I need a minute."

Chris side-eyed me and whispered, "Again?"

"Wait for me in the bar," I muttered, turning to face Tate with a carefree grin I wasn't really feeling. "Sure thing, sir."

The door shut, and it was just me and Tate. Funny how the man barely paid any attention to me before yesterday—and now he wouldn't leave me the hell alone. It was like he sensed I'd betrayed him, and fucked his baby sister in my kitchen. I wouldn't put it past him.

He was good.

Too good.

"How did things go last night?" he asked, pouring himself some more whiskey. "With the auction?"

I crept closer, shoving my hands in my pockets, trying my best to look as innocent as possible. "Good. A lot of money was raised for the charity. Your sister seemed pleased."

"Did she?" he asked curiously, offering me a glass of whiskey. "Did you speak to her last night?"

I took the drink, forcing my expression to remain bland. "For a bit, yeah. I introduced myself, told her I was there to fill in. She seems like a good kid."

"She is." Tate sat. I didn't. After all, he didn't invite me to. "I spoke with her earlier. She had nothing but good things to say about you. Said you brought in the most money, and were quite polite, and a perfect gentleman at all times."

My grip tightened on the glass. His gaze dipped down, so I forced myself to chill the hell out, and hoped it wasn't too late. "I tried my best, sir."

"Clearly you succeeded."

I shifted on my feet. "Would that be all, sir?"

"No. We've got credible intel that Bitter Hill is planning an attack on our loved ones, to strike us in the worst way possible. I've done a good job at hiding her from everyone, clearly, but she's my sister, and we see each other often enough I can't help but worry . . ." Tate chugged his whiskey and set the glass down. "I can't rule out the possibility they might have put two and two together."

Doubtful, since the DEA had never done so, and we were a hell of a lot smarter than Bitter Hill. Still, I understood his concern. I finished my drink with one swallow, but I held on to it. "Did you put some guards on her?"

"Yeah. Some guys I hired are watching the building." He tapped his chin. "But it's not enough. I want someone watching over her more closely than that."

I stiffened, knowing where this was going but hoping like hell I was wrong. "Sir?"

"She's alone in her apartment, without a roommate. I want someone inside the building with her." He pinched the bridge of his nose. "Someone like . . . you."

Well, shit. "What, exactly, are you asking, sir? You want me to sleep at her place as her—?"

"Hell no." He sat up straight, looking murderous.

"Okay, sir," I managed to say through my confusion.

He reached into his pocket and tossed a metal key at me. I caught it easily, frowning down at it. "I have a second apartment in her complex. It's right next to hers, and the walls are thin. I didn't want some lowlife asshole moving in next to her, so I rented it out myself."

I laughed uneasily. "Seriously?"

"Yes." He narrowed his eyes on me, clearly not giving a damn that he took the protective-brother role to a whole new level. "I want you to stay there, and watch over her. Don't talk to her, or draw attention to her. Just . . . watch."

Annnnnd here we go again.

It was coming at me from all angles.

I closed my fist around the gold key, its edges digging into my palm. Agent Torres would be ecstatic over this turn of events, because it would get me even closer to Skylar. Me? I felt nauseous. "Why me, sir? Why not any of the other older, more experienced men?"

"I'm not saying I don't trust the Sons, but . . ." He shrugged. "Are you trying to tell me I shouldn't place my faith in you, Donahue?"

"No. Absolutely not."

I left it at that.

"Good." He stood, smoothing his unwrinkled jacket. "221B. If she notices you and asks questions, tell her you're new to the area, and a short-term renter, but don't encourage her to be chatty. We don't want to draw attention to her. It's best if she doesn't see you at all, so try for that."

I nodded, setting my empty glass down. "Yes, sir. Anything else I need to know?"

"Never come straight from here to there, or vice versa, in case you're being followed. Play it safe." He tugged on his tie, watching me through his lashes. "And my earlier warning stands, of course. Don't touch her, or I'll kill you."

Does it count if I already did? I held my hands up. "Of course not, sir."

"Good." He made a shooing motion with his hand. "Off you go, then. I'll expect texts updating me every few hours, so I know she's okay."

Greeeat. "Yes, sir."

CHAPTER 10

SKYLAR

It had been two days since I went home with Scotty Donahue and lost my virginity. Two days of sleepless nights, lonely hours in bed, and a lot of longing on my part. While he . . . *he* was probably already two or three girls past me by now. He wasn't the type to pine away, or to try and keep a memory alive by keeping his penis firmly tucked inside his pants.

Which had brought me to this moment . . . with this guy. Steven, a boy I'd just met a few hours ago, smiled at me as we walked up the stairs to my condo complex. I smiled back, but glanced away quickly, my heart pounding. Not out of excitement, or lust, or anything even half as promising as that. No, it was pounding because I felt absolutely nothing for him.

I'd taken chemistry, and learned all about attraction and molecules, but this? Yeah. There was none of that. No pheromones. No pull. No chemistry.

He might as well be my brother.

I'd met him at the coffee shop near campus, where I'd been studying for my upcoming Advanced Neurological Sciences test. He'd come up to me and started flirting, opening with something about the brain and the most recent scientific research behind it all, and since I was feeling sorry for myself, I'd tried to keep an open mind. When he'd asked if I wanted to continue this discussion over a meal, I'd said yes . . .

Even though I didn't mean it.

In my mind, I was trying to enjoy the newfound sexual freedom I had, attempting to find another man who made me feel the way Scotty had. It was a fruitless search.

Clearly, my first instinct with him had been correct. We had an undeniable chemistry between us that couldn't be replicated, no matter how hard I tried. Still, I'd brought Steven home anyway, so the least I could do was try to forget about those green eyes and that wavy red hair, since I'd never be seeing them again.

"I'm right over here," I called over my shoulder, leading him up to the second floor, trying my best to keep my tone flirty. "221A."

"You live there alone?" he asked slowly, glancing over his shoulder. "No roommate or anything?" Suddenly, something about him felt . . . off. Damn Tate and his millions of lectures about the dangers of bringing strange guys home. "No boyfriend . . . ?"

I stopped outside my white wood door. "I have a brother." I glanced at 221B, which had been empty for as long as I'd lived here. ". . . and a very protective neighbor." I tapped my knuckles on the door gently, smiling. "Right here. Next to me. He watches over me."

Steven frowned and rested a hand on the wall, leaning

close to me, smiling. "Well, then, we'll have to be sure to be quiet. We wouldn't want an angry neighbor barging in, now would we?"

Actually . . . "I—"

Before I could come up with something to say, Steven lowered his face to mine and kissed me, pressing me backward against the door. I gasped, caught off guard, and he took advantage of the opening to slip his tongue inside my mouth. I placed my hands on his chest, giving him a second to woo me, or to blow my metaphorical panties off like Scotty had done. It wasn't awful, and he tasted nice, but it was about as pleasurable as a root canal. There was no wooing.

And my panties weren't going anywhere.

Unfortunately.

I pushed at his chest, but he just strained to get closer instead of getting the message. Turning my head to the side, I gasped for air and pushed harder. He latched on to my neck instead, sucking on it. "St-stop."

He froze, pulling back. He looked irritated, but he stopped trying to kiss me, even if he didn't let me go yet. "Is something wrong?"

"No, but I—" The door to 221B swung open, and then, as if by some weird twist of fate, Scotty Donahue stood there, looking tall, and handsome, and one hundred percent pissed off. For a second I thought I was hallucinating, but there was nothing fictional about the anger burning in those green eyes. "Scotty?"

Scotty frowned at the man who still held me, though in his defense, Steven was probably pretty distracted by the huge guy looking at him like he wanted to skin him alive; a man that he, more than likely, assumed was my overprotective neighbor. The one I'd made up.

"Is there a problem here?" Scotty asked slowly, his tone harder than a diamond.

Steven immediately released me. "No, man. No problem at all. I was just leaving."

"Excellent." He lifted a hand and wiggled his fingers. "Bye."

Steven practically ran off, and then we were alone in the hallway. I clutched my purse to my chest, and stared at him. He wore a pair of ripped jeans, a blue T-shirt, and a dark brown leather jacket. He looked dangerous, sexy, and angry.

At what?

I had a feeling I was about to find out. "What—?" I licked my dry lips, and took a step closer. "What are you doing here?"

"What are *you* doing here?" he shot back.

"I live here. You don't—"

"Who the hell was that asshole?" he growled, fisting his hands at his sides. I glanced down, and sure enough, he was slowly releasing his fingers, one at a time. So . . . definitely angry, then. "Did you even know him before you brought him home?"

"No . . ." I lifted my chin. "But I didn't really know you either, when I went home with you. And that turned out okay, if you ask me."

"Why did you bring him here? Why did you let him kiss you?"

I blinked. "Shouldn't it be clear what I was after?"

"Humor me," he growled.

"Okay . . . ?" I answered slowly, thrown off by what, for all intents and purposes, seemed to be jealousy. Which made no sense. Not coming from a guy like Scotty, who was a self-professed player who never double dipped—*and why was he here?* "I was hoping he'd kiss me, and make me feel good. I was hoping I'd want to do more than kiss him. I was hoping . . ."

One step closer, and his jaw ticked. "You were hoping *what*?"

"I was hoping he'd make me forget all about you, if we're being one hundred percent honest with each other." I lifted my chin. "Are we? Being honest?"

"You want to find out?" He released the last finger, and walked toward me, looking like he was seconds from jumping me, kissing me . . . or jumping me to kiss me. "Open your door. *Now*."

I turned, fumbling with the key as I slid it inside the lock. The second I opened the door, he was guiding me through it, shutting us in together, and locking it. He backed me up against the wall, pressing his body against mine, and caught my wrists in one of his hands, trapping them over my head. "You want to forget me, Sky? Want to get me off your mind?"

A small moan escaped me, and my pulse surged as my blood heated. And *there* it was. The lust, the attraction, I'd been so desperately seeking with Steven. Liquid warmth pooled in my belly, and my legs trembled, and I licked my parched lips. "I—"

"You can't forget me that easily, sugar." He slid his hand under my skirt, and up my thigh, stopping just short of where I ached for him most. I wasn't sure whether to be angry, relieved, or to cry. He lowered his forehead to mine, and his warm breath touched my lips. "Wanna know why?"

I nodded, not speaking, just letting out a ragged breath.

He crept his hand higher, running the side of his thumb over my folds, through the thin satin of my panties, which were now damp with my desire. "I'm gonna let you in on a little secret. One you can't tell anyone."

I waited, holding my breath as he traced my clitoris, teasing me with his barely there caresses. "Yeah?"

"There's been no one else since you." He scraped the side of his thumb over me. "I can't get you off my mind, and I can only think of one way to fix that. We need to fuck again. Get it out of our systems." His grip on me tightened. "I need you, sugar."

A groan escaped me, and I tilted my head back, staring up at the high white ceilings of the apartment. "Am I supposed to be flattered you want more?"

"No, if anything it should make you run. I never want more."

I said nothing.

He wasn't done.

"I can't stop thinking about you, and when I'm alone in bed, I jack off and pretend I'm with you," he said, his voice gritty and rough and oh-so-sexy. "I can't stop thinking about how amazing your tight pussy felt clamped around my cock, or fantasizing about how sweet you tasted, like sugar. Do you still taste that good? Are you still sweet? I need to know."

I lifted my chin, stopping just short of kissing him, even though I could have easily closed the distance between us. He's the one who had been adamant about not wanting more than one-night stands in his life. If he wanted another taste . . . he'd have to be the one to push for more. "Why don't you find out? *I dare you.*"

He let out a broken moan, and within a second of me issuing the biggest challenge of my life, his lips were on mine and he was showing me what a kiss *really* was. There was no hesitation as he slid his tongue into my mouth, washing away any memory of Steven's mediocre kiss. His hand was still wrapped around my wrists, and his other hand pushed my panties out of the way so he could slide a finger in between my folds, spreading my wetness out over my clitoris. When he pressed a thumb against me, teasing me, and thrust a finger inside my depths, I gasped and rocked my hips forward, trying to get more.

To *feel* more.

His mouth moved over mine, stealing my breath and all rational thought, until all that was left was Scotty, and how deliciously erotic he made me feel. It was like he had the power to make me forget about everything but pleasure the second he touched me.

Growling, he stopped his torture and lifted me up so he could step between my legs, thrusting his erection against me as he deepened the kiss. He'd let go of my hands, so I buried them in his hair, pulling on it as I strained to get closer. I had a feeling I'd never get close enough, never get enough, of him. Ever.

That was a *scary* feeling.

And thrilling.

He closed his palm over my breast, squeezing my nipple, sending a shaft of need piercing through me. I skimmed my fingers down his muscular back, remembering how hard he'd looked as he led me upstairs naked, and how I'd been so sure I would never get to see him again.

Yet, here he was.

Kissing me all over again.

He broke off the kiss, his lips moving down my jaw, over my throat, and to my collarbone. He let out a tortured groan as I rolled my hips against him. "Jesus, you're even sweeter than I remembered."

I opened my mouth to reply, but then he yanked my shirt down, shoved my bra out of the way, and closed his mouth over my nipple. Whatever words I would have said came out in a jumbled moan, and I threaded my hands through his hair, urging him closer.

The last time we'd had sex, it was fast and hurried, and I'd assumed this time would be as well, considering how we'd started. But now . . .

He scraped his teeth against me, and I cried out, arching my back as he rocked his erection against me, driving me mad. I thought he'd sent me over the abyss of pleasure before, but having his mouth touch me everywhere . . . there was something erotic and forbidden about it. He released my nipple and yanked my shirt over my head, throwing it aside. Within seconds, my bra was off, too, and his hands were free as he held me in place against the wall with his hips.

He tore his shirt off, muscles twisting and flexing as he stripped it away. All that black ink . . . I traced the Sacred Heart on his chest, barely touching his skin. I hadn't really gotten the chance to explore him that night, and I ached to get to know every inch of his body intimately. Every muscle, every hollow, every piece of artwork.

Even the one that claimed him as a gang member.

I kept trying to ignore that he used to be a criminal, kept telling myself he'd changed his life for the better, but knowing he'd once walked down that path, and maybe killed people . . .

It was terrifying.

But people could, and did, change.

I had to believe that.

Leaning in, I pressed my lips to the heart, breathing in his scent. He sucked in a breath and held it, standing completely still. "Sky . . ."

"May I . . . ?" I trailed my fingers over his pecs, and down to his six-pack . . . stopping at the waistband of his jeans, where I was pressed against him.

His brow shot up. "May you what?"

"Explore." I licked my lips, running my hands back up where I came from, dragging my palms over his nipples. The veins in his neck stood out, and he stiffened. "You. All of you. I want my turn."

"So polite, so proper." He cupped my ass, and stepped back, lowering me to the floor slowly. "Do your worst, Sky."

Biting down on my lip, I stepped closer, learning the feel of his skin, of his body pressed to mine. I held on to him for support, because my heart was racing, and I couldn't catch my breath as the room spun around us. When my fingers drifted lower again, I hesitated at his waistband, gripping the button and glancing up at him questioningly.

He held on to my hips, like he sensed my need for something grounding, and nodded once. "Go ahead. Do it."

I undid the button, carefully unzipping his pants. His huge erection pressed against the confines of his jeans, and his hold on me tightened as my knuckles brushed against him. I slid my hand in his jeans, brushing my fingers down his thighs as I pushed them off him. They hit the floor with a *thud* and he stood in tight black boxer briefs.

It was, hands down, the sexiest thing I'd ever seen.

Him standing there, waiting for me to "do my worst."

Knowing I needed to get out of my shell, I cupped his erection, testing the feel of him in my palm. He was huge and hard, and I ached to feel him without the fabric in my way. He gritted his teeth and thrust into my hand, his cheeks flushed. "You're going to kill me, sugar. Are you satisfied yet?"

"I've barely even started," I said breathlessly.

"Shit."

I pulled back, stepping away so I could admire him. He watched me, body hard, jaw harder. I made a circle around him, taking in the rear view, too, skimming my fingers over his back as I walked. He had a green-eyed dragon climbing up his spine, the green being the only hint of color on him.

I touched it.

"This one's nice," I murmured.

"It's for my brother." He turned his head, studying me. "Lose the skirt."

I came around the front of him, smiling slightly. Gripping the waist, I pulled it down, standing there in nothing more than a pair of pink panties. "Better?"

"Almost." He pulled me into his arms so our bare bodies touched. My nipples brushed against his chest hair, and I gasped, resting my hands on his shoulders. "Look, sugar, I wanna give you what you want. But I don't know how long I can stand there, letting you look at me. I'll be damned if I waste another second denying myself something I want. I'm not that kind of guy."

"Fine," I said quickly. "One more thing?"

He nodded jerkily. "You've got thirty seconds until I take over again."

I dropped to my knees, like he'd done the other day, and turned my face up to his. Sliding his boxers down, my mouth dropped open when I was literally face level with his erection. I skimmed my fingers over him. It was a weird sensation, his skin on mine. He was hard, yet smooth, and soft, but stiff.

Which made no sense at all.

Closing my fist over him, I slid it down his shaft, squeezing the base gently. "You like?"

He let out a short laugh. "Yeah, I fucking *like*."

I rose up on my knees, leaning in. After one last peek at him, I flicked my tongue over the tip of his erection, wanting to taste him like he'd tasted me. I wrapped my mouth around him and sucked, rolling my tongue over the head of his shaft and relaxing my throat to take all of him in.

I discovered I had an excellent gag reflex.

He groaned and grabbed my hair, tugging. "Jesus," he croaked, his voice raw and sexy as hell. When I wrapped my mouth around the base of his erection, he let out a strangled groan that kind of sounded like he was dying. *"Sky.* What—*oh God."*

I slid up his shaft, almost letting go, and then took him inside my mouth again, sucking harder. "Son of a bitch fucker shit . . ." He let out a long groan, his fingers latching on to my hair and pulling insistently. "Enough. Shit, enough, Sky."

I released him reluctantly, rocking back on my heels and wiping my mouth with the back of my hand. "But—"

"Thirty seconds are up," he growled, urging me up by the hair. I followed his lead, wincing slightly when I didn't move fast enough. "Where the hell did you learn how to do that?"

"Instinct?" I offered helpfully. "Also, lots of romance books, and one unfortunate incident where I tried it out in real life."

His grip on my hair tightened, and he pulled me closer until I was wrapped in his arms. "Why was it unfortunate?"

"He came all over himself, and passed out," I said in a rush. "It was sloppy, and gross, and I didn't get a turn like he promised."

He snorted. "After finding out what you can do, I don't blame the asshole for passing out happily—though he should have returned the favor first." He frowned, eyeing me curiously. "Though, I'll be honest. I don't like the idea of you with another guy like this. I was supposed to be your first."

"You were my first."

He lifted a shoulder. "Not in *that*."

I mimicked him, and raised a brow. "And you were a virgin before me? Never even went down on a girl before? Never had sex?"

His nostrils flared. "It's not the same thing."

"The hell it's not," I said, anger starting to pierce through the lust cloaked over me. "Just because I'm a—"

"Okay, you're right. *Shit*." He gently pulled on my hair until my chin pointed up and my neck was bared. "I'm a jealous asshole, and I'm sorry."

I stared at him, not accepting his words.

Not rejecting them either, but still . . .

"I take it all back. I was being a prick, something I'm unbelievably good at, as you'll find out firsthand. Forgive me?"

He ran a finger down my neck, all the way to my nipple, tracing a circle around the hard bud. Gently, he grasped it, squeezing and twisting in a way that made me forget all about what we'd been fighting over in the first place.

I bit back a moan, still not speaking.

He released my hair, and I collapsed against the wall, resting my palms against it for support. I watched him from lowered lids as he bent and pulled a condom out of his pocket. God, did he just carry those around at all times, in case someone threw herself at him?

Chances were women did.

All the time.

As he rolled the condom into place, his hands on his erection made my stomach clench tight as I remembered when I'd found him in the bathroom . . . touching himself while thinking of me. He'd done it in bed, too. So had I, but it hadn't given me the pleasure *he* had.

I had a sinking suspicion nothing could.

After he finished, he took a step toward me, somehow making even that undeniably sexy. "I know how to sweeten the deal. How to make you forgive me."

"Oh yeah?" I managed to ask, my gaze locked on his thick erection. It had a blue vein running up the side of it that I ached to trace with my tongue. "How?"

"Like this."

He grabbed my thigh, tossed it over his shoulder, and gripped my panties. With a jerk of his hand, he ripped them in half, and they hit the floor. Before I could so much as gasp, his mouth was on me, and my gasp turned into a groan. His tongue rolled over me, jabbing at my sensitive flesh. Pleasure coiled in my belly, bunching into a tight ball, and I dug my heel into his back, rocking my hips against his mouth wantonly. "Oh my—*Scotty*."

He palmed my butt, digging his fingers into the flesh there as he thrust his tongue inside me, growling deep in his throat. His teeth scraped my flesh, and when his tongue teased me again, I lost it. Everything inside of me coiled so tight it broke. The second I collapsed against the wall, chest heaving, he was on his feet, and his mouth was on mine.

His tongue curled around mine as he slapped his erection against my sensitive flesh, and I soared into the sky again, and I came harder than before . . . which I didn't think was possible. But it was. God, it was. I trembled and dug my fingers into his back, right above his hips, lifting my leg. He took my silent command, hoisted me against the wall again, and slid between my thighs.

He froze, seconds from driving inside me, and pulled back. His nostrils flared, and then he said something that blew my mind even more than his actions did, which was saying a heck of a lot. "I never take risks that won't pay off. I never threaten everything I've worked so damn hard for on a night of pleasure. But with you, I can't seem to help myself, or stop, even though I know you might end up getting me killed. And I don't know what to do about that . . . besides this."

I blinked. *Killed? Why would I get him—?*

He thrust into me, destroying that thought and the confusion that went with it, until I didn't remember anything but this. Him. Inside me. God, I'd missed it. It might have only been two days since I'd had him, but it felt like a lifetime. I was still a little tender, but the pain was manageable, barely there. The pleasure outrode it by far. *"Scotty."*

He cupped my head, holding me tenderly as his lips closed over mine, claiming me as his, even if he didn't know it. He moved, his hips rotating smoothly as he slammed into me, pulled out, and did it all over again. I wrapped my legs around him tightly, gasping into his mouth touching mine, his tongue moving in tandem with his hips. Everything he did, every move he made, was specifically designed to drive me crazy, and he was a genius at pulling at all my strings.

I couldn't breathe.

Couldn't think.

Couldn't . . .

By the time I came again, my body was humming with need, and all that pleasure just kind of exploded as I came, his name on my lips. He made a low, primitive sound, thrust into me one more time, and his whole body pressed against mine harder as he rode out his orgasm, too. When it was finished, his lips froze over mine, and his hands skimmed the curve of my thigh and hip gently one last time.

He let out a long breath before breaking contact.

When he looked at me, he glanced over my body, taking his time. By the time our gazes caught, my pulse was racing just as fast as before. I held my breath, waiting for him to say something impossibly hot and sexy, like he had before. Something that would make me tingle and want more, even as I forgot everything he said the second his lips touched mine. Or maybe he'd make excuses and leave.

My father—the man who was supposed to love me no matter what—had sworn that I wasn't his, and he'd walked away and never looked back, so what would stop Scotty from doing the same?

What would stop any man from doing the same?

He opened his mouth, closed it, and then said, *"Again."*

CHAPTER 11

SCOTTY

We collapsed on the bed together, breathing heavily, her sprawled across my chest, naked, and looking like some kind of goddess. Me, naked, trembling, weak from exertion, yet no less attracted to her. The early morning sunlight streamed in through the curtains, playing with her strawberry blonde hair, and I reached out to touch a curl hesitantly, in awe of her and the way she made me feel. Her hair was soft between my fingers, and slightly damp with sweat, which wasn't a huge surprise, since we'd started fucking last night and hadn't really stopped since. I was trying to bang her out of my system . . .

And failing miserably.

The more I had her, the deeper the craving went.

I didn't get that. Didn't understand what it *meant*.

I twisted her curl around my finger, frowning. I never stayed in bed after sex, and I sure as hell didn't play with a girl's hair. The only time I touched it was when I needed to yank on it to make her come. That was about it. I dropped the curl immediately, and glanced at the clock on the wall. "Shit."

She lifted her face, resting her chin on my chest. "What?"

"I have to go to work." In half an hour, I was due to meet with my team and Agent Torres about Bitter Hill, and I had to wash last night off before I went. "I gotta go."

"Wait." She licked her plump, pink lips, and placed a hand on my shoulder. "Can I ask you something first?"

I stiffened. Here it was. She was going to ask me if this meant something, if I was sticking around, all because I came back for more. Despite sleeping with her all night long, I was still hard with desire for her. She was like an all-natural version of Viagra, and if she didn't knock it off, I'd have to seek medical care—because she'd get me killed. And I'd have no one to blame but myself.

"Fine," I said, my voice harder than I intended. "What is it?"

"Nothing . . . just . . . Why are you living next door suddenly?" she asked, eyeing me cautiously.

Oh. No reason at all. Your brother asked me to guard you from a murderous gang we're trying to take down. "My house is getting fumigated, and my—"

She blinked. "*Fumigated?* For what?"

"Termites. Just started. Getting it right at the beginning of the invasion, thank God." I scratched the back of my head. "My buddy was traveling, and he said I could stay at his place while my house was taken care of, so it worked out nicely."

"No one lives there."

I shrugged. "He just bought it. Doesn't move in until next month."

"So there's no furniture over there?"

"There's some." I shrugged. "Enough. He had it delivered the day of the auction when you went home with me, which was probably why you didn't see it, or know you were getting a neighbor. I had no idea you lived here until you knocked on my door last night. When I saw you and that guy, the rest is history."

She studied me for a second, pursing her lips, then looked away, sitting up, letting go of the hold she had on me. "I . . . see."

I slid off the bed, bending over and grabbing my boxers. I'd put them on at some point throughout the night, and they'd come right the hell back off shortly thereafter. As I stepped into them, I watched her, taken aback that she hadn't mentioned the elephant in the room—me and my return to her arms, when I'd sworn I wouldn't ever sleep with the same woman twice.

Didn't she have questions?

Questions about the future?

Expectations I couldn't fill?

She hopped off the bed and grabbed a robe, shrugging into it seductively. The thing was, though, on any other woman, it would have just been a chick putting on a robe. She didn't even try, but she looked sexy as hell doing pretty much everything. I couldn't wrap my brain around it, or the strange hold she had on me. I stepped into my jeans, lowering my head. "You okay?"

"Yeah, why wouldn't I be?" she asked, sitting back down on her bed and rolling socks up her leg. "Should I *not* be okay for some reason?"

I stopped and stared, watching her cover her ankles and calves with the blue knit fabric. I stared at her ankles—her goddamn *ankles*, for Christ's sakes—for longer than I should have before I snapped myself the hell out of it. "No."

"Okay." She finished putting her socks on, and gathered her hair in her hand, pushing it over her shoulder and spinning to face me. She hugged her knees and rested her chin on top, offering me a small smile. "Last night was fun. Thanks."

I stared at her.

That was *all* she had to say?

Last night was fun. Thanks.

I buttoned my pants, feeling irrationally angry but not really knowing why. She was doing exactly what I wanted her to do. Not asking for more. Not looking at me with warm, needy eyes. Not asking me to stay. And yet . . . "Yeah. It was."

She stared at me.

I frowned back.

After a while, she cleared her throat and tucked her hair behind her ear. "Anyway, you better get going. Wouldn't want you to be late on my account."

I picked my shirt up off her light wood floors. They were shiny and clean, and the only things on the floor were our clothes. Clearly, I'd been dismissed. I didn't like it. I was usually the one who did the dismissing, damn it. "Yeah. Sure." I headed for the door, and froze after two steps. She needed to know that what we had was special, yes, but not special enough to make me break every rule I've ever lived by. "Sky, I—"

"I know," she said softly. "No need to say another word."

"You reading me again?"

She nodded. "Am I not supposed to?"

"What am I thinking?"

"That this was fun, but that's all it can ever be, because you don't want more than fun." She smiled, tucking her hair behind her ear. "Luckily for you, that's all I want, too. So we're cool. Okay?"

I opened my mouth, closed it, then nodded. The thing with her was she *did* seem to know what I was going to say, without me having to actually *do* so. Good.

There was no misunderstanding.

No hurt feelings.

Just us.

Leaning down, I curled my hand behind her head, and kissed her before breaking it off quickly. Without another word, I headed next door, not looking back. I didn't know what she was doing to me, but I knew it wasn't good. I'd hoped one more night would appease the need that wouldn't let go of me, and yet it hadn't. But if I was going to possibly be going after her brother at some point . . .

I couldn't mess with her.

Not like *this*.

I made quick work of brushing my teeth, took a second to comb my hair back, and shrugged into an Oxford shirt, doing up all the buttons. It was my go-to gear because it was respectable enough for the office, yet, with a few undone buttons, it could be casual enough for a day out and about as a Son.

After shoving my arms through the sleeves of my leather jacket, I stood there in front of the mirror, studying the image that stared back at me. Smooth red hair. Hard green eyes. Enough scruff to seem laid-back, but not so much that I looked like a damn lumberjack or hipster. Sick of staring at myself, I shut off the light, grabbed the keys to my truck, and headed out into the hallway. I spared a glance at Sky's door as I passed it, but I walked right the hell by, and I went to my meeting without thinking about her again.

Instead, I focused on work.

On taking down Bitter Hill, once and for all.

I walked into Fitness Headquarters, a gym bag slung over

my shoulder, and stopped at the front desk, signing in like any other patron would. After changing in the locker room, I spent thirty minutes working on my upper body, sweating and pushing myself harder than ever before. My muscles screamed and my heart raced by the time I let the weights hit the bottom of the machine one last time.

Releasing a shuddered breath, I swiped my forearm across my forehead, and glanced around. No tail. No suspicious lurkers. Just a few chicks, and one dude on the elliptical who was far too busy checking out the women to be watching me. Standing, I slung a towel over my shoulder and headed for the showers. After I showered and dressed, I pulled a key out of my pocket and unlocked the storage closet, glancing over my shoulder as I slid inside.

I descended the stairs quickly, heading down a secret hallway. The second I entered the office, I smiled as the familiar sound of typing and low voices surrounded me. On the surface, the gym was a legit business, but underneath that, it was all DEA. and the perfect home base for me to report to my handler. Anyone watching me would see a visit to the gym and not think twice about my long shower afterward.

I nodded at Agent Warren and headed into the back room. "Good morning, Warren."

"Morning," he said in reply, grabbing his phone and standing. He wore a hoodie and a pair of sweats. He was on the streets a lot, and played the part well. When not working, he mostly drank and fucked his way through life. Like me. "They're waiting for you."

"I know." I grabbed a notepad off my desk, tugging on my buttoned-up collar. "I was running late this morning."

"Chasing a lead?"

I headed for the conference room. "Something like that."

We entered, and I scanned the room. There was a rectangular table and Agent Torres sat at its head like always. He was in his midthirties and muscular as hell, and he loved control almost as much as Tate did. Both commanded a room and assumed the authority in it without hesitation or a hint of weakness. Both preferred to be the most powerful man in the room, but still respected strength. If not for the fact that they worked for opposite sides of the law, I bet they would even be friends.

"Sorry I'm late," I said the second I sat in my chair toward the opposite end of the table. "I was with Skylar Daniels."

Agent Warren sat across from me, next to Agent Gilbert—who I had every reason to suspect had once been an item, although now they hated each other. "The sister?" Warren asked.

"Wait." Gilbert shifted away from him, her mouth pressed into a tight line, and glowered toward me. "Tell me you're not using the angle I think you are."

I didn't quite meet her eyes. "Tate asked me to watch over her because things with Bitter Hill are heating up. I'm the only one who knows about her existence, and he'd like to keep it that way. We're currently next-door neighbors."

Agent Torres leaned closer. "Did she give you anything good?"

"No." I opened my notebook, picturing her soft smile and even softer kiss. *Shit.* So much for not thinking about her. "She knows nothing about his secret life, or who he really is. They were raised separately."

Torres perked up. "They were? Why?"

I choked back any guilt that I felt for sharing the information Skylar had given me in confidence. This was my job, and I had to do it, no matter how wrong it felt. "Her mother and father split, so their father raised Tate while the mom kept custody of her. She never saw her father again, so she has no clue what he was or what he did."

Torres leaned back, nodding. "Interesting. Think it's all an act?"

"No." I flattened my palm on the cool, smooth table. "To her, Tate's just an older brother who wants her to be a good person, and do well in school . . . which she does. Her record is as clean as her conscience. She's innocent. It's my professional opinion that we should leave her alone."

Agent Torres rubbed his chin, leaning back in his chair as he studied me. I met his stare without flinching. "I'd like to remain close."

"Why?" I dropped my pen on the pad, grinding my teeth together. "With all due respect, sir, we're after Bitter Hill, not the Sons. They deal guns, not drugs. There's no reason we should focus on her when she's not our intended target, and neither is her brother. It's my opinion that the DEA has better ways to spend their budget than chasing after innocent women . . . *sir.*"

Warren looked at me with wide eyes.

Gilbert smiled before looking away.

The two other men in the room—Agent Lawrence and Agent O'Donnell—glanced toward Torres, waiting to see how he responded to my criticism. I typically answered with "Yes, sir," or "No, sir," so my mouthful was probably a bit surprising.

But I had a lot to say about Skylar Daniels.

Torres grunted and readjusted his position. "And if we do decide to investigate the Sons? Is that going to be a problem for you, Donahue? Is that going to make your commitment to cleaning up our streets waver?"

I stiffened. "You know where my loyalties lie, sir. I've been clear about that since the day I walked into your office."

"I thought we were clear, yes." He slammed a hand down on the table. "Until you started to talk about Skylar Daniels, that is. Until you started questioning *my* orders. Is there something we need to know, Donahue? Do those loyalties now lie somewhere else?"

I shook my head, though I ached to slam his face into the table repeatedly until he saw that Skylar wasn't an asset to be collected. I admired the guy, and he was an excellent agent, but in this case, he was wrong. "My loyalties are and always will be here, sir. It feels wrong to target Ms. Daniels. She has no idea what her brother is, or what he does. However, if you want me to continue to keep an eye on her, I will."

"Good." He glanced at Warren, who had been uncharacteristically silent throughout all this. "We could send someone else, if you'd rather. Warren, perhaps."

Warren perked up, glancing down at Skylar's picture in the file. "I could do it, sir."

Gilbert stiffened. "No doubt," she said dryly.

Let *him* near *Skylar*? Hell no. He'd feel no qualms about using her. At least with me, she got a hint of the honor I used to feel. "No, sir. I've got her. I'm already undercover, and I don't mind staying. Besides, Tate has me living next door anyway."

"Then it's settled. We continue watching her and collect intel in case we need it in the future." He reclined in his chair again, looking laid-back when we all knew he was anything but. Gilbert shot him a quick look, her appreciation for the attractive man obvious. Warren frowned. "Now, what's their plan with Bitter Hill?"

"They're attacking when the clubhouse is full." I pushed a copy of Chris's sketch to him, then to the rest of the agents, too. They all glanced down at it, so I continued. "Block the back door, which they'll assume is open because it's a secret—"

"If it's secret, how was its location discovered?" Torres interrupted.

"Chris," I said simply. "He has connections."

"And the intel is good?" Gilbert asked.

"I believe so." I glanced at Gilbert, who bit down on her lip as she studied the drawing. She was the smartest one in this room . . . minus the whole Warren thing. "So does Chris."

She looked at me with shrewd eyes, and then nodded once. "All right. Go on."

"The ones who survive the fire will go out the front. We pick them off, one by one, till there are none left." I tapped the drawing. "Risk free. Easy. Problem solved. Then the DEA can swoop in and clean what's left of the mess, and take down any stragglers."

Warren whistled through his teeth. "That's awfully well thought out, and heartless, even for a criminal leader."

"They attacked us where we're weakest," I said slowly, tapping my fingers on the table. "Tate Daniels simply plans to give them a taste of their own medicine . . . and to take them down. He's as unhappy about the innocent lives being wasted as we are."

"How . . . noble," Torres said, watching me closely. Too damn closely. "Why, then, did he sell them guns?"

I lifted a shoulder. "He didn't know what they would become. Once he figured it out, we stopped our dealings with them, right around the same time when the feud with my brother started."

"I see." He rubbed his chin. "So that's why the Sons cut ties?"

"Yes," I said simply.

He nodded. "And you'll be there for this attack on Bitter Hill, since you're a lieutenant there, and Bitter Hill 'killed' your brother?"

He, of course, knew Lucas was alive.

Everyone in this room had helped my brother escape to start a new life. A clean life. And as far as I could tell, he'd lived up to that promise. Kept his hands clean. He had a mechanic's shop down in Georgia, and Heidi had a bar. They were engaged. And *happy*.

Whatever the hell that meant.

"Yes, I'll be there, sir, to avenge Lucas. It'll be expected of me to fight," I said.

He winced. "So we need to swoop in immediately after they set the fire, and after the first shot is fired—"

"With all due respect, it should be before the first shot is fired. We can't take the Sons down with anything we have, and to bring them up on petty gun charges would be ridiculous."

He shook his head. "Not to mention lots of paperwork . . . some of which you still owe me from the other day."

"I'll get on that right away, sir."

"But regardless, we need an exchange of gunfire to call it an active crime scene." He tapped his fingers on the table impatiently. "You'll take the first shot, Donahue. Then when we start to come in, you can sound the alarm, and the Sons can 'escape.' We gather as much evidence as we can against Bitter Hill, and they're finished."

Everyone nodded in agreement.

It was a solid plan.

"Understood. I'll make sure I don't hit anyone, while

appearing to try to do so for the benefit of the Sons." I closed my notepad and tucked my pen into the pocket on my shirt. "Are we good to go, sir?"

"Yes, I think so." He steepled his fingers. "Try not to get yourself shot," Torres said, grinning. "You're up for a promotion after the undercover years you've put in, if your SAPP scores are good enough. And now you're in deep with the Daniels girl, too, which'll help. You've proved to be a valuable asset to the team, and we don't want to lose you. If you manage to maintain your cover, then I suspect your position with the sister and the gang could carry on for years."

I forced a smile, ignoring the judgmental way Gilbert stared at me from across the table. "I'll try my best to stay alive, sir, and to not disappoint you."

We all cleared out, and I avoided everyone's stares as I made my way to my desk. After I opened my laptop to work on the reports I owed, the phone I used for undercover buzzed. I pulled it out.

It was Tate. Of course. I'd forgotten to text him an update this morning in my rush to get out of Skylar's apartment and back to my duplicitous life as a DEA agent/gang member.

How's Skylar?

I rubbed my forehead. Good. She spent the night at home, studying. Alone.

Excellent. She'll be out late tonight. I set her up on a date.

Stiffening, I rubbed my jaw and forced myself to take a second before I replied: A date? Do we think that's wise right now, sir?

It'll be fine. He's a cop.

Of fucking course he was. Tate was always looking for cops to add to his payroll. And a cop, even if he was a dirty one, would be perfectly adept at keeping her safe. I had no reason to object, and yet I did. Very much so.

Excellent. Does she know?

Why the hell do you care?

I let my neck rest on the back of my chair, staring up at the white tile ceilings with fluorescent lights, not answering. Maybe this dirty cop would be the guy to make Sky forget about me. Maybe she'd like him, and maybe they'd kiss after the date, and she'd like it this time. Maybe she'd be happy with the asshole, like Lucas was with Heidi. Maybe . . .

Maybe I'd shut the hell up.

CHAPTER 12

SKYLAR

After my last class ended at six, I spent a few hours at the library studying with Marco, until the words blurred and I couldn't focus anymore. Tate had called and tried to spring a last-minute date on me, but for once I'd had a legitimate reason to say no. I couldn't afford to lose studying time to go on a date with some guy I wouldn't like anyway.

Not when Scotty Donahue was one door over.

"Thanks for walking me home," I said, smiling at Marco.

"Sure thing," he said, nudging me with his elbow. "Where I grew up, a girl walking home alone is a welcome invitation for trouble."

I slowed my steps. Marco had told me a bit about his past, and his time homeless on the streets. A kind bar owner had given him a place to stay and a job, and had helped him get into college. Unfortunately, she died in a horrible fire. Marco still talked about her like she was alive. "I lived there, too."

"Kids of Steel Row," he said, his jaw tight. "Not to be confused with the Sons of Steel Row."

My mind immediately went to Scotty. "Right."

"I hate them." He ran a hand through his dark brown hair, his even darker eyes focused straight ahead on something only he could see. "They took her."

I blinked. "I thought she died in a fire."

"She did." His dark olive skin flushed. "With *him*."

"Who?"

He flexed his jaw. His black shirt and matching black basketball pants were as dark as his eyes. "Her boyfriend. He was a Son. Whoever attacked his place was after him, not her. She was just collateral damage."

"I'm sorry," I said, my heart aching. And I was. It hurt, knowing that the Sons had taken something away from him, for more reasons than one. My gaze wondered to Scotty's door.

He stopped at my apartment, not meeting my eyes. "I know."

Reaching out, I hugged him close. We'd originally bonded over our mutual past in Steel Row, but, over time, it had turned into a true friendship. He was a good guy. It hurt to see him look so sad. So alone. I knew that feeling all too well. He wrapped his arms around me, hugging me close, and pulled back, giving me a smile. "See you tomorrow?"

I nodded. "You bet."

With a wave, he walked off, his steps sure and steady. After he rounded the corner, I dug my keys out of my purse, but as I slid the key into the lock, I froze. I swore I could feel Scotty, standing just beyond the neighboring door. It was crazy, and I knew, logically speaking, you couldn't *feel* someone through a door. And yet . . .

I totally did.

He was watching me.

Pulling my key out, I sidestepped to his door, lifting my fist to knock. Before I could do so, it swung open and he stood there, wearing a pair of jeans and an open shirt showing hard muscles and a whole lot of ink. He gave me a once-over, lingering on my chest. "Did you have a nice date?"

I cocked my head. "What makes you think I was on a date?"

For a second, he looked worried. His brow furrowed, and his nostrils flared slightly as he rocked back on his heels. "I don't know. The dress, I guess. Answer the question."

"I was studying with a friend." I licked my lips, darting a quick glance at his face. "I didn't go on a date. Tate asked me to, but . . ."

He frowned. "But . . . ?"

"He wasn't you," I said simply.

He gripped the door tight, then asked, "Want to go to a concert with me?"

I blinked, caught off guard. "Right now?"

"Yeah, why not?" He buttoned up his top button before moving on to the next. "You're already dressed."

I hesitated, thinking of all the studying I still had to do before bed, but Scotty was standing there, with his bright green eyes, staring at me. It was like the beige walls of the hallway were closing in on me, and the only way out alive was with him. "Yes."

"Great." He finished buttoning his shirt, grabbed his dark brown leather jacket, shrugged it on, and caught my hand. "Let's go."

Three hours later, a woman stood on a stage in a big purple ball gown, holding a microphone with diamonds on it, singing so beautifully, it brought tears to my eyes. Her words were of loss, and pain, and moving on from something that had broken her—and I could feel the pain laced into those words with every syllable she sang. When Scotty had asked me to go to a concert with him, I'd expected some sort of punk group, or maybe a rock band that sang about fighting the government. But I'd gotten the Boston Pops and a Broadway star.

One whose voice was magical.

She held on to the last note of the song for an impossibly long time. I blinked rapidly, staring at her, convinced she was an angel. When she broke off the note perfectly, bent over, her hand on her chest, her face broken, the crowd cheered, clapping and shouting, some with tears running down their cheeks, some cool and calm but clearly impressed.

I stumbled to my feet, clapping, and Scotty stood, too.

The singer bowed, her brown hair falling on either side of her face, and blew kisses to the crowd. I turned to Scotty, about to say something about her amazing voice, but as he clapped, he stared at *me* with wonder. He looked at *me* as if I were the person who had done something amazing, rather than the woman on the stage.

My breath caught in my throat, and we locked gazes, staring at each other.

After a few moments of charged silence, he cleared his throat. "She's good, huh?"

"Yes," I said slowly, pushing my hair behind my ear. The lights turned on, and I grabbed my jacket. He took it out of my hands and draped it over my shoulders, his fingers touching my skin. "Thank you for inviting me."

His lips tilted into a smile. We were the last ones in the row, so we waited for everyone else to clear out first. "How surprised were you when we pulled up here instead of some club?"

"Very," I admitted, laughing. "I didn't know you were a Broadway fan."

He shrugged. "They said I was, in that auction."

"With a whole lot of stuff that wasn't true."

"This was, though. My ma used to listen to Broadway musicals, and sing along as she cleaned. I guess it kind of stuck with me. I go to listen to them every once in a while, and it reminds me of her." He ran his hand down his face. "Stupid, huh?"

"Not stupid at all," I said, my voice thick. "My mom used to sing when she cleaned, too."

He dropped his hand to his side. "Did your dad sing, too?"

"No. He never sang, or smiled, really." I tucked my hair out of my face. "Not when I knew him, anyway."

"When was the last time you saw him?"

"I was ten, and we were leaving. I remember crying because Tate wasn't coming, and he hugged me, and promised we would be together soon." I lowered my lashes, hiding my eyes from him. "He, of course, was wrong. I didn't see him again until I was sixteen, and Mom died."

He reached out and ran his knuckles down my cheek, his eyes soft. "What happened then?"

"My father still refused to help me. According to him, I wasn't his. He swore Mom cheated on him and I was the daughter of another man, and he never backed down from that stance. So as far as I'm concerned, he was never my father. I didn't even have his last name—I changed it after he died, for Tate. He wanted us to match. But, anyway, Tate helped me get emancipated since there was no one to be my guardian and I didn't want to end up in the system. He did his best to provide for me, since *his* father wouldn't." I watched the crowd around us file out. The room was mostly empty now. "He did what he had to do to make sure I was okay."

A muscle in his jaw ticked. "What does that mean? What did he do?"

I hesitated, my heart picking up speed. He was watching me intently now. Almost as if . . . "Well, I mean . . . I guess he got a job, or something. He never told me, but I know he struggled to support me. As soon as he was able to, he got us a tiny little place outside of Steel Row, and he moved out of the mansion. When his father died . . . well, everything changed."

He nodded, skimming his knuckles over my jaw before stepping back. "My brother was the same. He did what he had to do to keep me safe."

"Do you know what he did?"

"Yes." He grabbed my hand, scanning the crowd. "It's thinned out. We can go now."

We walked out of the concert hall in silence, and he held on to me the whole time. As we stepped into the cool night air, I shivered and moved closer to him, seeking his heat. He glanced down at me, and hesitantly put his arm over my shoulder. He did it awkwardly, as if he'd never done so before, and his hand settled firmly over my arm.

"Have you ever dated before?" I asked, pressing my mouth into a thin line. "Like, you know, had a real girl-friend?"

He tensed, his fingers tightening against my bicep. "No."

"Never?"

He shook his head. "Never."

I didn't say anything.

After a while, he asked, "Have you? Had a real boyfriend, I mean?"

"No." With a brother like Tate, dating wasn't easy. I was always on guard, and always careful that someone didn't use me to get to him.

"Why not?" he asked.

He'd asked me this before.

I'd avoided the answer. But now . . . "Tate is . . . different. Having a brother like him makes it difficult to date. He's very . . . protective. And I don't want to drag some poor unsuspecting guy into that, unless it's for real. Unless I . . . I don't know. Unless I love him, I guess."

He watched me closely, his brow furrowed slightly. "How is Tate different?"

"He just is."

When I didn't say anything else, he stared straight ahead. "Have you ever been in love?"

"No." I shrugged. "I'm not sure I really believe in it."

"What?" His head snapped toward me. "Why not?"

"My mom loved my dad with all her heart, and look what it got her. She lost her son, her house, her lifestyle." I lowered my head, staring at our feet as we walked. He wore brown leather boots. "I watched her fall apart, and up until the day she died, I'm pretty sure she still loved him. He didn't even come to her funeral."

He was silent for a while. "Maybe he didn't love her like she loved him."

"Maybe not." I lifted a shoulder, playing with my purse strap. "That seems to be the case most of the time. One person always loves the other person more, and that person is the one who gets left behind. The one who gets hurt."

"And you don't want to get hurt," he said slowly.

"Do you?"

He shook his head once. "No."

"Yeah. Me either."

He opened the door to his Escalade for me silently, watching as I slid inside and arranged my dress over my thighs. He closed it without another word before climbing into his seat, buckling up, and starting the engine. We drove home in silence, me watching Scotty, him watching the road. When we pulled up to the curb, he shut the car down and got out.

I opened my door, too, and he was there, waiting for me, offering a hand to help me down. I stared at it for a minute, because despite my words about not believing in love, and not wanting to get hurt . . . I had a feeling I was going to let him hurt me. And nothing I did would stop it, because he already had a hold on me I couldn't shake.

He frowned, staring at his hand, then me. "Sky?"

Shaking myself out of my thoughts, I placed my hand in his larger one and hopped down right in front of him. When he didn't let go, I glanced up at him, and caught my breath. He was watching me like he was thinking the same thing I was. Like *I* could hurt *him*. "Thanks."

He didn't say anything.

Just led me inside.

When we reached the end of our hallway, I hesitated. He still hadn't let me go. After a moment, he did, and unlocked his door. I watched him, heart racing. He pushed it open, stepped back, and asked, "Want to come in?"

I sucked in a deep breath, because I did. We stared at each other the whole time, and my heart raced faster and faster until I was sure it would burst. After I passed him, he came inside, too, and shut the door, locking it. I stood there, taking in the apartment. There was furniture scattered throughout it, and a big TV hung on the wall. There was something familiar about the place, but I couldn't put my finger on it. "Nice."

"Thanks. It's not mine." He dragged his hand through his hair, and let out an exaggerated breath. "What the hell are we doing, Sky?"

"I don't know," I admitted.

"Yeah. Me either."

He watched me with a hunger I knew all too well. "I like spending time with you. I like being your friend. I don't really have many of those, and certainly not ones that go to concerts like that with me. You make me . . . you make me happy. Something I haven't been in a long time."

His emphasis on the word *friend* was not missed, or misunderstood. It was a clear reminder that it was all we were, and all we would ever be. "I like being your friend, too. Tonight was nice. Can I ask you something?"

He opened his mouth, closed it, then said, "Sure."

"Why did you join a gang?"

"Because it was the only thing I could think of. My brother was already a member, and my mom was gone, and it just . . ." He lifted a shoulder, not meeting my eyes. "It just seemed like the right thing to do."

"And then you got out."

He rubbed his jaw, letting out a small, harsh laugh. "I didn't want to make the city worse. I wanted to make it better. There's so much crime and pain in Steel Row. I didn't want to contribute to it anymore. I wanted to be . . . better. Better than my brother. Better than the gang. Just . . . *better.*"

I nodded. "Balance out the spectrum a little bit."

"Yes." He locked eyes with me. "You're too good of a person to not believe in love. To not want it."

I blinked at the sudden change in topic. "Relationships involve risk, and reward, and heartache. Not to mention the endless dates you have to go on to find someone you want to be with, where you repeatedly have to talk about your crappy childhood and your dead parents with some dude your brother asked out on a date for you."

He didn't say anything. Just stared at me. He was silent so long that we passed the awkward territory and went straight on a nonstop flight to the land of embarrassing.

Clearing my throat, I said, "Well, I should go study. I have to work at the shelter day care tomorrow morning, and then I have class—"

"Shelter day care?" he broke in, blinking. "What?"

"I volunteer there. It's a shelter for abused women who are starting their lives over after escaping their abusive partners. I play with the babies while the moms go try to find jobs." I forced a smile. "What can I say? It strikes a chord in me."

He stared at me. "My dad might not actually be dead," he said casually, like he was talking about the weather instead of himself. "I don't know who he is, and even though I could probably try to find out, to see if he's alive, I haven't, because to me? He's dead. And I want it to stay that way. I know people can change, and that they can be better, but even if he's a goddamned saint now, he'll always be the guy who walked away from us."

I wasn't sure what to say. Was he telling me this because he thought I was making a passive-aggressive hint that *I* wanted to talk more, or because *he* did? I didn't do passive-aggressive. I preferred everything out in the open, for all to see. "You don't have to—"

"I know." He locked eyes with me, his gaze completely vulnerable, taking me even more off guard with his off-the-cuff admission. "But Lucas was more of a father to me than my real father could ever be, and, basically, I'm saying I know how you feel about Tate."

I bit my lip. "When I turned sixteen, Tate threw me a sweet sixteen. I have no idea where he got the money from, but he got me a dress, and a tiara, and invited my friends . . ." I turned away. "I felt like a princess that day. Because of him."

Scotty stepped closer, his expression warm with compassion and understanding—but no pity. Thank God. If he'd pitied me, I would have walked right out of the room. "I had no idea you went through all that horrible stuff with your dad. The guilt over Lucas, over what he *had* to do, kills me."

My throat ached, and I took a deep breath. His apartment smelled like aftershave and vanilla. It was comforting. "Yeah. I know that feeling."

Neither one of us spoke. Nervously, I tucked my hair behind my ear. My fingers trembled, and I hid them behind my back to hide it from him. We were crossing new ground here. I wasn't sure what it was, or what it meant, but we *were*. Maybe that's why I was so drawn to him. We were both so *alike*.

After a moment or two, he dragged his hands down his face. "Look, I like you, Sky. I like when you're here, with me, kissing me. And I like touching you. Being with you."

"I like you, too," I said quickly. "And everything else you just mentioned."

"But that's exactly why you shouldn't be here. I like you too much to hurt you, and believe me when I say this." He dropped his hands to his sides. "If you stay, if you keep coming back to me, I *will* hurt you. I promise you that."

I shrugged out of my coat, letting it hit the floor. I wore a tight black dress that hugged the curves of my hips perfectly, something I knew Scotty would appreciate. I grabbed the hem of the dress, locking eyes with him. "That's a risk I'm willing to take tonight. Still want me to leave?"

Scotty stayed still, neither retreating nor stepping closer, keeping his expression closed off to me. "Hell no."

"Good." I pulled my dress over my head, letting it hit the floor. "I was hoping you'd say that. I'm an optimist like that."

He didn't move, just stared at me like a haunted man running from the shadows. "I know. It's one of the many things I like about you."

"There's many things?" I asked.

"Mm-hm. Like . . ." He came up to me, walking around me in a circle. He kissed the back of my shoulder, where my neck met it. "This spot right here." His fingers ran over my butt before he palmed it, squeezing roughly enough to make my breath hitch in my throat. "And your ass is easily the hottest ass I've ever seen." He gently spun me, his hand still on my butt. When I faced him, he pulled me closer, running the back of his knuckles over my cheek. "And your skin is so soft, and the way your eyes light up when you look at me is addictive. And your lips . . ." He leaned in, kissing me gently. Pulling back, he added, "They're the sweetest lips I've ever tasted." His hand slid behind my neck, and he rested his other on my chest, releasing his hold on my butt. "And this? Your heart?" It sped up under his touch. "It's pure. Too pure for a guy like me."

His mouth melded with mine, stealing my words right out of my mouth. I fisted the fabric of his shirt at his hips, swaying closer. He swooped me up in his arms and carried me into his bedroom, his mouth never breaking contact with mine. As he lowered me to his mattress, he covered my body with his, easily slipping between my legs as if he belonged there all along. The way he made me feel—breathless, achy, and complete—was addicting.

And for the first time, I was worried about the way he made me feel.

Worried I might never get enough.

He broke off the kiss, leaving a trail of fire in his wake

as he kissed his way down my body. I lifted my hips to try and get closer to him, and realized I still wore my heels. I started to kick them off with the help of the mattress, but he gripped my ankle, lifting it to his mouth. After kissing the inside of it, he said, "Keep them on. They're hot as hell."

He nipped the skin there, and then placed my foot on his back as he crawled his way up my body, stopping to place a soft kiss on my inner thigh. By the time he pulled my thong off and tossed it aside, I was already a trembling mess. He flicked his tongue over me, and I moaned, writhing on his soft green comforter with no shame.

He closed a hand over my breast to play with my nipple while the other slid under my butt, lifting me so he could drive me crazy with his tongue. And he did.

God, he *did*.

His tongue moved over me in steady circles, resting over my flesh every once in a while to apply more pressure. Every time he paused, it sent me closer to the edge until he pinched my nipple, twisting slightly, and didn't just push me off the ledge—I flew. I saw stars, the sun, and the moon, and when I came back down, he was sliding inside me, cupping my cheeks in both hands, and kissing me tenderly.

Kissing me like I *mattered*.

I moaned into his mouth, and he thrust harder, his mouth increasing the pressure over mine. Every nerve in my body was tuned into his movements, and I lifted my hips higher, desperate to take more of him inside me. His movements quickened with each stroke and every time he moved, something coiled tighter and tighter until I was sure I'd die without him here, holding me. He groaned and tilted his hips, hitting a spot that made that pleasure snap, and I came.

Scotty lifted me higher as he thrust once, twice, and then *bam*. Letting out a few soft curses, he collapsed on top of me, cradling the bulk of his weight on his elbows so he didn't crush me. We didn't speak for a while. Just lay there, wrapped in each other's arms, letting our breathing calm down enough to speak. When he lifted himself up on his elbows and looked down at me, his lips were soft and his eyes were a gentle, warm green.

Just as I was thinking I could stay here forever, wrapped in his arms, he opened his mouth and said, "What do you need to study tonight?"

Oh. Right. Was that my cue to leave?

Back to reality, Skylar.

"Advanced Biology." I glanced at the clock, wincing when I saw it was already almost midnight, and I had to be at the shelter day care at eight. It would be a long night, with little to no sleep, but spending a short time in heaven with Scotty was worth the inevitable bags under my eyes tomorrow morning. "I should probably get going, actually."

He rolled off me, flopping onto his back. He was hard, and sweaty, and naked, and hot as hell—but I forced my attention from his body as I slid off the bed, or else I'd never leave. As I bent down to grab my panties, he said, "I like having you in my bed."

"Oh." I stepped into my panties. "I like being in your bed. It's . . . nice. But it's not exactly conducive to studying."

"It could be," he said, lifting up on one elbow. "I'll keep my hands to myself, if you want to hang here, and study in my bed. I'm in the middle of an amazing James Patterson book right now, so I'll be quiet."

I blinked. "You read for pleasure?"

"Of course." He frowned. "Don't you?"

"I don't really have time anymore."

"There's always time for an escape from real life," he said slowly. Reaching out, he caught my wrist and tugged me back onto the bed, giving me the most charming smile ever to grace this side of the earth. "Stay? Escape real life with me."

"Okay," I whispered, resting my head on his chest.

"You can study in my bed any night you want, even," he added, playing with a piece of my hair. "Or I could read in your bed."

My heart picked up speed. "One question, though."

"Yeah?" he said, his voice deep and rumbly because my ear was pressed to his chest, his voice hard. I'd learned he didn't like when I asked questions. They made him uneasy. "What is it?"

I ignored the millions of questions I had about us, and what his invitation to stay in his bed meant, and settled for, "Can you go get my books for me?"

CHAPTER 13

SCOTTY

I walked down Maple Street in the heart of Steel Row, whistling under my breath with my hands in my pockets, feeling like a happy son of a bitch. It wasn't a feeling I was comfortable with, but that didn't change the fact that my step was lighter, and my body was relaxed. For once, I was actually looking forward to going home because Sky was waiting for me.

With dinner.

She *cooked* for me.

We'd been sleeping together for a few days now, and that was a-okay with me. Tate and Torres wanted me to keep an eye on her, and it was a hell of a lot easier to do so when she was in bed next to me. That was the reason I hadn't ended things yet. The simplicity of having my charge close by.

Or so I kept telling myself, because anything else would be stupid as hell. Everything we had together was built on lie upon lie, woven together like strings, and if she tugged on one, it would all fall apart. And it was only a matter of time until someone, or something, tugged. I wasn't so far gone that I didn't see reality, or was completely ignoring the fact I was jeopardizing everything I'd so carefully built, just for a few nights with a woman.

But I finally understood why Lucas and Chris had risked it all for a girl.

Some girls were worth the risk.

Skylar Daniels was one of them.

We didn't stand a fireball's chance in the Arctic of making what we had into something real, but still. This was . . . Having her in my life was . . .

Nice.

"Dude." Chris elbowed me in the ribs hard. "What the hell is wrong with you?"

I snapped out of my head, scanning the streets for any signs of danger. A guy in my line of business couldn't afford to daydream like a kid. There were two blond teenagers behind us, on phones, and two more across the street staring at us. One had brown hair and one had a shaved head. Both were sporting ink and looked like they might be carrying.

"Sorry," I mumbled. "You were saying?"

"Last night, Gus's wife was attacked. She's okay, but they're attacking our families now. And Molly's at work today. High schools have metal detectors, but they haven't resorted to frisking kindergarteners yet, and all I keep thinking is that she's defenseless out there without me. I just want this damn thing to end."

Shit. Maybe Tate was right about being worried for Sky's safety. But if the DEA hadn't known about her up until now, how would Bitter Hill? She'd be fine. I'd make sure of it. I remained silent, surreptitiously checking out the men across the street again.

Chris watched me with concern, shoving his hands into his coat pockets. It was a chilly September morning, and his cheeks were flushed from the wind. "Is everything okay, man? You've been acting strange."

"I'm fine." I rested my hand on my holster. The two teens across the street stood up, tugging on their black leather coat sleeves. They didn't look more than nineteen or twenty years old. Kids, still. I'd been seventeen when I joined the Sons, but they'd kept me as a runner for years, and I never went on missions or sales. Not until they were sure I could handle myself.

Bitter Hill *couldn't* be sending these kids after us.

Not even they were that low.

I shifted my stance uneasily, ducking my head but keeping an eye on them just in case I was wrong. We were two blocks from the clubhouse, so as long as we hurried and didn't stop to chat, we'd be okay. "Five o'clock."

"What?" Chris frowned. "No, it's three. See what I mean? You're distracted, and smiling all the damn time. Why are you smiling so much—?"

"Dude. Shut the hell up." I gripped my gun. "Five o'clock. Two kids. They're—"

"Not the ones you should worry about." A trigger clicked behind us, and I froze. I'd been so busy watching the other boys, I hadn't heard the other ones behind us creeping closer, because they'd looked even younger than the two across the street. Classic rookie mistake. "Hand off the gun. Now."

I let go, gritting my teeth and shooting Chris a warning glare—who had the long-haired blond boy behind him. *Shit.*

"Who are you, and what the hell do you think you're doing on our turf?"

"Taking out the trash." The barrel of a gun pressed against the back of my head. "Bitter Hill wants to send a message."

The kid behind Chris did the same, pressing it against his skull, and leaning close enough to rest his chin on Chris's shoulder. He was trembling, and sweating, and his eyes were as shifty as his grip on his Sig. The kid was probably only seventeen, if that, and should be in school instead of holding a damn gun to our heads. Bitter Hill shouldn't have sent him to kill experienced fighters like me and Chris.

This was a suicide mission, and these fools were too damn young to know it.

I locked eyes with Chris, shaking my head once, silently telling him to remain calm and not to kill these kids. He tensed, but nodded. All Chris had to do was jerk to the side, spin, and grab the gun before this inexperienced boy could pull the trigger.

"See my buddies over there?" the long-haired blond boy behind Chris asked. He looked like he belonged on a surfboard instead of on the streets of Steel Row.

Chris nodded, looking entirely unconcerned about the gun pressed to the back of his head as he looked where he was told to look, playing along. I'd seen him survive worse, so it didn't surprise me too much that he hadn't lost his cool. "The ones I'm gonna kill? Yeah. I see them."

I nodded my head once, curling one finger into my palm, giving Chris the signal he'd been waiting for. "Look, you don't stand a chance in hell of walking away from this alive if you try to pull those triggers. Bitter Hill should stick to drugs, because guns aren't your thing. I bet you don't even know how to load that thing by yourself."

The shorter blond behind me pressed the gun closer to my skull, digging into my skin. "But I bet I know how to fire it. Want to find out?"

I focused on my breaths, keeping them calm and evenly spaced as I familiarized myself with exactly where we were on Maple Street. To our left was Pete's Barber Shop, and to the right was a cheap bar that made the Patriot look like the Grill 23 & Bar. The closest cops were at least ten blocks to the west. I didn't want to kill these kids, but if they wouldn't listen to reason, I wouldn't have a damn choice. "I'll let you walk away, I'll let you *live,* if you drop the gun and start walking right now."

Long-haired blond boy blinked the sweat out of his eyes, and tightened his finger on the trigger. He was going to shoot Chris if we didn't stop him, and that wasn't a loss I was willing to accept. "Whatever, man. Let's end this and go home, Bobby."

I nodded once at Chris. "Go."

"You should have walked," Chris said casually.

And then we both spun, taking the inexperienced boys off guard. The one facing me, Bobby, stumbled back, aimed, and pulled the trigger. Pain seared through my arm, and I launched myself at him at the same time as a gunshot boomed next to me. I had no idea who pulled the trigger— Chris or the blond boy—but I couldn't look yet.

I was too busy with my own fight.

When I landed on the sidewalk next to my attacker, the gun skidded away from both of us. I still had mine, but I wouldn't shoot an unarmed kid. I'd rather try to save him, and maybe show him that there was more to life than being a sacrificial lamb. So instead, I wrapped my arm around his neck, rolling him to the side as I choked him out. As I held the lanky, struggling teenager, who showed no signs of passing out any time soon, tight against me, I saw the kid across the street lift a gun and aim at me. *"Shit."*

The damn kids were everywhere.

Was Bitter Hill recruiting out of high schools now?

I ducked my head behind Bobby's shoulder. A shot echoed, and I braced myself for impact in case the kid could actually aim. But then I realized it came from behind me—and the young man fell to the ground, his backward hat tumbling behind him, red blood seeping across his white shirt. The other kid who'd been across the road, the one with the shaved head, got one look at his buddy and took off running.

Good. Then I wouldn't have to—

I glanced over my shoulder in time to see Chris take aim. He had blood running down his face out of his nose, and a split lip. His finger tightened on the trigger, and I knew he was a good enough shot to hit the running teen from this far away without blinking. "No!" I shouted, letting Bobby go once he finally went limp. "Don't. He's just a kid, and he's running."

Chris glowered, not letting go of his hold on the trigger. "I know. And soon, he won't be."

"You can't." I struggled to my feet. "He's not a threat anymore, and he's a kid. We don't kill kids. We're trying to save them, right?"

"Right." He shifted, staring at the dead body by his feet, his head lowered, shoulders stiff. "He tried to kill me."

"And you didn't have a choice." I gestured toward the running boy. "But with him, we do. We let him go. Let's hide this one before—"

A gunshot broke me off, and we both spun, guns raised.

The kid across the street covered his head, and kept running, so it clearly hadn't been him who'd tried to kill us. I scanned the area for whatever hidden threat I'd missed—and saw it. Brian aimed, fired . . . and didn't miss this time. Neither did Frankie. The teen with the shaved head went down in a spray of blood against the corner of a weather-worn cement building. I stumbled back, my chest tight, lowering my gun. *"Shit."*

Chris lowered his gun, his jaw tight. "At least it wasn't us, right?"

I didn't say anything.

Right now, I wasn't sure I could.

Bitter Hill was taking this too far, sending boys to kill men. If they wanted to take us down, they should be sending lieutenants who understood the risks, and accepted them.

Not *kids*.

Swallowing hard, I tucked my gun away and surveyed the rest of the damage, trying to take my mind off the carnage. I'd been grazed on the arm, Chris looked like he had a broken nose—*again*—and the long-haired blond kid who'd attacked us had been taken down with a bullet between the eyebrows. He sat up against the brick wall to our left, blood and brain matter dripping down the wall behind him, all empty stares and slack jaw.

Such a waste. Such a damn waste.

When was this going to end?

Was it even possible to change Steel Row?

I'd been so sure, once upon a time, that I could do it. But now . . . the violence was escalating, kids were dying, and I was nowhere closer to solving the gang issue than I'd been when I'd sworn in as an agent in the first place. These sense-less deaths . . .

They had to fucking *stop*.

"Damn it." I dragged my hands down my face, letting out a long breath. "Why did they send kids at us when there's no way they can win?"

"Because they're expendable." Chris tucked his gun away, looking down at the one I'd choked out, his jaw tight. "Is that one dead?"

"No." I stepped in front of him, grabbing the kid's ankles. "I wanna keep him that way. Help me drag him off."

Chris bent and grabbed the kid's shoulders, nodding once. We picked him up, and I glanced over my shoulder in time to see Frankie come up behind me. He stared down at the kid, frowning. "What are you guys doing?"

Chris flinched, and for a second, I saw the regret he held deep in his soul, hidden away from the world, just like me. He didn't like this violence any more than I did. It was why he'd joined me. To help stop this shit from happening. Being with Molly had changed him. "Cleaning up," he said immediately.

Brian came to our side, too. "What happened here?"

Frankie and Tommy went across the street to the other guys.

Chris faced him, any sign of regret disappearing. "We were on our way to the clubhouse when they attacked from behind." Chris touched his nose gently, flinching. "We took down these two, then the other one tried to help his buddies. I shot him, too."

Brian nudged the kid—Bobby—with the tip of his boot. We still held on to his ankles and shoulders, and he was suspended in air. "And this one?"

"He's . . ." I wanted to lie, but Bobby chose that moment to moan. "He's alive. But I thought it might be good to question him, and send him back with a message."

"I've got no questions to ask," Frankie said casually, spitting on the sidewalk at the kid's feet. I hadn't heard him come back. "Drop him."

Me and Chris let go, and Bobby hit the sidewalk hard.

Tommy stood behind Frankie, watching me closely. "What kind of questions do you want to ask?" His phone rang, and he pulled it out, turning his back and talking quietly.

"I don't know. Maybe ask where Bitter Hill is recruiting these days," I said slowly, knowing Brian was my only hope at saving this kid since Tommy was on the phone, more than likely talking to Tate, and Frankie had grown ice-cold during this war. But I couldn't push too hard. I wasn't supposed to have a conscience, after all. "He's just a kid."

"A kid who tried to kill you," Frankie pointed out, crossing his arms.

Chris stepped forward. "He had no idea how to fight. He's not a threat anymore."

"Until he comes back, and takes out one of us because we let him walk," Frankie snapped. He looked at Brian, holding his hands out. "Since when do we let people who try to kill us live?"

Brian hesitated, rocking back on his heels, eyeing me curiously. "We don't. They attacked on our turf. The message was clear."

"Exactly." Frankie lifted his gun, aiming. "And this is the best message to send back. We're at war. We can't afford to play nice because Bitter Hill keeps sending kids with guns our way."

Brian turned away, clearly uncomfortable with the situation, but still willing to do what needed to be done. I got it. I did. But still . . . "Do it."

Frankie pulled the trigger.

Chris stared at the sidewalk, his jaw tight.

I forced myself to remain still as dark blood pooled beneath the kid's striped shirt, staining the broken gray concrete. The white shoelace on his Nike sneaker was untied, and it dampened to pink as the blood from his fallen colleague touched it. The kid hadn't even bothered to tie his shoe before he tried to kill me. I didn't know why I found that so disturbing . . .

But I did.

I really fucking did.

He wasn't much older than I'd been when I joined, but the Sons had kept me safe. When you recruited new members, it was your job as a lieutenant to keep the newbies safe. To show them the ropes and make sure they could survive out there when the bullets started flying. But Bitter Hill hadn't given a damn. These kids were cannon fodder. Bobby looked impossibly young lying there, now that his tough-guy attitude had been stripped away by death.

Anger choked me.

This kid should still be alive.

Tommy waved from across the street, hanging up the phone and shoving it in his jacket pocket. "Let's go. Boys are coming."

We all walked, tucking away our weapons, our strides long and fast so we could be inside before the cops showed up. They didn't usually bother in this section of town, but I guess this time there were too many gunshots to ignore. I glanced over my shoulder, gritted my teeth, and quickened my steps.

"We'll have to sell the guns. Too risky to keep on us with all the slugs left behind," Brian said, his face ashen as we walked. "We'll get replacements at the warehouse later."

Across the street, a block away from the scene of the crime, a mother knelt in front of a child who was about six years old. He smiled down at her as she tied his shoe, hugging his teddy bear to his chest, and something inside my chest ached. Would this kid grow up to be like the ones behind us, lying in pools of blood?

"Scotty?" Brian said.

I snapped out of it, looking away from the child and his mother. "Yeah. Good idea."

Chris gave me the side-eye. "You okay, man?"

"I'm fine." I forced a grin. It hurt. "You're the one with a broken nose again. Molly's going to kill me, or you."

"Or both of us," Chris agreed, touching it again, his brown eyes shadowed. "I'll straighten it in the bathroom once we're inside."

"How many times is this?" Brian asked, his tone light, despite the tense way he held himself. Something told me he didn't like that dead kid we'd left behind either . . .

But it hadn't stopped him from giving the order.

Did that make the Sons as dangerous as Bitter Hill?

"Five," Chris admitted. "Maybe six."

Tommy laughed, and he didn't seem upset at all. Why should he be? We'd been attacked, and we'd lived to tell. In his book, we'd won. "Shit, man."

"I don't know why people like breaking my nose so damn much," Chris gritted out, glancing over his shoulder.

I did the same. No one followed us.

"It's big. That's why. Easy target," Tommy said, laughing.

Chris flipped him off with a bloody finger.

Brian laughed. "Watch yourself, O'Brien. Tommy's already geared up for a fight, and he ranks higher than you."

Frankie glanced at us. "No fighting. That's an order, and I rank higher than all three of you. We need to save our strength for the fight ahead of us—with Bitter Hill."

How many more kids would be killed before we put an end to this? If they'd grown up somewhere else, somewhere

where gang activity didn't run rampant, where there were options, would those kids have been different? Would they have been on a court with a ball in their hands, instead of guns? Would they have stood a goddamned *chance*?

I opened the door to the clubhouse, holding it for the others, still not speaking.

Frankie went in without a word.

Brian clapped me on the shoulder. "You did good today, man."

"Thanks," I managed to say, because I hadn't done good. If I'd done good, at least one of those kids would have walked away. And the fact that they thought I'd done good by killing . . . it had never occurred to me before, but these men—my brothers—were just as ruthless as Bitter Hill. They hadn't hesitated to kill an unconscious kid. They might die for one another, and they might die for me, since they didn't know my secrets, but underneath that loyalty . . .

They were killers.

What did that make me? Was I with them, or against them? Was I Scott Donahue, DEA agent, or was I Scotty Donahue, Lucas's little brother, who whored around and killed people without thinking twice?

Was I a good man . . . ?

Or a bad one?

When I remained silent, Tommy frowned and pointed to my arm. "Are you okay? Does that need stitches? I can call the doc."

I could have saved him. If only—

Chris cleared his throat. *"Scotty."*

I jumped slightly. "What?"

Tommy narrowed his eyes and spoke slowly. "I asked if you needed the doc."

The one on our payroll. He patched us up when we

needed it because hospitals reported gunshot wounds. Chris was pretty good with a needle, too, though, so I'd just go to him if it needed work. "Nah. It's just a graze. I don't even feel it anymore. Thanks, though."

"You're lucky," Tommy said, turning to Chris and frowning. "You're both lucky. No more walking in from wherever you two were until this is over, and that's an order. Drive here, and park out front."

Tommy outranked us, so we didn't have a choice in the matter. When you were given an order in the Sons, you followed it. Tommy's authority was only outranked by Brian, Frankie, and Tate. "Yes, sir," Chris said, saluting him cockily.

Tommy eyed me. "Where were you two, anyway?"

"Heidi's old bar." We'd gone to the Patriot to discuss the latest developments with the DEA, and the ambush plan. "Whiskey's half price on Wednesdays."

Tommy didn't say anything at first. Just stared. Then: "Well, no more bars, and no more cheap whiskey. You wanna drink, do it at home or here. Got it?"

"Got it," I replied.

He went inside, leaving me with Chris, who frowned at me the second we were alone. "I get why you're upset, I don't like what's happening either, but you need to pull yourself together, man. Molly's life could be in danger, and I'm not risking my girl's life for anyone."

"I agree. I wouldn't risk her life either."

Chris leaned in. "Then get your head in the game. You're distracted. You were distracted before all this shit went down, and now it's even worse."

"I'm fine. My head is fine." I inclined my head toward the men inside. "We should probably go in, before we raise suspicion."

"All right." Chris leaned in close, his tone soft but his eyes anything but. "But don't forget to mess up your hair, Scotty boy. It's still slicked back."

I gritted my teeth and didn't say anything.

He walked into the clubhouse. He was right, earlier. About my head not being in the game. I *was* distracted. I had four deaths that rested on my conscience. I'd been too busy daydreaming about Sky to pay attention to my surroundings. If my head had been in the game like it should've been, maybe I could have stopped the attack before it started. Maybe those kids would still be alive.

It was time to stop ignoring how ruthless the Sons really were.

Yes, they'd taken my brother and me in, and yes, they'd die for me. But they'd kill for me, too. And if they learned the truth about me, they would pull the trigger as effortlessly as they'd pulled it back there on the street. From now on, I had to make sure I was one hundred percent focused on the war at hand, on *both* wars, and on keeping me and Chris alive.

I couldn't be fantasizing about soft hair, smooth skin, and sweet kisses. I couldn't afford to be caught up in the false normalcy of a relationship, when my life wasn't even close to ordinary. And I sure as hell couldn't risk dragging Sky down with me if I messed it all up again.

Pulling out my phone, I jotted off a quick text. Can't come over. Sorry.

After sliding my phone into my pocket, I dragged a hand through my hair to mess it up, took a deep breath, and ignored the buzzing of a text message in my pocket.

It was time for me to choose what side I wanted to be on. To decide what kind of *man* I was.

CHAPTER 14

SKYLAR

The early dawn sky was beginning to lighten, banishing the darkness, and casting away the shadows overhead. September sunrises were the best, with that hint of autumn peeking through the orange-and-pink sky. I sat in front of the window inside Starbucks, watching, but I focused my attention down to my textbook instead, ignoring the early morning crowds around me. The words all blurred together into one unintelligible blob, making it hard to focus.

I'd hoped that by leaving my apartment, I would stop being so distracted. I'd heard Scotty come home two hours ago. He'd thumped around in his bedroom for a little bit before all went silent.

I'd never hated thin walls as much as I did then.

No matter how many times I told myself to knock it off, I kept straining to hear a feminine laugh. He'd told me he couldn't come over, and then ignored my texts for the rest of the night. They showed as read, but he hadn't sent a reply. Not a single one.

I might not be experienced in dating and matters of the heart, but it seemed to me like he was brushing me off. That his silence was an answer all on its own.

I was pretty sure we were done.

But I wasn't sure *why*.

Things had been going well. We'd developed a sort of silent understanding that we were together, and it would continue until one of us decided otherwise. Two nights ago, when he'd made love to me and then held me close, kissing my bare shoulder as he fell asleep, he'd shown no signs of wanting out of our arrangement.

Until last night.

What had sent him running? Maybe it had been the dinner I made for him. He'd mentioned offhand what his favorite meal was, and I'd decided to make it for him. It hadn't *meant* anything. I'd just been trying to be nice. But maybe it had been too much.

Too girlfriend-ish.

Yawning, I picked up my coffee and took a sip, forcing my mind off Scotty and whatever I'd done to make him pull away from me. A shadow fell on the table, and I glanced up. A red-haired man stood beside me . . . but not the one I was trying to get off my mind. "Hey."

"What are you doing out here so early?" Tate asked, sitting across from me and plopping his latte on the table, his back to the sunrise. He wore a black suit, a white shirt, and a blue tie that matched his eyes. His red hair was combed to the side and slicked down to perfection, and he was clean-shaven. He looked every inch the professional CEO he liked to present to the world. "You don't usually show your face around here till after seven thirty."

"I couldn't sleep last night, so I finally gave up and came here for some caffeine." I leaned back in my chair, cradling my salted caramel mocha and breathing it in. "Why are you here?"

"I crashed here last night, in my old apartment. I never cancelled the lease. I like having somewhere close to you, if need be," he said, smiling. "I have a meeting at eight, and this is closer to my office, so I figured I could sleep a little later. Big deal going down today, and I have to oversee it to make sure no one messes everything up, so a good night's sleep was essential."

"Micromanaging again?" I teased.

"Always." He reached out and tapped my book, his motions light and smooth. "What's all this?"

"That's what I'm trying to figure out," I said, smiling sheepishly. "My brain isn't working very well, though."

He lifted his coffee. "Drink faster."

"I'm trying," I said, my gaze wandering toward our apartment building. What would happen if Tate saw Scotty? Would he put two and two together, and figure out we were sleeping together? I could only hope he left before Scotty came out of the building. At least Tate had his back to the window, so he might miss Scotty if he appeared. "What deal are you working on?"

"Just boring work shit." He let out a sigh. "Nothing you'd be interested in. It's stressing me out, that's all."

"Why?" I asked, tearing my attention off the sunrise. I kind of wanted to go outside, feel the brisk autumn air on my skin, but I didn't move. Now that I looked closer, he had bags under his eyes and, his desire for a good night's sleep aside, he looked like he hadn't slept in at least a week. "What's wrong?"

He scanned the crowd around us like he searched for

some unknown threat in the shadows. He was always on the lookout for danger. He and Scotty had that in common. "Do you always wander around alone before dawn?"

I frowned. "I go where I want, when I want. It's one of the benefits of being an adult. Why?"

"No reason." He lifted his cup. "Crime has been rising lately, and I hate to see you out and about in the dark alone."

"You're out," I said slowly. "And alone."

"I'm also a black belt." He cocked a brow. "Are you?"

"I have black belts," I joked. "Does that count?"

He frowned at me.

I rubbed my forehead. "Tough crowd."

"I don't think you being hurt is funny."

"I'm not hurt." I gestured around us, pointing out everyone else who was either staring at their phone or just sitting there, trying to wake up. Boston ran on coffee, ever since we went and threw all the tea in the harbor. "No one here is going to do anything. We're all half asleep."

He didn't say anything.

"You look tired . . ." I reached out and covered his hand with mine. "Instead of worrying about me, worry about you. When's the last time you slept?"

He slowly turned to me. "I'll always worry about you. I'll never stop."

"I know." I licked my lips and lowered my head. "And I worry about you. When's the last time you slept?"

"I got a few hours last night. More than you, I'm sure. It's just this work thing. It's . . ." He focused on something over my shoulder, and stood. "Oh. Hi."

I glanced over my shoulder . . .

And froze.

Craaaaaaap.

Scotty stood behind me, wearing a button-up blue shirt,

a pair of gray khakis, and a frown. When he saw me, he stopped walking, one foot still in the air. His brow was furrowed as he spotted me sitting with Tate. I couldn't help but feel like this was some kind of setup. A way for Tate to see us together and make sure I wasn't messing around with the wrong guy.

"Sir?" Scotty said, still staring at me. He had a hint of suspicion in his expression, like he thought maybe *I'd* set this up. He should know better. I didn't want my brother on my case any more than he did. "How are you this morning?"

"Good," Tate said. His eyes, though, were narrowed, as he studied Scotty. "Oh, how rude of me. Skylar, Scotty, do you remember one another, or should I make introductions again?"

Scotty smiled, and it was just as fake as Tate's introduction. "Yes, of course I remember your sister, sir." He hesitated, then held a hand out to me. "How are you, Ms. Daniels?"

"Excellent." I slid my hand into his, jerking back as soon as I could. His skin still made mine tingle, which wasn't fair. "It's nice to see you again. How have you been?"

Scotty fisted his hand. "Great. Busy with work."

"So I hear." I tucked my palm in my lap, safely out of reach. Tate watched us, more than likely waiting to see if we slipped and showed something we shouldn't. So . . . he *was* suspicious. Great. Once he was on to something, he was like a dog on a scent. We wouldn't be able to shake him off. "Well, I guess you two are headed in now?"

"Yeah, I am, at least. Not sure about you, Scotty," Tate said, putting his hands in his pockets, turning his back to his intern. "Though I don't like leaving you out here alone, Skylar."

"I'll be fine," I said stiffly. "I'm going home soon, anyway, to get ready for school."

Now that *he* was leaving.

"How about you go up now instead?" Tate asked. "I'll walk you up."

"Stop worrying, I'll be fine. I'm going to try to catch some sleep before class."

Scotty eyed the red leggings and black sweater I'd tossed on. I'd had them on yesterday when he kissed me good-bye. I'd been too busy pacing and not sleeping to change clothes. "Just coming home from a night out?"

"No." Tate frowned at me, then Scotty. "She doesn't stay out all night."

I stiffened. "Actually—"

Scotty smiled, laughing lightly. "I was just teasing." When he turned to me, all signs of laughter faded. "Going home now, Ms. Daniels?"

His tone was light, but his gaze was demanding. I refused to run home because both men said I should. "No. I'll stay here until I finish with my coffee. It was nice seeing you guys, though."

Tate's nostrils flared, but he leaned down and kissed the top of my head, knowing I wouldn't give in if I didn't want to. "Love you."

"I love you, too," I muttered, turning away from Scotty. Saying those words in front of him, even though they weren't to him, felt *weird*. "See you later. Good luck."

"You should go home, Ms. Daniels," Scotty said, his voice hard. "There's a lot of stuff going down in the city right now. You're safer inside."

"I haven't seen anything on the news," I said slowly, closing my book, staring up at him and blinking. "Funny, how you both keep talking about this 'danger.'"

"You'll just have to trust us on this," Scotty said, glancing over his shoulder quickly. Tate watched, frowning.

Something silent passed between Scotty and me. Something I didn't fully understand, but it didn't make it any less real. "Please?"

We had a tiny stare down.

Tate watched, stiff.

The longer we glowered at each other, the more his curiosity grew.

I could *feel* it.

Finally, I looked away, simply because I knew Scotty wouldn't back down. He brought stubborn to a whole new level. Hoping to take the focus off us, I turned to Tate. "You're seriously that worried about me?"

He nodded once.

"Fine." I cleared my throat, ducking my head, and checking Scotty out one more time. "I'll go home."

Relief crossed Scotty's expression, and he flicked a quick glance at Tate—who looked about as happy as a cat caught out in pouring rain. Tate held his coffee out for Scotty to take, and then grabbed my books off the table for me. I could carry them by myself, but it made him happy to help, so I let him. "I'll be right back down. Hold this for me?"

"Yes, sir. It was nice seeing you again, Ms. Daniels," Scotty said gently.

"Yeah." I lowered my head. "You too, Mr. Donahue."

Tate threw his arm around me, and led me toward our building. "I know you think it's stupid, but I still worry about you." He paused. "Apparently, Scotty does, too."

I lowered my head. "I don't know what you mean. He was simply backing up his boss, I'm sure."

"Is there something going on I should know about?" he asked, not accepting the excuse I'd given for Scotty's behavior as easily as I'd hoped

"What? No." I laughed. "God, no."

There went that brow again. "Okay."

"I'm serious. I haven't seen him since the night he was at the charity event in your place. And I barely spoke more than a word or two to him that night, as well." I stepped away from his arm, facing him. The last thing I wanted to do was get Scotty in trouble . . . even though I hated lying to Tate. "Don't go getting all protective older brother on me. There's nothing going on between us that you need to know about."

That, at least, was true. He *absolutely* didn't need to know about what we'd done.

His lips twitched as he held the door to my building open for me. "Yes, ma'am."

"I love you, but you need to relax." I walked past him, into the lobby, and started up the stairs to my floor. It was faster than waiting for the elevator. Tate followed me as I added, "I'm not a little girl anymore, you know."

"I know," he said dryly, taking the steps two at a time. "If you recall, I tried to hook you up on a date just the other day with a perfectly suitable guy. One who could take care of you. How's your schedule looking, by the way?"

"Full," I muttered. "Really full."

He groaned dramatically.

"It is," I said defensively as I turned down the hallway toward my place. "Besides, he's probably not my type anyway, and we both know it."

"But Scotty is?" Tate asked caustically.

We'd reached my door, and I crossed my arms, giving him my best annoyed look. "I never once said he was, or wasn't, my type." I pointed at his chest, poking him gently. "Don't go putting words in my mouth, Tate William Daniels."

He winced at my use of his full name. "He's not for you. He's too much like our father."

"Your father. I didn't have one."

His brow furrowed. "Skylar—"

"Just drop it. I never said I wanted Scotty to be my type, so stop worrying about whether or not he is."

He nodded, not looking at me. "Yeah. Okay."

"I love you, Tate." I fixed the collar of his suit jacket, then rested a hand on his shoulder. "And I appreciate everything you've done for me."

"I feel the same way about you." He smiled, his blue eyes soft and tender instead of guarded and alert. "You're the only good thing left in this world, and I just want you to be happy."

"I am." With Scotty, and the rest of his colleagues, he was cold and callous, but to me, he was the best brother a girl could ask for. I'd fight anyone who suggested otherwise. "Why wouldn't I be happy with you as my brother?"

He twisted his lips into an almost smile. Lifting his wrist, he checked his watch and sighed. "I really do have to go. Dinner tomorrow night? I have another big meeting next Friday, and it's gonna run late, so I'll miss our normal night."

We went out to dinner together every other Friday. It had been our thing ever since I started college. I nodded, smiling. "I wouldn't miss it for the world."

"Oh, and my lawyer will be coming by to see you later today, around five. You need to sign a few papers for me," he said, stepping back. His shirt was crisp and free of wrinkles. "Should be quick and easy."

"What kind of papers?"

"Nothing. Just my will and living testament." He lifted a hand. "Don't look at me like that. It's just a precaution."

Yet . . . I felt like it wasn't.

"Okay. Sure." I hugged myself, swallowing hard, knowing something was up. Something he was trying to hide from me. He should know better. I could read him easier than anyone else in the world. "Everything's okay, though. Right?"

"Of course." He smiled again, but it didn't reach his eyes this time. "Why wouldn't it be?"

He clearly had no idea that I knew more about him than he'd ever want me to. So I didn't say anything, just smiled. "Love you."

"Love you, too."

I watched him go, swallowing hard. My phone buzzed and I pulled it out.

It was Scotty. Everything okay up there?

I slid the key into the lock and slipped inside my apartment. Yeah, it's fine. He's on his way down now.

Does he know about us?

I dropped my purse and locked the door behind me. I didn't tell him anything. I told you I wouldn't.

Good.

I bit my lip, staring at the short replies he was giving me back. It was like our first date all over again. There was my confirmation I'd been seeking that he was pushing me away. Even so, I stupidly put myself out there, and typed: Will I see you tonight?

It showed up as read instantly, so I waited for an answer I knew wasn't going to come. He didn't answer. Of course he didn't. Even if he hadn't actually broken things off last night, this morning would have served as a wake-up call. Tate suspected something was up, and nothing good would come if he learned he was right.

I rested against my door, knowing Scotty was right to end things, but hating it anyway. I lost track of how long I stood there, staring at my phone, waiting for a reply. But after a while I shook off the cloud of sadness hanging over me and pushed away from the door, heading to the bathroom. Time to shower, and study, and then study some more . . .

And time to forget all about Scotty Donahue.

He'd already decided to forget about me.

CHAPTER 15

SCOTTY

"That'll never work. They'd spot us coming from a mile away," Brian growled, shaking his head. "No way, O'Brien."

"But they'll all be in the meeting," Chris argued, pointing at the square on the drawing that represented the room the men would be in. "We could open this door, scare all the women out of the room at gunpoint, and take the men down without worrying—"

Frankie shook his head, looking murderous. "And let the chicks sound the alarm? No way. You're high if you think I'll allow that."

Tate stood back, watching everyone argue, rubbing his chin. He had his other hand on his hip, and his brow was furrowed. His red hair was as immaculate as ever, but he looked . . . *tired*. Like his heart wasn't really in this fight. Sure, he wanted to win, and he was pissed at Bitter Hill, but something like this wasn't Steel Row, and he seemed all too aware of that fact.

"They'll run at the first sign of danger," Chris said at the same time. "Or we can set a small fire in the front, giving the women a chance to see it and run, and then put a damn bomb at the other end of the club's escape route, and blow the Bitter Hill assholes up. We pick off the ones that survive and make it out the front. It's perfect," Chris argued, glancing at me quickly. "Back me *up*, Scotty."

Putting the women in danger sat wrong in my gut. I wanted to minimize the potential loss of life even though I was fairly certain we'd be able to pull this off without a hitch. I had the DEA at my back, and we were all locked, loaded, and ready to swoop in to stop this war, once and for all. Furthermore, the more witnesses we had against Bitter Hill, the better. But if those women were armed, and they shot at us, it could all go south really fast.

There was no clear "right" answer here.

Just as I was about to speak, the door burst open, and an older member, Roger, stumbled in. We turned incredulously toward the man. No one ever interrupted a closed meeting. *Ever.* It was unheard of.

Tate's hand dropped, and his face flushed with the murderous rage I saw burning in his eyes. "You better have a hell of a good reason for opening that damn—"

"I'm sorry," Roger said quickly, searching the room till he found who he was looking for. "But . . . Chris."

Chris stiffened, straightening. "Yeah?"

"It's . . . It's your girl. Molly."

Chris stilled, his face going ghostly white, his fists rolling at his sides. "What?"

"The hospital called repeatedly, so I finally answered your phone for you. She got in a car accident . . . but we don't think it was an accident. I sent one of the recruits to check it out." Roger flicked a glance at Tate, wringing his hands. "Word is, she was on her way home from school, and a car hit her. Witnesses say the driver got out and started for the car, a gun in his hand, but a cop showed up, and he fled the scene."

Chris stepped forward, jaw working, then stopped. "Is she . . . ?"

"She's alive. At Boston West Med."

Chris didn't say another word. Just started for the door. I followed after him, brushing past Tate without a thought. He caught my arm. Locking eyes with me, he said, "Don't let him do anything stupid. Not yet."

I nodded once, gritting my teeth.

He let me go, and I hurried after Chris, ignoring everyone else. If he lost his shit over this, there would be no holding him back. And if Molly . . .

No, she was fine.

She'd be fine.

I caught up to Chris. "Hey, she's okay. Don't—"

"She is not okay," Chris growled, shoving through the door into the late afternoon sunlight. We'd been at this all morning, meeting after meeting, going over every possibility for every scenario so we could attack Bitter Hill fully prepared. "And it's my fault. They're dead. Every one of them. *Fucking dead.*"

I grabbed his shoulder and spun him around. "Yeah. Next Friday."

"No." He shook me off, quickening his strides and pulling his gun from his holster. He stared down at his gun, checking the mag. "Right now. Don't even think about trying to stop—"

I shoved him into the car, pressing him against it. "Stop being stupid. We need to keep our heads in the game. You told me that yesterday."

He aimed his gun at my head, pressing it into my temple, his face perfectly composed. "Get off me. *Now.*"

"No." I didn't back off, even though he could easily blow my brains out in his anger. "I understand you're upset, and I am, too. I like Molly. But you can't—"

He took a swing at me, and I lurched back, knowing all too well how much power was behind that fist. "Fuck you, you don't understand anything. You don't love her. You don't love *anyone*!"

I slammed him back into the car, easily disarming him since he didn't actually intend to shoot me. I slid his gun into my back pocket, casting a surreptitious glance toward the clubhouse to see if anyone watched us. No one did . . . yet. "You need to pull yourself together. Take a deep breath, maybe two, and then I'll get you to Boston West. To Molly."

He struggled to free himself, but I didn't budge. Too much was at stake to lose him now. "She's my life. My world. She's why I breathe. Why I fight. Why I stayed. And she . . . she . . . I . . ." He deflated in front of me, his eyes closing as he said, "It's my fault. This happened because she loves me. Because hurting her hurts me."

"And you'll get your vengeance. I swear it. They'll either die or get caught by the DEA and never be free men again." I backed up and held my hands up in a nonthreatening manner. Chris might be strong, and a hell of a fighter, but if push came to shove, I'd take him to the ground. "But, first, let's go check on your girl. Okay?"

He let out a deep breath, and covered his face. The sun was shining in an impossibly blue sky, a complete mismatch for this situation. It should have been pouring. Chris spoke, dropping his hands in defeat. "I never should have gone back to her place that day. Never should have told her I loved—"

I opened the car door for him. It was his Mustang. I'd drive him there before hitching a ride home, so he'd have his car there. "Don't say something you'll regret. She loves you, and you love her, and Bitter Hill shouldn't have the power to change that."

He didn't say anything.

Just lowered his tall frame into the car.

"Besides," I added, watching as he settled into his seat, staring straight ahead with a hard jaw. "She'd kick your ass if she heard you say that."

I slammed the car door shut, palming his keys, which I'd taken out of his pocket without him even noticing. As I settled into the driver's seat, I buckled in, then started the car. He stared at me as I sped out of the parking lot and onto Monroe. He held on to the door, cursing under his breath. "This is my car. Why are you driving?"

"Because I don't trust you to drive right now."

I swerved around a parked car, narrowly missing the Buick coming our way. "Says the man who almost crashed my car. Put one scratch, one *damn* scratch in it, and I'll—"

"Kill me. I know." Opening the glove box, I tossed my personal phone at him, using my thumbprint to unlock it instead of the passcode. We'd driven to the Patriot together the day before and I'd stashed it in his car, and then promptly forgotten about it. In our rush to leave the clubhouse, we'd left behind the other cells. "Call the hospital. Try to get ahold of her."

Chris dialed first Molly's number, and then the hospital. As he spoke to someone, his voice low, I stared at the road ahead of us. It was weird, seeing Chris like this. So scared. So unsure. So damn vulnerable. It was something I would have sworn he'd never allow.

Weakness got you killed in this life.

And, apparently, it got your girl killed, too.

Not that Molly was actually dead, but it wasn't for lack of effort on Bitter Hill's part. It was because a cop had been too close for comfort. That was the only reason she was still breathing, and there was no guarantee that her lungs would continue to operate. She'd only be truly safe when this war was over, and then I'd try my damnedest to make sure the Sons didn't start another.

We needed to end this, before more innocent people were taken down. Immediately, my mind went to Skylar and the way I'd left things. There was no doubt in my mind she was pissed at me for pushing her away, but if she knew the dangers of being with me, if she fully understood what it meant, she would be thanking me, not giving me the evil eye. It wasn't that *she* wasn't worth the risk—it was that *I* wasn't worth the risk.

She just didn't know it yet.

One of the things they taught me at my accelerated program in Quantico—because a long absence wasn't easy to explain to the Sons—was that while you were permitted to have relationships once you graduated, you had to remember that anyone you loved was dragged into your life, and that you'd have to keep secrets from them—and they'd have to be okay with that. Plenty of agents had wives, and children, and they were perfectly safe from harm. But I wasn't *just* an agent. I was also in a gang, and Skylar was the gang leader's sister . . .

Nothing was simple with us.

I stopped at the parking garage gate and grabbed a ticket, handing it off to Chris. "For later."

He pocketed it and hung up, his face filling with color a little bit more. "Thanks."

"Any news?"

"She's on the fourth floor, under general observation. I didn't get to talk to her, but she's conscious and stable." He undid his seat belt and opened the door. "I need to see her, man."

I followed, locking the car and trailing him silently. Chris pushed the button on the elevator that would take us to ground level, so we could cross the road and go into Boston West. It was an upscale hospital, not a place Steel Row guys like us were usually sent, so hopefully she'd be safe here. I was fairly certain Chris would ensure that.

Knowing him, she'd have a full security detail from now on.

He and Molly could certainly afford it.

"If she's in the hospital awhile, you can sit out next week." I dragged a hand through my hair. "We can take care of Bitter Hill without you."

"Hell no. I'll be there."

"I figured," I said dryly. I wished he wouldn't come, though. It would be one less person for me to worry about. The only reason he was helping me was because of his guilt over attempting to murder my brother. Now he was dedicated to making sure I lived, even at the expense of his own life. I'd seen it come into play enough times to know he'd die for me.

And that's not something I needed on my conscience.

I had enough damn shit there already.

"Don't be stupid, though," I added.

He snorted. "And by *stupid*, you mean don't try to save your ass if you're about to be eighty-sixed. Right?"

"Precisely."

"I swore to keep you alive for Lucas, and I stand by that."

He crossed his arms and leaned against the wall, frowning. "I've already broken enough promises to Lucas. I won't break this one."

"He doesn't know you made this promise," I pointed out pragmatically. "He was gone when you decided to become a goddamn knight in shining armor."

"Doesn't matter," Chris said, stubbornly jutting his chin out. His brown hair stood on edge, and he had a light to his eyes that suggested I was getting nowhere with him. "I made it, and I'm not breaking it. End of story."

"You also made a promise to Molly, to love her for the rest of your life." I walked into the elevator, holding the door open for him as he came in. "You know how you feel right now? How scared and pissed you are that she got hurt?"

He shot me a *no shit, Sherlock* look.

"Well, if you do something stupid and get yourself killed, Molly will be going through this for the rest of her life. This empty, angry, churning feeling in your gut?" I pushed the fourth-floor button. "That'll be her. Sad, and angry, and alone, all because you wanted to pay back a debt to a man who is happier now than he was before you tried to kill him."

Finally, doubt shadowed his eyes. But, stubbornly, he persisted. "I won't stand back and let you die."

"I never said you should." I rubbed my jaw. "Just don't do some crazy savior shit for the sake of being a hero. I don't need that from you. Just have good aim, cover my back, and be smart. That's all I need. And if I go down, then so be it. I know the risks I run in my line of work."

"I won't be stupid, but I won't be a damn coward either." Chris locked eyes with me, his dark brown ones torn with indecision. "That's all I can promise you."

It wasn't enough, but I guessed it would have to do.

The elevator doors opened, and he charged through them, heading right for the desk with a nurse in scrubs behind it. He set his hands on the flat white top. "Where is she?"

She flinched away, instinctively sensing danger, and scooted her chair back, resting her hand on the phone on her desk. "Can I . . . help you . . . sir?"

"Molly Lachlan." He gripped the edge of the desk. "Where is she?"

"Who are you, sir?" the woman asked, her cheeks paling. "We can't just give out information to nonfamily."

"I'm the only family she has. I'm her fiancé."

My jaw dropped, because he hadn't said a damn word about *that*. Maybe he was just making it up, to ensure he could get back to her room without a hitch.

"Your name, sir?" the nurse asked hesitantly, giving Chris the once-over all girls like her gave to guys like us. Half terrified, half turned on.

"Chris O'Brien."

She clicked her mouse, staring at the screen. "Yes, I see you here, listed as her fiancé."

"Chris—" I started.

"Not now." He gave me his back. "What room is she in?"

"406. I can take you there."

The woman stood up, watching Chris carefully, before scrutinizing me. She looked at me with the same fear-slash-attraction. She was wasting her time. I might be a man-whore, but right now there was only one woman on my mind, and this nurse wasn't about to change that.

We followed her, and I trailed slightly behind Chris, guarding his back since he was too fucked up right now to pay attention to his surroundings. When we stopped in front of her open door, his hand trembled as he rested it on the door frame, letting out a shaky breath. The tenderness in his eyes, the absolute terror and love, was enough to floor even a cynic like me.

"Princess," he whispered, his voice cracking.

Molly turned her head toward him, a soft smile lighting up her face, despite the bruise already forming by her eye and the split lip cracking her smile. "I'm okay."

"I . . ." He rushed across the room, falling to his knees at the side of her bed, resting his head on her chest. He didn't say anything else, just wrapped his arms around her, and she rested her left hand on his head, running her fingers through his hair, her diamond engagement ring twinkling in the fluorescent lights.

Damn it.

It wasn't a lie.

He'd *proposed* to Molly.

I watched the tender scene between the two of them, knowing I was intruding but unable to look away. I heard the soft squeaking of her shoes as the nurse backed out of the room, giving us privacy. Chris tipped his head toward Molly's, and he looked at her like she was his whole world, the only thing that mattered, and I knew him well enough to know that's exactly how he felt. That his whole life revolved around this one tiny woman. And yet . . .

He'd still give it up for me.

I had underestimated Chris O'Brien.

He was a hero, and he deserved to live the life of one.

This war with Bitter Hill *would* end, and we *would* win, and then I'd find a way to get him free from this life, too. I'd find a way for him and Molly to be happy and live a normal life, just like I'd done for Heidi and Lucas. I had to give them that, even if it cost me everything.

Because I had less to lose.

My mind went to Skylar, and the way it felt when I held

her in my arms, but I shook that thought off. That completion, that happiness, was nothing compared to my duty to this man.

Swallowing hard, I walked away, my heart heavy and aching in my chest as I called a taxi. I gave the driver the address of the Danielses' apartment building, and made the ride in silence. We passed tourists bundled in winter jackets, holding hands and laughing as they explored Boston, carrying on with their lives like normal people did. No worries of gang wars, or maintaining your cover so you didn't get yourself shot. No car crashes that weren't really accidents at all. No matter how hard I tried, I couldn't shake the way Chris had looked at Molly, and the way she'd looked at him, and the warmth that had made me feel in my chest. And I couldn't stop thinking of Skylar . . .

And how she made me feel that way, too.

Warm.

Tossing a twenty at the driver, I got out of the cab and made my way up to the second floor, my heart pounding as I climbed the stairs two at a time. I walked right up to her apartment and stopped, pressing my ear against her door. I needed to hear something. I knew she was safe, that no one knew she existed or that she was mine. But Bitter Hill was striking our women, and I *needed to know she was okay.* I listened, holding my breath.

There was silence, no hint of life, or anything else inside the room. I flattened my palm against the cool wood, pressing against it harder. If she didn't sneeze or cough—

I heard it too late.

The sliding of a latch.

The door swung in, and I stumbled inside her condo, falling into her arms. She caught me, stumbling backward under my weight, and I caught both of us, locking my feet into position and pulling her close until we ended up in each other's arms.

Right where we damn well belonged.

It might be stupid, and it might be a horrible idea, but the way Chris looked at Molly? That's how I felt about Skylar. She was *my* world . . . and tonight, I needed to be with her.

She let out a small sound, steadied herself, and looked up at me in surprise, dropping the bag of garbage she'd held. "Scotty? What—?"

"I just wanted to make sure you were okay. I didn't mean to . . . to . . ."

She cocked her head to the side. "Didn't mean to what?"

Fall for you. Care about you. Let you in. "Knock."

"You didn't," she said slowly.

"I know. But I would've." We stared at one another, with nothing watching us but the white walls of her home, both of us breathing heavily, and I didn't let her go. I didn't step closer either, but still. I should have let go. I should have walked away. I curled my hands over the fabric of her shirt tightly. "I have to go."

She breathed in, slow and deep. "Okay."

When I didn't move, she blinked.

"Are you okay?" she asked, her eyes soft with concern, and with something else I was too much of a pussy to admit.

I stared at her, trying my damnedest not to say anything.

To admit nothing.

I shook my head once. Visions popped through my head. Bobby's bloody shoelaces. The kid with the shaved head running for his life before Brian and Frankie shot him. Chris, clinging to Molly, terrified to lose her. Lucas, fighting for Heidi's life, and his own.

I was done denying myself the one thing that would make it all go away.

The one thing that made me better. *Her.*

"No," I said, my voice raspy as hell. "I'm not okay. Nothing is okay."

And then I kissed her.

CHAPTER 16

SKYLAR

I curled my fists into his jacket, holding on for dear life. Scotty Donahue was, hands down, the most confusing man I'd ever met. He told me he wasn't the guy for me in one breath, then proved he was. He told me I shouldn't be with him, then pulled me closer. He ignored me, then kissed me like he couldn't breathe without me. When he held me in his arms like this, his kiss made everything better. I didn't know what that meant yet, or why he had so much power over me, but he did.

And I had a feeling that wasn't changing any time soon.

Not even when he walked away for good.

He cradled my face in his hands, backing me toward my couch as his mouth ravaged mine, no mercy—and I was totally okay with that. His mouth continued to claim me as he pressed his body against mine, slipping a hand under my butt as he slid between my legs. His hardness pressed against where I needed him most, filling me in ways only he could.

We were destined to be together, him and me, and the sooner he accepted that, the better. I had. I *did*. He was mine. And I was his. We just made sense.

He nodded, almost as if he heard my thoughts, and broke off the kiss long enough to rip my shirt over my head, tossing it on the living room floor. The second he had that off, he undid my bra and then closed his mouth over my nipple, sucking on it deeply. I moaned and threaded my hands through his hair, arching my back as a short breath escaped my lungs. *"Scotty."*

His hand slipped in between my legs, giving me what I wanted. He released my one nipple with a popping sound, and went to the other, giving it the same attention he gave the first. At the same time, he circled his fingertips over my core, teasing me, giving me what I needed, but not enough of it. I groaned and tugged on his hair impatiently.

He scraped the edges of his teeth over my second nipple, sending pleasure rocketing through my body to pool in my belly. He kissed a path down my body, taking his hand with him, stopping at the small patch of skin directly over my waistband. As he rolled my leggings down, I lifted my hips to help. He made quick work of the panties I wore, too, and then I was naked under him.

Thank God.

He leaned back, staring at my body with heated eyes, trailing the tip of his finger from the base of my throat down to the top of the tiny triangle of hair at the juncture of my thighs. "You are the most beautiful woman I've ever met, Sky. So soft. So gentle. So . . ." He locked eyes with me, dipping his finger between my legs to touch me. ". . . *good.*"

I let my eyes close, opening my thighs more, pushing his head slightly down so he'd get my message. "I'm not that good. Right now, I wanna be bad. Really bad."

He chuckled, the raw sound washing over me like his fingertips on my skin as he slid lower over my body, dropping a kiss on my inner thigh. "Lucky for you? I happen to excel at being bad. It's all I know."

I opened my mouth to argue with him, to tell him that a guy who worried he was bad wasn't bad at all, but then he closed his mouth over me and all coherent thought left. I arched against his tongue and closed my eyes, offering myself to him in the most intimate way I knew. He palmed my breasts as his tongue moved over me, squeezing my nipples and driving me insane with pleasure, and need, and . . . and . . .

Crying out, I squeezed my legs on either side of his head, writhing against his mouth, desperate for the pleasure I knew he could give me. He made a low, sexy sound, and released a breast so he could thrust a finger inside me, slashing his tongue over me harder as he did so. I screamed something incoherent, straining against him, and then he did it again . . .

Sending me to heaven and back.

He pushed off the couch and tore his shirt over his head, his muscles flexing as he undid his jeans, kicking out of them impatiently after taking a condom out of his back pocket. I dropped an arm off the couch, letting it hang there as I came back down from the high he'd sent me on, watching him from under my lashes. He pushed his boxers down his hips, rolled the condom over his erection, and squeezed it once.

"It's almost a crime to touch you right now," he said, locking eyes with me. "You look so pretty lying there, cheeks flushed, nipples hard. If I could draw like my buddy Chris, I'd make a picture of you. Right here. Like this. You're the prettiest picture I've ever seen."

A car honked outside, and another one honked back. Voices rose in anger, and a police siren wailed, but Scotty didn't even hesitate as he stepped closer to me, ignoring everything else. He was looking at me like he would never get enough, and it was dangerous to think that. To believe he needed me like I needed him. "I'm yours, Scotty, even if you're never mine. And that won't change, whether you like it or not."

"I like it too much."

I didn't say anything because I wasn't sure what *to* say.

"I shouldn't say this. Shouldn't be honest." His chest rose and fell fast. "But I've been yours since the second you touched me, and I'm done pretending that's not true. Done denying it," he admitted, his voice raw. "You and me, we've got something special."

It was a big admission, coming from a guy like him, and we both knew it.

Without saying anything else, without *needing* anything else, I opened my arms to him. He hesitated, then slid into them, wrapping his under me so he held me close. I locked my legs around him, knowing this was different somehow. That what we were doing wasn't just sex, or just fun, or meaningless. It was real, and we were crossing a line we'd sworn not to cross.

His mouth sought and found mine, and we groaned in unison as he pushed inside me, filling me in ways no other man had . . . or could. I knew fully well that he was going to hurt me in the end, and I didn't care. I couldn't think of any cold, logical reason why I would be so stupid unless . . . unless . . .

Oh God. Oh no.

It couldn't be that. Anything but that.

If I was that stupid, that crazy, to give him my heart when

he clearly didn't want it . . . I totally was. I'd gone and done it. I'd fallen in love.

I *loved* Scotty Donahue.

And he was going to break my stupid heart.

My mouth stilled under his, and he held me tighter, reassuringly holding me close as he moved inside me, making my pulse race as fast as my mind. I held on to him tightly, burying my face in his shoulder when he broke off the kiss, hiding from him, to prevent him from seeing what I felt.

If he knew . . .

His lips brushed against my temple, and he moaned, moving faster, his arms going tighter around me. As he drove himself deep inside me, I climbed up that mountain with him, and when we both came, there was so much emotion and intensity behind it that it took my breath away.

He collapsed on top of me, resting his face in the crook of my neck, his arms not loosening. "Jesus," he breathed. "What the hell was that?"

Love. It was love.

I closed my eyes, remaining silent. If I opened my mouth, I'd say something stupid, and I'd send him running so far away that he'd never come back.

"Hey." Scotty reared back on his elbows, looking down at me with concern. His lips were soft, and his green eyes were glowing with something I couldn't quite place. "You okay?"

I nodded, biting down on my lip. "More than okay. I'm great."

And I love you.

He smoothed my hair off my face, then dragged his thumb over my lower lip. "I don't know what you're doing to me, but every time I close my eyes, I see you. And when I see you, I need you close by, to fill an emptiness I have a feeling will never stop." He gave me a soft smile. "I need you, and I'm not sure what I should do about that, because I've never felt this way about someone before. I've never been unable to walk away, even though I know I should."

"I . . ." My heart raced as I cut myself off, because I didn't trust myself to say anything else. Those three little words, those dangerous words, were on the tip of my tongue, dying to be released. I'd never been in love before, and now that I was, I ached to be as honest in this as I was in everything else. I wanted to say it. Wanted to *tell* him.

When it became clear I wasn't going to say anything else, he pushed up off me and stood, picking up his shirt and tossing it at me as he gave me his back. "I'm starving, are you?"

Sitting, I shrugged into his shirt, nodding even though he wasn't looking at me. Didn't matter. He didn't really need an answer anyway. I watched him step into his pants, his movements smooth and assured as he walked to the trash to remove the condom. I buttoned up the last five buttons, then pulled my panties on. Standing, I ran my fingers through my hair, which was crazy and knotted, and probably resembled a lion's mane more than actual *hair*.

He walked up to me and cradled my head tenderly, studying me with bright green eyes. "Leave it. It's sexy as hell."

"I . . ." And then I opened my mouth and did the worst thing possible. I told him the truth. "I love you, Scotty."

He stared down at me, mouth open, and didn't move. Just *stared*.

Footsteps pounded down the hallway, followed by a door banging against the wall next to us. *His door.* I jumped, looking past him toward mine. Someone tried to turn the knob.

He froze, nostrils flaring, and paled. "Shit. Get down!"

I blinked. *"What?"*

Without another word, he pushed me backward, taking me off guard. I fell on my butt, skidding across the hardwood floor toward the dining room, behind the wall that separated the two rooms, and slammed my head against it hard enough to see stars. The skin on the backs of my legs burned from the friction, and my head felt like an anvil had been dropped on it.

I rolled to my side, groaning, and clutched my aching head. Blinking, I searched for Scotty, my view partially obstructed by the wall. He knelt behind my couch, breathing steadily, staring at the door like he was waiting for . . . whatever was out there.

"Scotty? What—?"

Someone kicked the door in, and a masked man stood there, holding a gun. I screamed and tried to struggle to my feet, but my limbs were like jelly, and I just went limp. There was nothing solid in my body except for *fear*. It pounded through me like a locomotive train, barreling through without hesitation, and I was so sure I was about to watch the man I loved die.

Scotty let out a terrifying battle cry—there was no other word for it—and charged the gunman without even a hint of fear, and the boom of a bullet being discharged from the barrel filled my home. They went down in a tangle of limbs and the gun skidded across the floor uselessly.

I scooted farther away on my butt, breathing heavily, eyes wide as they struggled against one another for control of the weapon. Blood smeared the wood as they rolled, and I gasped, covering my mouth, unable to stop looking at the streaks. Not even after they rolled again, smearing the blood into discernable blobs.

Someone was bleeding.

God, had Scotty been shot?

Since the gun had slid toward my hiding spot behind the wall between the living room and dining room, I reached for it, but the attacker's foot hit it before I could close my hand around it, sending the weapon skidding out of my reach. Scotty managed to get on top of the shooter, and I found out where the blood was coming from—*Scotty*.

He'd been hit in the shoulder, and yet he was still fighting like it was nothing.

Like he felt no pain.

He lifted his fist and plowed it down into the man's face mercilessly, bone crunching under the force of his punch. As the man struggled to reach the gun, he shoved his forearm into Scotty's throat, forcing his head backward. Scotty's long fingers, the same fingers which had stroked me into heaven, closed over the grip of the gun, and he aimed it at the man beneath him, braced himself, and pulled the trigger.

Blood splattered all across Scotty's face and chest.

The scream I let out was almost as loud as the gunshot.

I covered my ringing ears as I stared at the intruder. Blood seeped out of his throat where the bullet had hit, spurting as he stared at the ceiling with wide, horrified eyes.

Within seconds, it was over, and I had a dead man in my living room.

Scotty struggled to his feet, ripping the mask off the man. I covered my mouth when I saw how young he was. He didn't even look old enough to drink, let alone murder someone. Scotty cursed, tossed the mask on the floor, and swiped a bloody forearm over his forehead.

It didn't help.

If anything, he looked bloodier than before.

He was breathing heavily, and there was a murderous rage burning deep in his eyes, but it chilled as he focused on me. He softened, right in front of my eyes. Glancing at the dead man at his feet, he stepped between us, blocking him from my view as he held a hand out, the other one still firmly wrapped around the gun. "Skylar . . ." he started.

I backed up a step, heart pounding, fear still coursing through me because of what I saw behind him. It wasn't over. None of this was over.

Something crossed his expression at my retreat. He held his hands up higher. They were stained red. I swore I could smell it. The blood. All over him. "Don't be scared. I'm a—"

He cut himself off as two more masked men came up behind him, both holding guns. One was aimed at me, one at him. He tensed before they even spoke, somehow sensing them.

"If you know what's good for you, you'll turn around and keep going, before I have to kill you both," he warned. "If you're the same age as the first one, you have too much to live for to die fighting a fight that's not even yours. Run. *Now*."

The chill factor in his voice was enough to set off an arctic freeze. However, the men didn't so much as hesitate. If anything, they got even more confident. "You might be stupid enough to risk your life, but I'm guessing you won't risk hers. Lower the gun."

Scotty locked eyes with me, and what I saw there—the anger, fear, and vulnerability—sent the same coursing through me. He lowered his gun to the floor, a muscle ticking in his jaw.

Something told me if he were alone, he would take on both these guys and win, and would walk away with a few scrapes. But because I was here . . . he was going to die.

We were *both* going to die.

CHAPTER 17

SCOTTY

This was why guys like me shouldn't fall in love, or give ourselves over to the weakness that came along with it. But I'd stupidly let my heart guide me, and now I was going to get her killed with my selfishness.

Chris was right earlier.

I never should have come back.

Instead, I should have watched her from a distance, like Tate requested, and I should have kept my dirty hands to myself. I held them up, staring at the bloodstained tips. It was under my nails, in the cracks of my skin, and there was still more bloodshed to come, because I would die before I let them touch a hair on her head. By the time this was over, I'd never be clean again.

She watched me, eyes wide, lips parted. "Sc-Scotty?"

"You're going to regret this," I said, forcing my attention off of Sky and keeping my voice low. The kid behind me smelled like Old Spice cologne and Axe aftershave. "You have no idea who you're messing with."

"We know exactly who you are." The kid behind me crept around, heading for Sky. I tensed, my fingers itching to wrap around his throat. "We followed you from the hospital, and waited to see where you went. Our intel said you were next door, but apparently you're fucking the neighbor." He licked his lips and swaggered forward, laughing. Sky stiffened. "I can see why. Damn, girl. Stand up so I can see all of you."

Sky didn't say a word.

And she sure as hell didn't stand.

"Let me rephrase that," he said, aiming the gun at her head. "Stand up or I'll shoot you, and my buddy will kill your lover right in front of you, *after* I make him watch us together."

Sky paled, her gaze flitting to me, and struggled to her feet.

She stumbled, but caught herself.

Rage rushed through my veins, and I took a step forward. A gun pressed against the back of my head and I froze, my pulse racing. That was his first mistake. Getting so close. The second was in thinking I froze because I was scared. I wasn't. I was *pissed*.

They *dared* to threaten my girl.

"Don't hurt him." She rolled her hands into fists and lifted her chin. She looked so defiant, standing there in nothing more than my shirt. "Don't even touch him."

The man approaching her laughed. "I don't take orders from chicks." He walked behind her, touching her shoulder. She flinched, but otherwise remained still. "No matter how pretty they are."

"If you're looking for a protection fee, I can pay it," she said in a rush. "Just put the guns away."

"This isn't about money. It's about him." He pressed his gun against her temple, closing an arm around her waist. "You should have picked a better lover. One who wasn't a Son."

Her gaze slammed into mine. "He's out."

"No. He isn't." The guy behind her laughed. "Tell her."

I didn't say anything. I wouldn't speak on command.

The kid cocked the trigger. "Whatever. Take your secrets to the grave. But first . . . ?"

His hand crept up Sky's shirt, groping her breast. She flinched, but she didn't cower away or make a sound. A small tear escaped her eye, and that was the end of it for me.

They'd made my girl *cry*.

Spinning, I grabbed the other man's gun out of his lax grip, since he was too busy drooling over Sky, and shot him without a hint of the regret I'd felt with the other kids. He collapsed to the ground lifelessly, like a broken marionette. I spun to take the second one out, knowing this would be trickier since Sky was in front of him.

Just as I was about to launch myself at them, Skylar slammed the back of her head into his nose, stomped on his foot, and then leapt out of the way when he released her to clutch his nose. As she rolled across the floor, I pointed the gun at him and pulled the trigger.

My aim was true.

The kid hit the floor, red spreading across his chest. He twitched, lying on his side, and then stilled, his brown eyes staring vacantly straight ahead, his black ski mask twisted and half off.

I fell to my knees, clutching my shoulder where I'd been hit. It stung like a bitch, and the room was starting to blur a bit from blood loss. Guess it was worse than I originally thought. I gritted my teeth, blinking against the unconsciousness trying to take me down, and focused on Sky's pale face. Immediately, a calm took over, like she had a medicinal effect on my nerves.

She sat on the floor, eyes wide, hugging her knees as she rocked back and forth.

"Are you okay?" I asked quietly, blinking away the blackness.

She didn't answer. Just stared straight ahead.

Shit. She was in shock.

"Sky?" I said, struggling to stand, to get to her. "It's okay."

"I know. I'm fine. Sandra Bullock saved the day," she said, laughing. It came out hysterical sounding. She covered her mouth, still staring. "She . . . I . . ."

I steadied myself on my feet, swaying slightly, trying to keep her mind off what happened, and Sandra Bullock seemed a good enough way to do that as any. "How'd she do that?"

"Huh?" Her head lifted up, and she blinked at me. "Oh. I learned that move from my favorite movie. When you didn't come over, I binge-watched her movies last night. She teaches people to defend themselves in one of them."

I took a step toward her, pressing my palm to my shoulder to slow the bleeding, forcing a reassuring smile. The room spun, and I wasn't sure if I'd make it to her side before passing out, but I was determined as hell to try. She stared at the guy who'd been holding her. The one she'd helped me kill. The horror in her eyes would haunt me forever. "Which movie?" I asked softly.

"*Miss Congeniality*. It's S.I.N.G. Solar plexus, instep, nose, groin." She let out a small laugh, then covered her mouth, staring at the man who had been holding her captive. "I . . . I . . ."

I fell to my knees in front of her, reaching out and cupping her cheek. I left streaks of red behind on her pale, perfect skin, and that's all I could see. "Sh. I've got you."

She closed her eyes, tears streaming down her cheeks, smearing the blood streaks. A tear landed with a splat on the hardwood floor, and I tried to pull her into my arms, but she pushed back, staring at my shoulder. "You're shot. We have to call the police. Report this."

She was right. There was no way we could avoid this mess. Someone had probably already called it in. We hadn't been attacked in Steel Row, so there wouldn't be a whole lot of time before the cops showed up, and then I'd have to go through all the shit of being treated like a gang member, while secretly contacting my superior and getting him to haul my ass out of jail. I was exhausted just thinking about all the bureaucratic hoops I'd have to jump through, but, more important, I had to make sure Sky was okay.

"They're on their way, I'm sure." I grabbed her hand, but my vision was starting to fade. "I might pass out, Sky. I'll be okay, but I lost a lot of blood, so I don't think . . ." I cut off, because footsteps came pounding down the hallway, rushing toward us. *"Shit."*

She looked up at me with fear-filled blue eyes. "Oh God. It's not over?"

"It's probably just the cops, but stay down just in case." I struggled to my feet, turned, lifted the gun, and took aim. My grip was firm, even if I was barely conscious. "I won't let anyone else hurt you again. I swear it, Sky."

If this wasn't the cops, if this was another attack, they'd find they picked the wrong target. I wasn't fighting for my life—I was fighting for *hers.*

When it came to Skylar's safety, I had no mercy.

Tate skidded into view, almost tripping over the first dead

body. He surveyed the scene, counting the corpses, and his face went paler than I'd ever seen before. He was always so calm. So collected. But not tonight. He turned in a slow circle, taking in the carnage inside his sister's usually pristine apartment with horror, like he couldn't put the violence in place with the location. She wasn't supposed to be touched by this life, so it was almost as if his brain couldn't deal with it.

Brian came up behind him, gun drawn.

I wasn't sure whether to be relieved it was them, or start running for my life now, before Tate realized why I'd been here for the whole attack. But at least Sky was safe now. That was all that mattered. I lowered my gun, releasing a breath.

"Skylar?" Tate croaked, tucking his gun into his waistband, under his fancy suit, scanning for his baby sister. "*Skylar!*" he called frantically.

"H-here," she whispered. "I'm here. But Scotty's hurt."

Tate ran into the room, totally ignoring me and everything else, sliding on his knees to her side. He pulled her into his arms, lowering his face to her hair, and breathing in deeply. His hand trembled at he cradled the back of her head. "Jesus Christ. I'm sorry. Are you okay, Skylar?"

She nodded, clinging to him. "Scotty saved me. He . . . he saved my life."

Brian shook his head, staring at me, and came to my side. "You need the doc."

"Yeah." I turned my head to look at my shoulder in surprise. For a second there, watching Tate and Skylar, I'd forgotten about the pain. Now, though, I clutched my shoulder. "I think I do."

"Thank you for getting here so fast. I . . ." Tate glanced at me, over Sky's head, and broke off. His focus shifted to my shoulder, and the blood smeared all over it, and then to the fact that I wasn't wearing a shirt. It didn't take long for him to put two and two together as he lowered his lids and took in what his sister was wearing—and, more important, what she *wasn't*. When he met my eyes again, there was a quiet rage in them, one that promised much more than a gunshot to the shoulder when he was finished with me. *"You son of a bitch."*

I fell back against the wall, blinking in an attempt to keep my consciousness, and heard police sirens in the distance. "Sir, I can explain—"

With a blur of speed that the Flash himself would envy, Tate launched himself at me, taking me down. My head slammed into the wall behind me, and I saw nothing for a few seconds. When my vision cleared, he was on top of me, his face red with rage and his blue eyes blazing with hatred. He grabbed my hair, lifted my head, and slammed it into the floor again. "I *trusted* you. You were supposed to fucking *protect* her. *You promised me you wouldn't touch her.*"

Sky lurched to her feet, pulling on Tate's arm. "Stop!"

Tate shook her off and lifted his fist, slamming it into my nose. Pain burst over my skull, and I pushed at his shoulders, trying to get him the hell off me, but it was useless. I was already weak, and my body was done taking a beating for the day.

Skylar screamed, and it sounded like it came from a distance, even though I knew she was next to me. "Stop it! You're hurting him!"

"Damn right I am," Tate growled.

I opened my eyes, having every intention of assuring her I was fine, but I couldn't find the energy to speak. Huh.

Maybe I wasn't okay after all. She pulled on his elbow, falling on her butt when he shook loose of her hold, and I growled when she fell back.

"I . . . I love him!"

Tate froze, his eyes going wide, and turned to her slowly. "What did you just say?"

"You heard me," she shot back stubbornly.

I blinked, and a strangled groan escaped me. "*The ops re oming*," I managed to warn.

Brian cleared his throat, eyeing me nervously as he stepped forward. "Mr. Daniels? He's right. The sirens are getting closer. What do you want to do?"

Tate leaned in and whispered, "You're dead, Agent Donahue. *Dead*."

At first I thought I was hearing things, that the blows to my head had messed with my hearing, but then I saw the way he looked at me. The only thing stopping him from pressing a gun to my temple right now and pulling the trigger was the fact that the cops were minutes away, and his baby sister was right there. The same one who thought he was a saint, and not a killer.

He pushed off me, leaving me where I lay.

Skylar stared at me with horror, trembling. She scrambled to my side, touching my chin gently. "Oh my God. Scotty?"

I tried to smile. "I'm okay, sugar."

Tate made a choked sound and turned to Brian, ignoring us both. "You go. I'm staying here with her. Go to the office and continue to take care of the preparations for next Friday."

Brian hesitated. He had a record and couldn't afford to be caught with a bunch of dead bodies. Tate was squeaky clean, so he had nothing to worry about. Not to mention the fact that his sister would seriously question his need to run from the police. "But, boss—"

"*Understood*?" Tate growled.

Brian nodded, cast one last look at me, and then was gone.

Skylar sobbed, brushing my hair off my forehead, glaring over her shoulder at her brother. "You *hurt* him. He was already shot."

Tate grit his teeth, his upper lip curling. "I don't give a damn."

Her soft fingers touched my chest. "But I love him," she said softly. "You can't just *hit* him."

Tate stiffened, not speaking.

Cops rushed in, guns held up, and screamed, "Nobody move! Hands on your head."

Tate put his hands on his head.

I didn't move. I couldn't.

Skylar choked on a sob, lifting her hands and entwining them behind her head. Her strawberry blonde hair was knotted and straggly, slightly damp with blood and God only knew what else. "Please help him. He saved my life."

Tate stiffened even more. "These men broke into her apartment, and shot at her and her . . . boyfriend."

"And you are?" the cop asked, his voice hard.

"Her brother." He opened his mouth, closed it, and then looked at me. "And his boss."

The cop knelt beside me, pulling his radio closer to his mouth. "This is Walker 1-F reporting. We have a GSW victim and need a bus. Also three DOA. Send the ME and transport."

I blinked against the blackness, and the last thing I saw

was Skylar's face, pale, worried, and hovering over mine as everything faded away. She was probably the last thing I'd ever see, because as soon as Tate got a chance, I would be a dead man . . .

Whether I was awake enough to know it or not.

CHAPTER 18

SKYLAR

I paced the confines of the tiny, poorly lit waiting room for the millionth time, hugging myself and purposely avoiding my brother's eyes. He'd been frowning at me all night, ever since I told him I loved Scotty, and quite frankly—it was getting a little old. As if his silent disapproval wasn't enough, the police made me tell my story over and over again, until even I didn't believe what I was saying, and I *lived* through it. And Scotty . . .

God, Scotty.

I didn't even know if he was alive.

Did people die from a shoulder wound and a beating from an angry brother? Or was he lying in a hospital bed somewhere, healing? Or even worse . . . was he currently being arrested? Those men had said he was still in the gang, and if he was, then the chances of him walking away from this without punishment were slim to none. Would this be his first offense?

I eyed Tate, wanting to ask him for more information, but I knew now was not the time. Running my fingers through my knotty hair, I let out an agitated breath. They'd finally released me from questioning twenty minutes ago, and we'd rushed over here to check on Scotty without changing or showering first.

Well, *I'd* rushed here.

Tate refused to leave my side, so he was along for the ride, even though he clearly didn't care whether or not Scotty was okay. When he passed out on my living room floor, and I thought he'd died . . .

Yeah. I kinda lost it.

Tate had held me back as the paramedics hauled Scotty away, his skin ashen and his jaw hard as he watched me freak out. I'd never seen him so pensive. So disapproving of me and my choices. I had a million questions for Scotty, and he had a lot to answer for, but first I had to make sure he was alive to *answer* those questions.

Tate grabbed my bicep as I passed him, halting my pacing, an unopened bottle of water in his hand. "Jesus, Skylar. Calm down. Sit and take a drink of—"

"I'm perfectly calm," I snapped, pulling free. "I just want to know if he's okay."

He leaned back in the chair, frowning so deeply his creases had creases. I resumed my pacing because it was the only thing keeping me calm right now. My mind replayed what happened earlier in my apartment, and I bit my tongue hard enough to make my eyes sting. What I'd done back there . . .

I was becoming a doctor. It was my duty, as a future healer, to make people better . . .

Not *kill* them.

Logically, I knew what I'd done was self-defense. But I also knew that if I hadn't opened the door for Scotty, they wouldn't have come to my place. That didn't make the outcome any different, but it did open my eyes to the truth of what Scotty had been saying this whole time. I understood what he meant now. All this time, he'd been warning me away, telling me that being with him would hurt me. And it *had*.

Just not in the way I'd expected.

"He'll be fine. Guys like him always are," Tate said, rubbing his forehead.

I shook my head. "But what if they arrest him?"

"Then they arrest him . . ." Tate crossed his ankles, and shrugged. "And you move on to someone more appropriate for you."

I stiffened. "Just like that?"

"Just like that," he agreed.

The hypocrisy choked me. He was so . . . "How can you be that cold toward a man you work with? A man you clearly trust?"

"Trust*ed*," he said, his voice hard. "Big difference."

"And he broke your 'trust' because he likes me?"

"Among other reasons," he said slowly. "Reasons you'll never understand, or know. He lied to me about more than just you, Skylar. And *you* lied to me, too. Right to my face."

I never picked a fight with my brother. Never yelled at him. Always tried to be considerate, and understanding, and everything he taught me to be. But now . . . I was done with all that crap. "Why did you do it?"

He looked bored. "Why did I do what? You'll have to be more specific."

"Why did you send him in your place that day?" I asked, turning back to him, finally standing still. "At the auction."

He blinked, clearly caught off guard by my question. "Because you needed a guy there, and I couldn't go."

I shook my head. "No matter how many times I try to figure it out, I can't make sense out of why you'd send *him* to me that night, if you disapproved of him like you say you do." I held my hands out, palm up. "Why *him*, out of all the people who work for you? Why not a normal guy, like the ones you constantly try to hook me up with? But, no, you send Scotty, and then get upset when I fall for him."

"At the time, he was the only man available who had the proper age and looks. Unless you wouldn't mind me sending a sixty-year-old in his place?"

"That's what you're going with?" I asked angrily. I'd been to his office. I *knew* he was lying. "Seriously?"

He tugged on his collar, sitting up straight, and didn't look directly at me. Instead, he lowered his head and stared at the bottle he still held, turning it in his hands. He'd washed Scotty's blood off them hours ago, but I could still see it. Still see him on top of the man I loved, slamming his fist into his nose. Could still hear him yelling about breaking promises . . .

"Yep. I'm going with that."

I pointed at him. *"Liar."*

"No, I'm not." He shifted in his seat. "I—"

The door to the waiting room opened, and I whirled on my heel, breath held. A nurse in white scrubs stood there, an iPad in her hand. "Are you the family of Scotty Donahue?"

"I'm his . . . girlfriend. He doesn't have family." I stepped forward, biting down on my lower lip. "I'm all he has, that I know of."

The nurse glanced down at the iPad. "Your name?"

"Skylar Daniels."

The other woman nodded. "He has you listed as a contact. Follow me."

"Wait." Tate stood, putting his hands in his pockets. "Is he okay?"

"Your name?" she asked.

"I'm sure he didn't list me as a contact," he said dryly.

The woman stared at Tate. "I cannot discuss the condition of a patient without the permission of said patient. So . . . your name, sir?"

He flushed, rocking back on his heels. "Tate Daniels."

"You're listed."

"Wait. What?" Tate asked.

She nodded once. "Follow me, too, if you'd like."

I stared at Tate. He looked surprised Scotty had listed him as a contact. Even more surprised than me. "Still don't trust him?" I whispered furiously.

Tate remained silent, staring straight ahead.

We trailed after the nurse, side by side. We passed rooms filled with beeping machines, and nurses made their way through the halls, looking about as enthusiastic as the one we followed. Some had more of a pep to their step, and I suspected they were at the beginning of their shift. We stopped in front of room 312, and she knocked on the wall. "We good?"

"Yes," a masculine voice replied.

One who wasn't Scotty.

The nurse went inside, and we followed. A man with brown hair and brown eyes stood there, looking down at Scotty. He wore a police uniform, so it didn't take a whole lot to figure out why he was here. "If you think of anything else . . . ?"

"I'll let you know." Scotty glanced at Tate quickly, then away. "Thank you."

The officer nodded once, and then walked past us, nodding at Tate once. Tate nodded back. He held his hat to his chest as he inclined his head my way. "Ma'am."

"Officer," I said quietly.

He left, and the nurse checked the screens showing Scotty's heart rate and blood pressure before pressing her fingers to his wrist. Scotty stared at me, looking a little out of it. I didn't blame him. He nodded at something the nurse said, and then she headed our way. "Visiting hours end in thirty minutes."

And then she left the three of us alone.

Tate shifted on his feet. "You made it?"

"Yeah." Scotty cleared his throat. "I made it."

"The nose?" Tate asked casually.

"Broken."

Tate snorted. "About time someone besides Chris took a hit to the nose."

Scotty didn't reply. He was so pale, he almost looked like a ghost. He had tape across his nose, and bruising was already forming all around his eyes and his cheekbones. His shoulder looked puffy under his hospital gown, and his hair stood up all over the place.

"Scotty . . ." I walked up to the side of the bed, my fingers itching to touch him.

He turned away from Tate, and tilted his face up to me, smiling faintly. "Hey."

"Hey," I echoed back, my voice cracking. I reached out to push his hair off his forehead the way he liked it, but stopped halfway, dropping my hand at my side. Seeing him like this, in a hospital bed, did things to me. *Bad* things. Memories of my mom lying in a hospital bed, breathing her last rattling breath, hit me hard. I'd been alone. Our father hadn't let Tate come, so I'd been the one to hold her hand as she left this world. And I'd been the one to make all the arrangements by myself, since that man couldn't be bothered to come and say good-bye to his ex-wife. And Tate hadn't gotten to see Mom one last time.

I forced my mind off my mother, and onto what mattered right now.

Scotty.

"I . . . Are you okay?" I asked.

He nodded slightly. He had wires sticking out of him, and he looked grayer than a corpse, but he was still breathing, so that had to be enough for now. "I told you, I'll be fine. I've had worse than this. Give me a few days, and I'll be back on my feet, causing trouble like usual."

"Not *too* fast," I argued. "You need to heal."

Scotty nodded, his jaw flexing, and stared at Tate.

Tate cleared his throat and looked my way. "Can we have a minute, Skylar?"

Leave him alone with Tate? "No way. Whatever you have to say to him, you can say in front of me."

"It's okay." Scotty touched my arm. "Could you go ask the nurse for some water? I'm thirsty."

"But—"

He squeezed reassuringly. "Sky? Please."

"I just want to ask him a few questions, that's all. Then I'll give you two some privacy to say what needs saying, and wait for you in the waiting room until you're done," Tate said dryly.

Scotty nodded. "Go on, sugar. I'll be here when you come back, I promise."

Tate stiffened even more at the pet name.

I hesitated, but nodded. "All right. I'll be right back."

He smiled at me, the skin under his eyes shaded with gray exhaustion.

I walked out, glaring at Tate as I went. After I closed the door behind me, I walked out into the hallway, and covered my face, taking a deep, long, shaky breath.

Because, God, I needed it.

CHAPTER 19

SCOTTY

The second the door closed behind Skylar, I felt her absence. It was a feeling I'd have to become accustomed to. No matter what happened from this point on, I wouldn't be by her side.

I locked eyes with Tate.

He walked to my side of the bed, staring at the IV pumping fluids into me, looking all casual and calm, even though he was probably plotting my death right now.

"Sir, I know you're upset, but I really—"

"*Upset* doesn't begin to cover my feelings on this subject. I gave you specific instructions when it came to my sister and you failed to follow them. Now there will be consequences," Tate said, his voice eerily calm and cool.

"It's not like you think. Skylar and I—"

"There is no you and Skylar. When she comes back in here, you are going to break her heart and make sure she never wants to see you again."

His voice was still perfectly calm.

Like he didn't really give a shit, when we both knew he did.

I shook my head. If he wanted to kill me, he could damn well try, but he couldn't force me to hurt her like that. "No."

"No?" he asked, raising his brows in surprise.

"No." I squared my jaw. "I'm not scared of you, and I'm not scared of dying. There's nothing you can do to get me to fall in line, nothing you can threaten me with, that will make me hurt her with more lies. From now on, she gets nothing but the truth from me, no matter what you say."

He made a choked sound. Maybe it was his pride cutting off his air circulation.

I stared at him, not saying anything else.

There was nothing more to say.

He rolled his shoulders back, and even such a simple gesture was filled with cold arrogance. "All right. I see how this is going to play out."

I stared at him, waiting for his next move.

He shoved his hands in his pockets, pressing his tongue against his inner cheek thoughtfully. "I'm not an evil man, Scotty."

"I never thought you were, sir." That was the truth. He was a complex man, sure, but evil? Nah. He was a guy who did bad things, just like I did, but there was good there, too. All you had to do was look at Sky to see it. He loved her.

"We live a dangerous life, Donahue. Tonight only proves my point." He gestured toward the closed door. "I've fought hard to keep Skylar safe and *out* of this life, and you just want to bring her right into it."

My chest tightened. "This war will end soon, and things will calm down. Until then, I'll protect her better than any other man could. And I'll—"

"We both know what you really are."

I gripped my blanket with my good hand. Outside my window, I could see the lights of the Cathedral of the Holy Cross. Out there, people were laughing, not fighting for their lives. In here, the walls closed around me, trying to finish me off for good. "I don't know what you're talking about, sir."

"Let's not play games anymore, *Agent* Donahue."

I tensed. I'd really wanted to believe that I'd imagined that little addition to my name, to just attribute it to a hallucination brought on by the blood loss, but there it was again. He'd called me Agent Donahue. I couldn't even blame the morphine. My head was clear. Painfully so. "Is this the part where you kill me?"

"Here? Now?" He scoffed. "You know me better than that, Agent Donahue."

He was right. I did, and apparently he knew me all too well, too. "How long have you known?"

"Since the second you applied to the DEA." He rocked back on his heels. "Do you honestly believe I don't keep tabs on my people and their families?"

"I thought I covered my tracks pretty well. Lucas had no idea," I said.

"True. But just as the DEA has people in my group, I have people in theirs." He cocked a red brow. "Did you think I didn't? That federal agents wouldn't jump at the opportunity to gain a little bit of extra cash here and there, just like the Boys? When I took over from my father, I made sure to make friends in high places."

There was nothing to say to that.

I knew firsthand how easily a soul could be corrupted.

At my silence, Tate continued, "The second your application was approved, I knew about it. Hell, I found out you got in before you did, I'd wager."

"And yet . . . you didn't kill me?"

He lifted a shoulder. "You're DEA. The Sons don't traffic in drugs, so when you let Lucas put you forward as a recruit, I knew the intention was to solidify your cover and to position you to gather intel. Because every drug dealer needs a gun, and drug cartels need even bigger guns. You could put faces to names, keep track of any rising stars, get addresses of delivery locations, and so forth. Your presence *protects* the Sons, because if we go down, the DEA loses access to all that information."

I choked on a laugh, but ended on a groan, because it hurt like hell.

"It didn't take long before I realized you cared more about following your code of honor rather than strictly obeying the law. I liked that." He rubbed his chin, considering me. "That's why I didn't look too closely when Lucas and Heidi died."

I froze, my heart stopping painfully. "There was nothing to look closely at. They died. End of story."

"Now, a guy who would risk so much for family, I thought, that's a guy I need by my side, watching over mine." He twisted his lips. "I thought surely you were the man to trust to do the job honorably."

I swallowed hard, my mind still locked on his mention of Lucas, and stayed silent. He'd caught me off guard, and I wasn't sure where he'd go next. It wasn't a good feeling.

He glanced over his shoulder. The door was still firmly shut. "366 Walnut Street."

My heart dropped to my stomach, and dread crept up my spine like a spider going in for the kill. "Excuse me?"

"366 Walnut Street." He leaned down, nostrils flaring. "Athens, Georgia."

I gripped his shirt at the collar, not letting go. I didn't

give a damn if he was my "boss." Not when he was threatening my family. I only knew where Lucas had ended up because I used the DEA's resources and I hadn't told anyone, not even Chris. If I doubted Tate had a mole in the DEA, well, here was the proof I was wrong.

"Where did you get that information?" I growled.

"I have my ways, just like you do," he said slowly, lowering his lids until he stared pointedly at my hands on his pristine white dress shirt. "Let go. *Now*."

I yanked him closer. "You go near him, and you'll have more to worry about than your goddamn shirt," I snarled, refusing to show how much that small action hurt me. "I could arrest you, right here and now, and no one would stop me. Then I could tell Skylar the truth about her big brother, and how he really got the money to send her to college for her fancy degree, and see how she handles that information."

"Just like *I* could have killed you at any point, and I didn't. I suggest you keep a cool head, for the sake of your brother . . . and O'Brien." He gave me a tight smile. "Yes, I know all about him and his attempted coup, which is an offense punishable by death, by the way. You know, I heard through the grapevine that Molly—his fiancée, is it?—is pregnant. They just found out today. Did you know? You would be like an uncle, after all. Uncle Scotty."

That right there?

It was the nail in my damn coffin.

Too many people were counting on me.

Lucas. Heidi. Chris. Molly. Their *baby*.

I let go of him, my chest aching because I knew what came next, and it hurt already. "What do you want from me?"

"First, let's talk about the DEA. You've got two choices." He stepped back and smoothed his jacket, his mouth tight. "You maintain the status quo and keep protecting the Sons while taking out our competition, but now when I need intel, you get it for me, no questions asked. Or, if you're feeling like dying, you come clean with the rest of the Sons and face the consequences."

There was no way I was going dirty.

And we both knew it.

At my silence, he continued on. "Second, you're going to break it off with Skylar. Make her believe you don't want to be with her, and make sure it doesn't fall back on me. If she thinks you were coerced into breaking it off with her, she'll keep showing up on your doorstep."

I gritted my teeth, continuing to say nothing.

He had me by the balls, and we both knew it.

"Break her heart, cut her loose, and I'll keep your secrets. And your family's, too. When this is all over, regardless of your decision concerning the gang and your role in it, they'll be safe. If you break it off with Skylar today, no one will get hurt. No matter what. You have my word."

"And if I don't break up with her?" I asked slowly.

He shrugged, looking like he wasn't planning his sister's heartbreak, but I saw the hesitation in his eyes when he turned back to me. He couldn't hide it. "Then I can't guarantee anything. It's not personal, Donahue. I just need to protect my sister."

"And I've got to protect my family," I gritted out.

"I'm counting on as much."

I stared at him, heart beating against my ribs.

Yeah, I knew why he was doing this, and I even admired it, to some extent. There was nothing I wouldn't do to protect Lucas, and he felt the same way about Skylar. But I owed Lucas too much. Chris, too. So I had to choose them, not her.

I had to let her go.

"It'll be done," I said, my voice low.

A soft knock sounded, and the door opened. Skylar came in, her eyes immediately seeking out mine. My chest hollowed out when we locked gazes. "My turn?" she asked quietly.

Tate squeezed her shoulder. "I'll be in the waiting room."

"Boss?" I called out.

He stiffened, clearly certain I was about to blow his cover. If not for the threat on my family, I totally would. "Yeah?"

"I'll be there for the meeting next Friday."

He glanced over his shoulder. "That's not necessary."

"Still. I insist."

Chris would be there, and I'd be right there with him, guarding his back.

Tate nodded once. "All right. Until then, lay low. Recover."

"Yes, sir."

He left, closing the door behind him softly. The second we were alone, Skylar rushed to my side, a glass of ice water in her hand. She looked at me like I was her world, and here I was about to make that world explode. I turned away, unable to meet her eyes, because I was about to do the unthinkable.

I hoped Tate rotted in hell.

"Are you okay? Did he do anything to you?" she asked quickly.

"Nah." I sat up straighter, heart pounding, stomach clenching, forcing myself to do what needed to be done, no matter how much it hurt me . . . or her. "I mean, he doesn't like that we're sleeping together, but he acknowledged that at least it put me in the right spot at the right time. So he wants me to keep playing bodyguard."

She froze, her fingers on the cup tightening. "Wait. What?"

"Tate's afraid you're still in danger, so I'll be hanging out next door for a while." I rubbed the back of my neck. "My water, Sky?"

"Oh. Right." She held it out, and I took it, making sure not to touch her fingers. If I felt her skin on mine one more time . . . "So he's fine with us being together?"

"Yep," I answered casually, lifting the water glass to my mouth. "We get to keep fucking for now."

She reared back, her lips parted in surprise. *"Scotty."*

"What?" I reached out and dragged a finger down her arm, leaving a trail of goose bumps in my wake. "Just because I'm your babysitter doesn't mean we can't be together. It'd be a waste otherwise. Christ, we burn up the sheets, sugar."

"Did . . . ?" She crossed her arms, rubbing the spot I'd touched. "Did Tate make you spend time with me?"

I called on every ounce of acting talent I had, keeping a cocky smirk in place. "He *is* my boss, sugar. I'm not going to jeopardize my job just for great sex. Of course Tate ordered me to keep you safe."

"So . . ." She pressed her mouth into a tight line. "That's why you said all those things to me. So you could stay close."

Those weren't questions, but I answered anyway. "Well, yeah. I mean, termites, Sky, really?"

She recoiled, and I could *see* her drawing into herself, could *see* the pain pierce through her. "I thought . . ."

"That I was in love with you?" I asked, laughing. It hurt. "I was up front about that: I don't come back for seconds and I don't do love. I'm a one-and-done type of guy."

Her eyes were dry and empty, and her face, Christ, her *face.* "And those things you said, about not being able to shake me . . . ?"

I laughed again. The physical pain from my injuries was nothing compared to the emotional pain I was experiencing. "Were just that. Pretty lines to keep you manageable. If I was going to be stuck watching you, I was damn well going to make it easier on myself by keeping you in my bed."

"I . . . see." She hugged herself, stepping back, out of reach.

I hated Tate. Absolutely hated him. "Look, don't be so offended, sugar. I was going to stick to just being your friend, but you're such a hot piece, I couldn't resist getting you into bed. That's a compliment."

She paled even more. "But—"

"No *buts*. I know you thought you 'read' me as some kind of beast you could turn back into a prince, but you were wrong." I leaned closer, smiling at her even though she was pale and clearly distraught, and I pushed on, showing no mercy because I couldn't afford to have any. "You delude yourself into thinking you can read the world, giving you the illusion of control. But, baby, except for Tate, every man in your life leaves you. Why would you think I'd be any different?"

She gasped, and I immediately wanted to take it back. She'd given me the perfect ammunition to use against her, and I hadn't hesitated to take a kill shot. Forget Tate, I hated *myself.*

Shaking her head, she wrapped her arms around herself. "Stay away from me," she said, her voice broken, but somehow strong, too. "Don't come near me again."

I shrugged, even though it hurt like hell. "Hey, I got my orders, but if you don't want to fuck me, there's plenty of other willing pussy out there. I'll still keep you safe, even if you take away the main perk of the job."

"Go to hell," she snarled, curling her fists at her sides, pain burning in her eyes as she stepped back. "If I ever see you again . . . I'll shoot you myself, and save my brother the trouble."

Agony burst through my chest, but I saluted her, acting like her words didn't strike deep at all. "All right. I'll just watch over you from a distance, but let me know if you change your mind and want an orgasm or two, for old times' sake."

She opened her mouth, closed it, and shook her head as she backed away from me, toward the door. "I . . . I *trusted* you."

She could have said a million things to me. Could have cursed me out. Wished death and agony upon me. Sworn to shoot me one more time. But that, right there, hit home the hardest.

It would never leave me alone.

The *guilt.*

Shrugging, I locked eyes with her. "Well, you shouldn't have. I warned you I would hurt you. You should have listened. It was the only honest thing I said to you that whole time."

She made a choking sound and covered her mouth. Without another word, she turned, opened the door, and left me on the bed alone, not looking back. I sat there, pain blinding me, biting back the urge to shout her name until she forgave me for what I said.

"Good-bye, sugar," I said softly.

CHAPTER 20

SKYLAR

Six days.

Six long, miserable, lonely days.

That's how long it had been since I'd visited Scotty in the hospital. Since I walked away from his room, and didn't look back. I'd put on a good show, and told Tate that if he insisted on watching over me for no damn reason, he'd have to find a new guy, because if I saw Scotty near me again, I'd kill him. And I'd meant it. At the time, I really wanted to kill him.

But now . . . now it just hurt.

Everything hurt.

Tate tried to pry for details about what had happened after he'd walked away, but I'd shut him down, saying it was none of his business. He didn't need to know how wrong I'd been about Scotty. I knew it well enough for the both of us. Heck, for the entire world.

Originally, the anger had been a lifesaver. I'd been able

to focus on it. Live in it. Breathe it in like air. But the second I locked my apartment door behind me, and took in the freshly clean floors and walls, the rage faded away. Thanks to my brother, there were no traces of blood, a fight, or Scotty.

It was all gone, like I'd imagined the whole thing.

When I lay in my empty bed and smelled his cologne on my sheets, the only thing I had left of a man who'd played me like a fool, an emptiness filled me. I hadn't cried yet, despite the pain in my heart, because I refused to let myself succumb, but still. I *missed* him.

Every night, I hugged his pillow until I fell asleep.

And every night I cursed myself for that weakness.

But the time for mourning was over. Instead of focusing on Scotty, and how much he'd hurt me, I was going to throw myself into my studies. I was going to take that energy and put it where it belonged—to my future. All my life, I'd wanted to be a doctor. I'd wanted to help people—kids, specifically. I'd wanted to be successful. Powerful. Independent. Never once in those dreams had there been a guy at my side. I'd always been alone.

It was time to go back to that.

To trusting no one. To *needing* no one.

I'd just returned from an intense study session with Marco, but I planned to spend at least a few more hours cramming. I needed to ace this test after the mediocre grade I'd gotten on my last exam thanks to being distracted with Scotty. I flipped open my Advanced Biology book and turned to page 213 at the same time as someone knocked on my door.

I tensed, staring at it.

Slowly, I crept to the door. I squinted and peeked through the peephole, letting out a sigh of relief when I saw who it was. At least my brother wasn't going to try to kill me, but I was still mad at him for bringing Scotty into my life.

Unlocking the door, I cracked it open, saying nothing.

"Hi," he said cheerfully.

I raised a brow at him impatiently.

"How are you?" he asked in that fake tone again.

I tapped my foot.

He shuffled his feet. "I . . . uh . . . brought dinner." He held up a box of pizza from Galleria Umberto. "And beer. Your favorite."

I glanced down at the six-pack of Peroni in his other hand, and shut the door in his face, like I did every other time he knocked.

As I walked away, he called out, "I have a key, you know."

"I know," I yelled over my shoulder. "But you won't use it."

He jiggled the knob again. "Please let me in."

I said nothing.

He let go. "I'm sorry, Skylar."

I froze midstep. It was the first time he'd said those words to me . . . *ever.*

He wasn't the type to admit wrongdoing, not even when caught red-handed. One time I found him stealing my last Reese's cup, and he refused to say he was in the wrong, even though he'd literally been shoving it in his mouth when I walked in. Even when he found out I planned our mother's funeral alone, he hadn't said he was sorry. He'd just hugged me, and promised to make it up to me.

"Skylar . . . please." He tried to turn the knob again. "I love you."

After letting out a breath, I walked to the door, unlocked it. When I saw him standing there, looking pitiful, I stepped back, clearing his path.

Tate walked past me, scanning the interior of my home. "You alone?"

"Scotty isn't here, if that's what you're asking." I closed the door and followed him slowly, tucking my messy hair behind my ear. "I told you, we're done."

"I know. But he's not the only man alive," he said gently. "You could have company of a different sort than Scotty."

Yeah. Funny, though. It felt like he was the only man in the world sometimes. "Nope. I was just studying," I said, gesturing to my book.

He set the pizza and beer down, pulled a bottle out, and twisted the lid off. He handed it to me, watching me closely. "You look tired. Are you sleeping?"

No. I missed Scotty, the way he made me feel and the what-could-have-beens of our relationship, too much to sleep. I hated that I missed him. And I hated that I didn't hate him, no matter how hard I tried. "Yeah, a bit. But I've been cramming for tests. I have four this week, then a clinical lab in a hospital the week after. Just making sure I'm prepared for all of that."

He nodded, opening his own beer with a quick twist. "Done anything fun lately?"

"Why don't you ask your spy?" I shot back.

He had the good graces to look ashamed. "Skylar . . ."

Sighing, I sat down, tucking my foot under my butt. "No. Nothing 'fun.' Just schoolwork, and studying, and working at the shelter. The usual."

He flexed his jaw. "What happened to Marco?"

"He's still around. We studied earlier today, and then grabbed lunch before I came back here." I cocked my head. "Why?"

"No reason." He turned the dining room chair around,

straddled it, and rested his forearms over the top of it. "I talked to Officer O'Hare today."

I frowned. "Who?"

"The cop I tried to hook you up with last week."

"Oh. Right."

"He's going to be calling you." He scratched the back of his head. "To ask you out."

"What?" I stood. "No."

He looked up at me. "But—"

"*No.*" I slammed my beer down. "I'm done going out with these guys because I want to make you happy. I found one I liked, and it was nothing but a lie . . ." I broke off, pressing my mouth into a tight line, because, *God*, I refused to cry over him. "I'm *done.*"

He stood, rubbing the back of his neck. "Done with what, exactly?"

"Dating. Trying to find something special. Pretending that love is something you should want in your life, when all it does is break you." I walked past him, sat down, and stared at my book. "I got off track for a little while, and I learned a valuable lesson, but now I'm back at it, doing what I do best. I'm back to being me."

He shifted his feet. "I don't think you need to be alone to be dedicated to work, or to be yourself. You just need someone a little more . . . more . . ."

"Clean?" I asked helpfully.

"Yes." He smiled. "Clean."

I smiled back sweetly. "No."

His smile turned upside down really quick.

I opened the pizza, pulled a piece out, and took a big bite, chewing thoughtfully.

He watched me, his brow furrowed. "You seem so . . . so . . ."

"Different?"

He frowned, not replying.

"I am, I guess. But it's not a bad thing." I took another bite. "You should be happy. You were right. You love being right."

Raising a brow, he rubbed his jaw. "I do. But what was I right about this time?"

"Scotty was no good for me." Focusing on my textbook, I tapped my foot on the floor and read, taking another bite of pizza.

He sat across from me, pulling a slice out of the box for himself. I could feel his eyes on me, but I didn't stop reading. I had too much to do, too much to catch up on. "You really loved him, didn't you?" he asked slowly.

"I said so, didn't I?" I answered distractedly.

He picked up his beer, taking a long drink. "Why him, out of all the men I sent your way? Why not Patrick, or—"

"Or Steven, or Gary, or Michael?" I cut in, finally lifting my head.

"Yes. Any of them." He rubbed his face, setting his beer down again. "Why *him*?"

"I don't know. There was just something about him. It was like . . . like I knew him the second I met him. He had a sense of honor that I thought I could trust, even though he told me not to . . ." I lifted a shoulder. "He told me not to trust him, and I didn't listen, and that's on me."

Tate turned away, staring out the window toward the Hancock tower. His grip on his beer tightened. "I'm sorry."

Two apologies in one night.

"Why did you ask him to watch me?" I held up a hand when he opened his mouth. "And don't tell me it was because you were worried about me. You're always worried about me. I know it was something bigger. Something that made you send a lawyer here so I could sign a bunch of paperwork and forms, for God's sake."

He rotated the bottle in a circle, leaving a trail of condensation in his wake. "I've done things, Skylar. Bad things. And those bad things are coming to a head tomorrow night."

I bit down on my lip, my heart racing. If he admitted what he'd done, where that money had come from . . . heck, was *still* coming from . . . I would become an accomplice of sorts. Despite that, I wanted him to be honest. To trust me with his secrets. "Things like . . . ?"

"I'd rather not say."

"Then don't say." I reclined in my chair, grabbing my beer and pressing the side of the rim to my lips thoughtfully. Maybe it was time for both of us to be honest. For both of us to make a change. "What if I told you, hypothetically, that I already know your secret? What if I told you, again, hypothetically, that I figured it out when I was a senior in high school?"

He rested his elbows on the table, his eyes narrow. "Bullshit . . . hypothetically."

I gave him a look.

His nostrils flared. "No. You don't have a clue about the things I've done, and I don't want you to."

"You can keep telling yourself that, if it makes you feel better."

"Did Scotty say something?" he growled. "I'll kill him."

"Scotty didn't say a word, and I didn't need him to." I shrugged. "I've known what you are, *who* you are, for years."

He chugged the rest of his beer, setting the empty bottle down on the table, and then leaned back, his face pale. "I don't believe you. There's no way you've known that long. If you did, there's no way you could . . ."

When he didn't finish, I reached out and covered his hand with mine, squeezing. Despite the things he'd done, despite his crimes, I loved him. He was my *brother*. "No way I could what?"

"Love me," he finally said, glowering down at his empty bottle.

"Tate . . ." I shook my head. "Our father wasn't . . . discreet about his chosen profession. Mom told me the truth about him, about why she left, and how he accused her of cheating on him with the undercover cop assigned to investigate him. And she told me why he refused to let you come with us. You were his heir to the world of darkness he'd created."

Pain crossed his eyes. "Mom . . ."

"She never stopped loving you, even though she wasn't allowed to see you. It killed her that she couldn't save you, too. But he threatened her life . . . and mine . . ." I stared at the picture of my mother and me. It had been the last photo ever taken of us. She had bags under her eyes, her blue eyes were not shining as brightly, her red hair had thinned out a bit with age, and she was far too pale, but she looked like the most beautiful woman in the world. She'd *always* been beautiful. "Anyway, when you suddenly started showing up with wads of cash after months of struggling, it didn't take a genius to figure out where the money was coming from. You took over the family business, because you had no choice. You did what you had to do."

He ducked his head. *"Shit."*

"Hey. None of that."

"But—"

"I was there when our father refused to take me in after Mom died and you refused to live there either. I watched you go on job interview after job interview, only to come back to me deflated and holding a stolen box of spaghetti for us to eat. I saw you sitting up at night, worrying that I was going to get kicked out on the streets when the landlord got sick of waiting for the rent money that was never going to come."

He swallowed so hard I heard it. "I tried not to be in this life. I wanted to do things the right way. But then . . . I did what I had to do. And I'm still doing it. I've become him."

"You're only like him if you walk away from everything that matters in life. You're only him if you let the darkness win." I pushed my hair out of my face, forcing a smile. "You tried so hard to rebuild us as a family. To give me the best chance in life. How could I not love you for that?"

Tate lifted his head. His eyes were haunted by memories, and shadows, and so much more that I'd never fully understand. "I went to him after months of struggling to support us," he said slowly, rolling his hands into fists on top of the table. "Begged him to step up and take care of you. To let you come home. Asked him to take a DNA test, at the very least. He laughed, said he didn't need a piece of paper to confirm our mother was a cheating whore. I walked then, went right for the door, when he said, 'You can go to her, and be poor for the rest of your life, or you can stop trying to make an honest living, come work for me, and give her everything you stupidly believe she deserves. Your choice.'"

I glanced out the window, seeing nothing.

"I did my best to keep you away from this life, just as hard as he tried to keep me in it. No one in the gang knows you exist. Dad told the ones who knew about you that you died. When I took over, I let that continue, so you'd be safe. I kept you a secret . . . until Scotty."

I pulled back, settling on my haunches. "Why did you trust him?"

"Same reasons as you." He pinched the bridge of his nose. "He seemed the type of guy I could trust to take care of you, and he did. He just also . . . you know."

I shifted back. "Yeah."

"I—" Tate's phone dinged and he picked it up, frowning. "Shit."

"You have to go?" I asked, my heart picking up speed. All these confessions came because something huge was taking place tomorrow. Something big. And if it was something that endangered Tate, it would endanger Scotty, too.

"Yeah." He pushed his chair back and stood, walking up to me, holding out the key to his apartment. I stared at it, confused. "Can you do me a favor?"

I crossed my arms, tilting my head. "What?"

"Go to my place tonight. Stay there and don't open the door for anyone that isn't me. Skip class. Wait for me to come back tomorrow. I want you there when this is over."

I nodded once, taking it. "Yeah. Okay." I closed my fist around the key, the edges digging into my palm. "What's tomorrow?"

"War. If we win, it's over, and you won't have to worry. No more spies. No more danger." He didn't say what would happen if they didn't win, but it didn't take a genius to figure it out. "But I want you safely locked away, just until the dust settles."

I nodded, forcing another smile. "Okay." He started for the door, and I grabbed his arm. "Please be careful. Don't take unnecessary risks. I need you to come back to me. Okay?"

He tensed, rolling his shoulders. "I'll do my best. Go to my place, lock the door, and don't come out. I have a guy watching for you. He'll stay outside once you're in."

And with that, he was gone.

I wrapped my arms around myself, holding on tight.

If I knew how, I'd totally rush to the front line, gun in hand, and start shooting to protect him. But I didn't even know how to hold a gun, let alone shoot one. So instead, I did the one thing I could do—give my brother peace of mind so he'd survive this "war." I made quick work of gathering my things, shut off the lights, swung the front door open— and then froze.

Scotty stood outside, his hand on the knob of the apartment next door, and his arm in a sling.

He wore a plaid button-up shirt, a pair of jeans, his dark brown leather jacket with the usual upturned collar, and a frown. His five o'clock shadow was more of a full-on beard, and he had an overnight bag slung over his good arm. He looked . . . tired.

Like he hadn't been sleeping.

At least I wasn't alone in that.

"God. *You're* the guy?"

I was going to kill Tate.

He looked at me, his eyes narrowing as he focused on the bag I held to my chest, and pressed his mouth into a thin line. "What guy?"

"The one Tate has watching over me."

He let go of the knob. "No. That job's not mine anymore. I was just grabbing some stuff out of the apartment. Where are you going?"

"None of your business," I said simply.

I started down the hallway, leaving him behind me.

Unfortunately, he fell into step with me. "Does Tate know you're leaving?"

"Yes."

He continued walking next to me, his jaw hard.

I ignored him, until he took a right when I did outside

our building. I stopped, shooting him a glare. "What are you doing?"

"Watching you."

"It's not your job anymore," I shot back, heading for my car.

"Do you see this other guy? The one who's watching you?"

I glanced over my shoulder, searching the darkness surrounding us. "No."

"Then I'll continue on as I am."

Since it was apparent he wouldn't leave me alone, I walked toward my car faster. The sooner I got away from him, the sooner my heart would stop aching. Or so I told myself, anyway. "Fine. Whatever."

"Where are we going?"

"Tate asked me to go to his place tonight, so I'm going." I got in my car, and he opened his car door, too. "I don't need you guarding me. Go home."

I slammed my door shut and locked it, pulling out of the spot without checking behind me first. I was too busy side-eyeing him. He stepped on the gas, following me. When he turned down Market Street, following me toward Tate's place, I gritted my teeth. The guy wouldn't take a hint.

The second I pulled into Tate's driveway, he was behind me. I got out of the car, and so did he. "What are you *doing* here?" I immediately asked, grabbing my bag.

"Talking to you," he answered, shutting his car door. "Watching over you."

"Well, stop. I don't want to talk to you," I managed to get out through my swollen throat. I swear to God, if he made me cry, I'd make him join me. I was a medical student. I knew lots of ways to make a grown man cry. "I think we said all we needed to say to each other, don't you?"

He shoved his hands in his pockets, his jaw flexing. "Yeah, I guess we did. We don't have to talk, if you don't want to. I'm just doing my job."

I had a very specific place I thought he could shove his job, but I didn't say so. If I showed him anger, he'd know he could still get to me. And I refused to show him I *still* cared. We walked in silence, and his heat burned me with each step we took. By the time we got to Tate's door, I was a nervous wreck, simply because Scotty stood next to me.

When would his weird hold over me end? You'd think him breaking my heart would be enough. But *noooooooooo*. I felt him to the bottom of my soul. It was infuriating.

I slid the key into the lock and opened the door. I walked inside my brother's place, prepared to close the door in Scotty's face, but he pushed in after me, switching the light on and walking through the living room like he owned it. When I saw Tate's old couch that he'd bought five years ago, something clicked in my brain. The love seat in Scotty's apartment was the match. So was the end table. They were part of a set.

"Did Tate send you to live in that apartment? Is it his?" I asked.

Scotty nodded once. "Yeah."

"Son of a . . ." I broke off, gritting my teeth.

Nope. Not gonna show my anger.

When he realized I wasn't going to continue my sentence, he shrugged and headed for the bedroom, turning the light on as he entered. When he came back out, he walked past me. "You're good. Stay inside. Don't open the door for anyone."

"Was any of it real?" I asked, my voice choked and cracking. I hated that tiny little crack, but whatever. I couldn't help it that I wasn't a cold robot like him. "One kiss, one word, *anything*?"

He stopped walking, his back to me, and curled his hands into fists. He released his fingers slowly, telling me more than words ever could. "Nothing about the man you knew was real. Everything he said was a lie, because *he* is a lie."

"And the things you didn't say? The things you felt?"

He released his pinky, let out a breath, and said, "Lock the door behind me, and don't let anyone else in."

And then he was gone. He walked away from me as easily as my father had.

Only this time, it hurt more.

CHAPTER 21

SCOTTY

I sat on the leather chair in the clubhouse, the one that was in the corner with the wall at its back, and rested my AR-15 on my lap. My shoulder still ached a little bit, but I refused to acknowledge the weakness. My head was pounding, my eyes hurt, but my heart was as calm as the sea on a warm summer day. We were going to war, and I might end up getting my fool ass shot, but I'd already lost the one thing in my life I'd actually wanted to keep.

Nothing else mattered.

The hurt laced in her voice had sent a knife of pain through me, but if nothing else came from our failed romance, at least she'd reminded me of what I was fighting for all along. I wanted to be a good guy, and to do that, I had to take down the bad guys.

Starting with Bitter Hill . . .

And then the Sons of Steel Row.

Right and wrong had to be black and white from now on.

The Sons, brotherhood and loyalty aside, were *not* the good guys. They sold guns to people who had no business having guns, which in turn got good people out there killed. They had to be stopped.

And I'd help, if asked.

Chris leaned on the wall next to me, resting his hands against the gun slung across his chest. His gaze skimmed over the room, which was filled with Sons. They were all here, ready to wage war. Even the older members, like Chris's asshole father, were present. "You're looking awfully pensive over here. Anything going on that I should know about?"

I hadn't told him about what happened with Skylar, Tate's ultimatum, none of it. He didn't need to know. "Nah, man. Just thinking. How's Molly?"

And the baby?

"Okay." He rubbed his jaw. "She's home and resting, with a guy to keep her safe."

I cocked my head. "A new recruit?"

"No, a legit bodyguard. An ex-SEAL. We hired him."

I whistled through my teeth. "Damn."

"I'm not fucking around with her safety again." He ran his hand through his hair. "I might keep him around indefinitely, after that attack."

"Hopefully once this is over, you won't need a guard on her."

"Yeah." Chris stared at his father, looking like his mind was somewhere else. Back home with Molly, probably. "How's your place? Do you need help repainting or refinishing the floors to get rid of the bloodstains?"

We'd told everyone the attack had taken place at my house, so Tate didn't have to tell everyone he had a sister. It was best for all involved. "Nah, I already cleaned it up. Thanks, though."

"At least we match now," Chris said, touching his nose.

I pressed my finger to mine, too. "Yeah, we do."

Tate came over to us, his AR-15 held against his shoulder. He had dark bags under his eyes, like he hadn't slept for a week. He frowned at Chris, then focused on me, his gaze falling to my shoulder. "Are you sure you're ready to do this, Donahue?"

"I'm sure," I said, my tone even, meeting his stare. There was no way in hell I was sending Chris out there alone, knowing what I knew now, and Tate was fully aware of where I stood on that matter. "My arm is fine, sir."

"And I bet it'll feel even better after we take these assholes down," Chris interjected.

"Yeah," Tate said dryly. "Revenge always looks nice on paper."

I frowned at him.

Brian came over, nodding at us once. "You ready, boss?"

Tate headed for the door without a word.

"Guess that's a yes." He grinned at us. "And you guys? You ready to kick some ass?"

"I was born ready," Chris said, cracking his neck. "The second they attacked Lucas, I was ready to take them down."

Hopefully I was the only one that noticed Chris didn't meet Brian's eyes as he spoke. His guilt over his part in this whole mess was written all over his face.

I stood. "Let's do this."

We headed for the door together, following the rest of the crowd. Everyone—Tommy, Brian, Frankie, Tate, Chris, Gus, even Pops O'Brien and every other damn member of the Sons old enough to fight—started to leave the building, intent on putting an end to Bitter Hill. The young recruits were left behind to protect the families of the men fighting.

I let out a soft breath, pulled my phone out, and shot off

a quick text to Agent Torres, who I had listed in my phone as Ricky. *It's supposed to rain for the Red Sox game tomorrow night.*

That was code for "the shit is about to hit the fan."

I'll bring an umbrella, he replied quickly.

That meant they were on the scene, hidden in plain sight, and had our backs.

Mine and Chris's.

"We're all set." Chris, of course, knew all about the DEA's involvement in this attack. I tucked my phone away and rolled my shoulder, wincing. "Here's hoping all goes as planned."

He frowned. "Are you sure your shoulder is up for this?"

"Yes."

He gestured to my wound, which admittedly still stung like a bitch. "Maybe you should just sit this one out. Go to my place and hang with Molly."

"No."

A muscle in his jaw ticked. "Fine. Just make sure you don't get us both killed with your stubbornness. Molly will be pissed if I come home in a body bag instead of the Mustang."

We settled into his car, and waited for the vehicles in front of us to go. There were fifteen heading for the Bitter Hill clubhouse. *Fifteen.* The Sons had too many members to get away with less. Six of them had already left, and each one would go a different way to avoid suspicion.

Two more cars pulled out onto the road. Shortly after, another two left, going different ways. Everyone was under strict orders that if some people didn't make it, for whatever reason, the attack was still supposed to happen. That way, no matter what happened, Bitter Hill would go down tonight. The contingency plans had contingency plans.

And yet . . .

I couldn't shake the uneasiness that settled at the base of my neck. I looked out the window as another group of men left. Ours was last in line, behind Pops O'Brien. Then it was Tate, Tommy, Frankie, and Brian—who were all in one truck together. I'd argued that keeping all the lieutenants so close was asking for trouble. If someone attacked the last part of the procession, the Sons' entire leadership would be in jeopardy, but Frankie and Tate hadn't listened to me.

Brian beeped his horn impatiently. "Yo, Pops! Let's go!"

Chris's father came out of the clubhouse with his best friend, flipped off Brian, and headed toward his pickup truck, swaggering cockily even though his truck was blocking us in. We were all waiting on them to get out of the damned way so we could go.

"Do you see these jackasses?" I asked Chris, gesturing at his pops.

"Yeah." Chris watched his dad, too, his jaw tight. "Jesus, could he go any slower? I've seen a fucking snail move fast—"

A boom filled the parking lot, and I jerked back in surprise. Pops O'Brien fell to the ground right outside Chris's door, spitting out blood as he collapsed to the ground.

For a second, no one moved.

We just stared, because *what the fuck happened*?

But then another boom filled the silence of the night, and Pops O'Brien's best buddy fell, too, his brains exploding out in a spray of skull and brain matter all over the window of his truck.

That was enough to snap me the hell out of it.

Bitter Hill was here. And my backup *wasn't*.

"Shit." I threw my door open to take cover, and aimed my gun toward where the shot could have originated, breathing heavily, trying to find the sniper since we were all just sitting ducks here. The rest of the Sons remaining in the lot did the same, taking shelter and aim.

Chris didn't move, just stared at his dead father, his knuckles tight on the wheel. Pops O'Brien had been an abusive son of a bitch who'd made Chris's life hell, but seeing your father killed in front of you?

Yeah, it was bound to make a man need a second to recover.

But a second was all he had.

"Chris!" I shouted.

He shook himself, his eyes blank. "Yeah?"

"Move."

He threw his door open, stepped over his father's body, and lifted his gun, his hands as steady as ever, taking cover with me, behind his car.

Brian backed his truck up next to us, squealing his tires, giving us cover on either side, and then jumped down beside us. Tommy, Tate, and Frankie all jumped down, too. "It's coming from up high. A roof, maybe."

"Can you see the shooter?" I called out, heart racing, blood rushing.

Another shot boomed, hitting the side of Brian's truck instead of us.

"Second window from the left, third floor," Chris called out.

Tommy slid into position beside us. When another bullet grazed by us, narrowly missing his head, he cursed and fired off a spray of bullets. The gunfire stopped abruptly, and I let out a breath of relief. "Got him. We need to—"

Another shot boomed from behind us, and Brian fell back, clutching his shoulder, his blood blending in with the red of his truck. "Son of a bitch."

"Shit." I whirled and squeezed the trigger, aiming for the sound. I was pretty sure it had come from the roof of the empty warehouse next to our clubhouse. "Brian?"

"I'm alive," he growled. "But it's my shooting arm. I'm out."

"Then stay down," Chris said, sliding in front of him.

I did the same, resting my finger on the trigger, guarding the man who had once been my brother. "We've got you. Be our eyes."

Tate crept closer, gun aimed at the building to our left, breathing heavily. "Brian?"

"I'm alive," he called out. "They got my shoulder."

"They're fucking with us," Tate said, his hair sticking up and his shirt showing a line of blood on his forearm. "They have us surrounded, and we can't find them. They waited for us to be alone, and now they're picking us off one by one."

I cleared my throat. "This hits a little too close to home for comfort."

"Yeah." Tate looked at me. "It's almost like someone tipped them off to our plan, and they executed it before we could. They're trying to take out the leaders."

Which was why I'd suggested we split up. Tate probably hadn't trusted me out of his sight—a mistake he was paying for now. I glanced past him. "Where'd Tommy go?"

"He's on the other side of the truck, scoping out that building." He cocked his head to the right. "Frankie's with him."

Another shot, and an older member who never joined in fights anymore fell to the ground, staring sightlessly up at the sky. For the life of me, I couldn't remember his name. Don? Dan? Tate growled, stood, and fired off three shots. At the same time, I saw the glint off a gun on the rooftop where I'd been aiming earlier. "Get down!" I called out, firing off shots.

He didn't hear me. Just kept shooting, his anger having apparently turned him into a reckless leader. The asshole was going to get himself *killed*. He stepped even more out of the cover, pulling the trigger again. "Tate!"

Skylar's face swam in front of me, and I locked eyes with Chris, who shook his head. I ignored him, because if Skylar lost her brother, she'd have no one left.

I threw myself at Tate.

He hit the ground hard at the same time a bullet buzzed right over us, shattering Brian's driver's-side window. I heard it whizz past my head, almost putting an end to all my lies for good. Tate's eyes were wide, his cheeks still flushed with anger.

"Roof!" Brian called out. "Eight o'clock!"

Chris turned, aimed, took a breath, and pulled the trigger before I could pick my gun back up. I'd dropped it while saving Tate's life. The shooter fell off the roof, hitting the pavement. "Thank you," Tate said after a moment's silence.

I nodded once, not meeting his eyes, and pushed off him.

Tate rolled to his knees, handing me my gun.

Chris aimed for the same roof again. "I saw another guy up there. Check the other roofs. I've got this one."

We all repositioned ourselves accordingly. I stayed where I was, even though I had worse cover here than where I'd been before. I felt too exposed on the end like this, but I wanted to keep an eye on Tate and make sure he didn't pull another stunt like the last one.

I took the left.

Tate the right.

Tommy, wherever he was, hopefully had the last shooter covered, if he could still hear us. But we had no way of knowing right now whether he was still alive and fighting. Too many men had fallen. "Tommy?" I called out.

No answer came.

"Frankie?" Tate yelled.

Again, no answer.

"Shit," he muttered.

Chris squeezed off a shot. A thump, and then an AR-47 fell from the roof. Another one down. We all knelt like that, circled around Brian, watching for any signs of life.

None came.

Tate tightened his finger on the trigger, and another Bitter Hill guy fell from the roof, landing on the ground with a thump.

Brian grinned. "Do you think they're all gone?"

Chris fired off a shot, and an answering boom filled the air at the same time, echoing through the darkness of the night. Pain seared through my thigh. I clutched it, glancing down, and saw blood painting my fingers red. The sniper must've been aiming for one of us when he was taken down, and he'd fired off one last shot . . . at *me*. "Son of a—"

"Scotty!" Chris yelled, his voice strangled, as he tossed his gun aside and crawled to me, his face pale.

"It's fine. I'm fi . . ." I pressed on my wound harder, frowning because the blood showed no signs of stopping. *"Shit."*

Tate came over to me, gun still raised at the enemy, eyes on the roofs surrounding us. "Are you okay, Donahue?"

Chris pushed my hand aside, cursing, his face pale. "Damn it. That's an artery. They nicked an artery."

Laughing, I fell back, the world spinning. "Of fucking course they did."

Chris grabbed my phone out of my pocket, punched in my passcode, and dialed. I was in too much pain to be impressed by the fact that he'd figured out my code at some point.

Brian sat up more, still holding his shoulder. "What are you doing?"

"Calling 911."

"*What?*" Brian grabbed for the phone weakly. Chris lurched back, easily holding it out of reach. "The hell you are. You can't call the Boys here. We'll just bind it good, and take him to Doc—"

"We can't wait that long." Tate ripped his shirt off and wrapped it around the wound, pulling it tight and applying a painful amount of pressure. When I groaned, he shot me a concerned look. "Do it. Call them."

Brian's jaw dropped. "But—"

"He's going to die if we don't do it," Tate growled, pressing harder. "Everyone else can clear out, but he needs help, and I'm not letting him die here."

Brian frowned. "I'm not leaving you."

"Clear out," Tate barked, still fussing over my leg. "That's an order."

Chris talked quietly into the phone, his back to us. I had a feeling he'd called Agent Torres instead of 911. Smart move. They'd get to Steel Row a hell of a lot faster anyway.

But at the rate I was losing blood . . .

It wouldn't matter anyway.

Brian struggled to stand, holding his shoulder. "They're going to arrest him, *and* you."

"I'll be fine. I have no record. I'll tell them I heard the shots from my office down the street, and came running to help." He lifted his chin, glaring at his right-hand man. "Go. Find Tommy, and Frankie, and get the hell out of here. *Now.*"

Brian staggered away, calling out for Tommy.

I tried to catch my breath, and failed.

The world started simultaneously spinning and fading away.

"Don't you die on me," Tate growled, pressing on my leg even harder and slapping my face gently. "*Scotty*. Skylar will kill me if I let you die."

I choked on a laugh, because she didn't give a damn about me anymore. "I really do love her," I said, the world rapidly fading away. "I . . . I . . ."

And then everything faded to black.

CHAPTER 22

SKYLAR

I rubbed my face, blinking away the exhaustion trying to claim me. Rubbing my forehead, I tried to focus on the TV, but there was no use. I stood up and paced toward the stairs, glancing up them at Tate's bedroom door, which had been shut ever since he staggered home covered in blood, shot me one look, said, "Don't leave," and then walked up the stairs into his bedroom.

That had been three hours ago.

He hadn't come out since.

There had been something in his eyes that told a story of the things he'd seen, and done, and that were going to haunt him for a long time. God help me, I didn't want to know what those things were. That emptiness in his eyes stayed with me long after his bedroom door shut behind him.

And even though I tried to pretend I wasn't worried about another red-haired man in my life, I couldn't help it. I needed to know if Scotty was still breathing. I glanced down at my phone, unlocking it, looking at the last text I'd sent. Are you okay?

I'd sent it to Scotty shortly after Tate had come home, despite my better judgment. He hadn't opened it yet. Hadn't read it. That could mean a million and one things. Or nothing at all.

The bedroom door swung open and Tate stood at the top of the stairs, wearing a pair of sweats and a loose white T-shirt. His hair stood up like he hadn't even bothered to run a comb through it after he'd showered. His jaw was tight, and there was determination in his eyes. "We need to talk."

I stood, swallowing as I smoothed my sweater over my stomach, which knotted with fear. "I agree. What happened out there?"

"That's not what I need to talk to you about." He headed into the kitchen, and I followed him. As he pulled a mug out of the cabinet, he sighed. "It's Scotty."

"Oh God. No." Fear struck my heart. Icy, cold, unforgiving. I gripped the edge of the island, a hollow noise echoing throughout my head. "Is he . . . ?"

"No," he said quickly. "He's alive. But—"

I collapsed into the chair by the entry of the kitchen, my legs trembling. "Maybe next time, open with that? *Jesus.*"

"Sorry." He slid a coffee pod in the Keurig and hit the brew button before turning back to me. His jaw was hard. "I made Scotty tell you he didn't love you."

Blinking in shock, I pressed a hand to my racing heart, pain twisting in my chest so sharply for a second that I couldn't breathe. Out of all the things I could have imagined him saying, this was pretty much last on the list. "Wait. *What?*"

"All those things he said in the hospital. It was me. Not him." He rubbed his jaw, letting out a long, slow breath. "I made him break up with you because he's not good enough for you."

I stared at him, not speaking.

Truth be told, I had no words.

None. At. All.

"I'm sorry."

I blinked.

Knock, knock, knock.

I didn't move.

Neither did Tate.

"I was trying to protect you," he said, his tone hushed.

Still I said nothing. Just gripped my thighs.

He ran his fingers through his hair. "Today, he was h—"

Knock, knock, knock.

Tate had a butler. Where the heck was he?

"Skylar? Are you in there?" a deep voice called out.

Tate stiffened, rage filling his expression. He stalked to the door, yanking it open. "What the fuck are *you* doing here, asking for *my* sister?"

I stood on shaky legs and walked into the living room, trying not to focus on the fact that my brother, the one man I trusted to never let me down, had just broken my heart even worse than Scotty had. A man in a Sons of Steel Row brown leather jacket, a pair of bloody jeans, and a gray sweater stood in the hallway, glowering at Tate. He had a five o'clock shadow that went on for days and eyes that said he was comfortable with violence. As I watched, he rubbed his forehead, letting out an agitated breath. He had a dimple in his chin. I don't know why I noticed that, but I did.

"Where is she?" he asked.

Tate stepped forward aggressively. "None of your damn business."

"Who are you?" I asked, ignoring my brother.

The stranger stiffened when he saw me, giving me a once-over. "You're Skylar?"

"Maybe." I crossed my arms in front of my chest, ignoring my brother. "Who's asking?"

"Chris O'Brien." He rested a shoulder on the door, seeming to be as determined to ignore my brother as I was. "I'm a friend of Scotty's."

"Chris—" Tate warned through clenched teeth.

"Stay out of this," I snapped at him, fury making me tremble. "You say one word—*one frigging word*—I'll walk out of here. And I'll keep walking until you never find me."

Tate stiffened and closed his mouth, his nostrils flaring. Chris whistled through his teeth.

"Why are you here?" I asked him.

He straightened. "Scotty didn't tell me much, but I know he's been with you these past few weeks. I've known the kid a long time. He can't hide shit from me. Not anymore."

I raised a brow, imitating Scotty when he was playing it cool. "And your point is . . . ?"

"He's been asking for you ever since he got out of surgery," Chris replied, his tone short.

"Surgery? *Why* was he in surgery?"

"He was injured badly in a . . . a . . ." He hesitated, glancing at Tate. ". . . an accident. He's lost a lot of blood. Between that and the painkillers, he's not thinking straight. . . ."

I uncrossed my arms and stalked over to Tate. "Were you going to tell me? Or were you going to keep *this* from me, too?"

Tate stared straight ahead, his hands fisted at his sides. "I was about to tell you when he knocked."

"Yeah. Sure you were." I turned back to Chris, swallowing, heart racing, stomach rolling, bile climbing up my throat. "Is he . . . is he going to . . . ?"

"He's still alive, for now." He looked directly at Tate, then gave him his back. "Do you want to go see him or not?"

"She's not going anywhere with you," Tate warned, stepping between us. "If she wants to go see him, then *I'll* take her."

"No, you won't," I said, my voice dripping with only a fraction of the anger consuming me right now. "You won't be going *anywhere* with me."

He flinched. "Skylar . . ."

"I'd love to go see him, Chris," I said sweetly, cutting Tate off. "Let's go."

Tate grabbed my arm as I walked past him. "I was just trying to protect you. You don't know what's at stake here. What he really—"

"And I don't want to know," I snapped, yanking free, pointing an angry finger at him. "And if you want to think you have *any* chance in making this up to me, *any* chance in earning my forgiveness, you'll stay here, and leave me alone until *I* decide if I want to talk to you again."

Chris watched, eyes wide.

The blood drained from Tate's face, giving him a ghostly appearance. *"Skylar."*

"Not. Now." I walked right past him. "Let's go."

Chris saluted Tate, then followed me.

"We'll talk about this later, O'Brien," Tate called out angrily.

"Yes, sir," he said over his shoulder.

I didn't look back. Just walked faster. I shivered. It was wet outside, and there was a chill to the air. Chris shrugged his jacket off and wrapped it around my shoulders. I hugged it gratefully. "Thank you."

"You're welcome," he said gruffly.

I licked a raindrop off my lips. "Where is he?"

"Saint Mary's. Outside of Steel Row."

I nodded. "Your car?"

"Here." He led me up to a Mustang. There were bullet holes in the body, a broken window, and something that looked like blood smeared all over the driver's side, as if someone had tried to clean it off before giving up. Chris walked over to the passenger door and opened it for me. "Sorry for the mess. It's been a long day."

Hugging myself, I slid into the seat. I breathed deeply, because I could smell Scotty's cologne in the car. It wrapped around me comfortingly, as I was still reeling from what Tate had told me. Though, in a way, it made a lot of sense. Scotty had never been so cold as he'd been on that day, when he broke me.

It had all been because of Tate.

What did he threaten Scotty with?

Chris got in the car and the engine roared to life, peeling us away from the curb instantly. When I shivered, thanks to cold air pouring through the broken window, he turned the heat all the way up and pointed the vents at me. I watched him out of the corner of my eye, nodding my thanks. After a few moments of silence, I cleared my throat. "Is it over?"

"Is what over?" he asked, flexing his fingers on the wheel. "The surgery?"

"No. Whatever war you guys got yourself into."

Chris laughed uneasily. "I think that's something you need to ask your brother."

"He won't tell me," I said quietly.

"Even more of a reason for me to keep my mouth shut. I'm already gonna get shit from him for taking you away like I did." As we pulled into Steel Row, Chris glanced at me, then returned his attention to the road. "You shouldn't be so rough on him."

I blinked. "On who?"

"Tate. He's got a good reason to keep the two of you apart." Chris turned left on South Harold Street. "Scotty's got secrets."

I lifted a shoulder. "We all have secrets."

"Absolutely." He stopped at a red light and faced me, his eyes serious and his jaw hard. "Scotty's got more than your typical guy."

My pulse leapt. "What's that supposed to mean?"

He shrugged, not speaking.

We pulled into the hospital's visitors' lot. After parking, we got out of the car silently, and as we walked away, he locked the doors with the remote. I found it amusing that he bothered at all, considering the broken window, but whatever.

"This way." Chris waited for me, then placed a hand at my lower back to guide me forward, scanning the shadows. "Scotty's on the second floor."

I hurried toward the door, eyeing the second story. "Why'd you come get me, if it'll get you in trouble with Tate?"

"Because." He lifted a shoulder. "I respect your brother, but I respect and love Scotty more. He's like my little brother, and he needs you at his side."

I nodded, walking through the automatic doors. "Have you always been close?"

"Not always," he said gruffly, pushing the up button on the elevator.

I sensed a lot of history behind those two words. It was weird that he seemed to know Scotty so well, yet Scotty had barely mentioned him. I studied Chris as we waited. He had a few scratches on his face and hands, and a lot of scars. He was clearly no stranger to violence and didn't seem inclined to stop any time soon.

The doors opened, and we stepped on. The only sound

was the chiming of the floor indicator as we ascended. The antiseptic smell so unique to medical facilities tickled my nose as I urged the elevator to get me to Scotty faster. Chris's phone buzzed, and he pulled it out.

After reading a text, he smiled slightly and typed a quick reply. The smile softened his face, making him seem more . . . more . . . *human*. When he saw me staring, he lifted his phone and wiggled it under my nose. "My fiancée."

I wondered what kind of woman a guy like him loved. Probably someone with as much ink as Scotty. Someone tough and unbreakable. "Everything okay?"

"Yeah." He stared at the second-floor number as it lit up. "She was in a car accident recently, and I told her to text me every hour so I know she's okay, till I can come home."

The doors opened, and I followed Chris into the crowded hospital hallway. Nurses rushed past us, heading to our left with crash carts and urgent voices. Chris cursed and ran after them.

My heart wrenched, because if Chris was running . . . *Scotty.*

I chased after him, my stomach hollowing out, every nerve in my body humming with tension as my heart pounded impossibly fast. When Chris skidded into a room, bending over and taking a deep breath, I crashed into him. He didn't even notice.

"Shit, man, I thought they were racing to you," he said, his voice hard.

A soft chuckle, and then Scotty slurred, "Nah. I'm cool. We're cool. It's all cool." He sounded half dead, half high. Mostly just high. "Hey. Did you see Superman in the hallway? 'Cause I did."

Chris straightened, a crooked smile tipping up the corner of his mouth. "Nah, man. I must've just missed him."

"It was awesome," Scotty said, slurring the word.

"I bet," Chris said, chuckling. "How's that morphine treating you?"

"Excellent," Scotty said, drawing the ls out really long.

"Good." Chris glanced over his shoulder at me. I stood there in the hallway, unable to see the man I loved, wringing my hands. I was okay with not seeing him, because I had a feeling once I did, I'd never forget it, or how bad he was feeling. "I brought you a surprise."

"Is it Wonder Woman?" Scotty said.

Chris stepped aside, and there I was.

Not Wonder Woman.

He looked as pale as the white sheets on his bed, and he was limp, lying there with a dull smile on his face. And his eyes . . . they were empty. Like he had no idea where he was and why.

Until he saw me.

Then he came to life.

He struggled to sit up straight, blinking away the fogginess. "What the hell did you do?" he snarled.

Chris raised a brow. "You were asking for her. I brought her to you. It's pretty straightforward."

"No. She can't be here." He finally gave up on trying to sit up, and pointed to the door. "Get out. Get her out. Take her home."

My throat ached, and my eyes stung as I moved closer to him, unable to look away. Anger shone in his bright green eyes. And that anger was focused on *me*. "Scotty—"

"Take her home," Scotty demanded again, his voice slurred, but not lacking command. "You have no idea what you're fucking with."

Chris stepped backward toward the door. "Yeah, well, you're too weak to argue or kick my ass, so since I brought her all the way over here, I'm gonna give you two a few minutes together, and *then* I'll take her home."

"Chris."

Ignoring his buddy, he locked eyes with me. "That okay with you, Ms. Daniels? Would you like a few minutes alone with him?"

I nodded once, wrapping my arms around myself. I had a few things to say to him, whether he wanted to hear them or not. "Thank you."

Scotty stared out the window, not speaking.

Chris walked out, leaving us alone.

"You shouldn't be here," he said slowly, finally facing me again. "I'm seeing superheroes in the hallway, so, clearly, my brain isn't functioning properly."

I stepped closer, unable to resist the pull that was always between us. I had so many things to ask him, *so many frigging questions*, but right now he was high, and weak, and in pain, so it wasn't the time to call him out. "I saw him, too."

"Was Wonder Woman with him?" he asked, frowning.

I nodded. "And Batman."

He opened his mouth, closed it, and pressed his lips into a thin, tight line. "I'm going to say something stupid. You need to go before I do."

I licked my lips. "Like what?"

"Like . . ." He flexed his jaw. "How much I've missed you, Sky. Because I have. I've missed you so damn much, it hurts."

"It hurts me, too," I whispered.

He held his hand out. "I can make it better, if you want. I know how to make it better."

I walked up to the side of his bed, one slow, heavy step at a time. My heart pounded so loudly, it echoed in my head, drowning out the small voice in the back of my mind that screamed for me to *stop*. That small, quiet voice was all too aware that Scotty did have secrets, that there was so much to talk about, but I didn't care.

Because I still loved him.

CHAPTER 23

SCOTTY

The hospital light flickered overhead, but neither of us looked at it. She looked so goddamn beautiful standing there, staring at me with worry in her eyes. Worry for *me*. Her eyes were watery, too, but no tears fell, which was a good thing because I didn't deserve her tears. If she cried over me, every tear that rolled down her cheek would be a tear wasted. But I'd almost died today, and she'd come to see me, so the last thing I wanted to do was send her away again.

Damn Chris for bringing her here.

And damn me for letting her stay.

She crossed the room, her hands clasped in front of her, and sat on the bed right next to me. It reminded me of the last time she came to see me in a hospital. I'd broken both our hearts then, and now I'd have to do it again. I didn't even realize I'd stretched my arm out until she bumped into it. When she reached for me, I slid it under the blanket quickly.

"You should go," I said again. "Tate won't like you being here."

"I don't care." She rested a hand on the blanket, not touching me, but it felt like she had. "You look like awful."

"You look beautiful," I said immediately. "I'm sorry."

She blinked. "What for?"

"For saying you're beautiful. Or maybe for not saying it sooner," I said, blinking away the haze of the drugs. Or trying to. It didn't work. I was high as a goddamn kite. "Damn it, I can't think. I don't know what to say to you right now."

Slowly, hesitantly, she reached out and brushed my hair off my forehead. "You don't have to say anything at all. I just wanted to make sure you were okay."

"You're here, and I know you shouldn't be, but I can't bring myself to give a shit. Other than that . . ."

She frowned and took her hand back. I caught it, and didn't let go. After glancing down at our hands, she locked gazes with me, her mouth parting on an indrawn breath, and entwined her fingers with mine, holding on tightly. "Why shouldn't I be here?"

"Because we're done. We are." I stared at our hands. Hers was so soft. So pale. So flawless. Mine was covered in callouses and scars, and stained with dirt and blood that would never fully come clean. I'd tried, but I could always see it. "We have to be."

She nodded, swallowing. "Okay. But you were asking for me."

"I was," I admitted. "I shouldn't have. I'm high."

"You said," she agreed, a small smile playing at her lips. "How'd you get hurt?"

"I took a bullet to the leg. Grazed my artery." I glanced down. It still throbbed like a bitch, despite the copious amounts of pain meds. "It hurts."

She lowered her head, her focus locked on my leg—the wrong one. I didn't tell her. "God."

"It's okay. I'm okay." My vision blurred, and she faded away to nothing. I was too damn tired to keep my thoughts and my feelings straight—emotions I had no right feeling for her, of all people. "Sky . . ."

"Sh." She leaned in and cupped my face, smiling sadly. "Go to sleep."

I closed my eyes, taking a deep breath, still trying to fight off the darkness that grabbed hold of me. If I succumbed to it, she'd be gone, and I'd never see her again. That was the way it needed to be, but right now, I didn't want to accept that. I didn't want to let go. "You're beautiful, Sky. Too beautiful for a guy like me . . ."

The last word away slurred into nothing. Son of a bitch. I was falling into that damn black hole of unconsciousness, and I wasn't going to be able to fight my way out. She ran her thumb over my jaw, and pressed her lips to my forehead tenderly. "You take care, Scotty Donahue."

I opened my mouth to ask her to stay.

Wait. No. To *go*. She had to go.

Right?

But before I could say the words, I slipped into unconsciousness. When I opened my eyes again, I blinked into the bright room, and she was nowhere to be seen. So I closed my eyes, letting the darkness claim me completely. Every time I woke up, someone was always there. Chris. Brian. Tate. Agent Torres, wearing street clothes. Even Agent Warren had stopped by, in disguise. But not Skylar.

She didn't come back.

Five days later, I forced my eyes open again, with a grunt, and searched the room for her beautiful face like I always did. Instead of soft strawberry blonde hair and softer lips, I found Brian. He sat beside me with his dirty Nikes resting on the side of my bed. He had a gossip magazine opened, and was apparently learning the reasons behind the divorce of a Hollywood It Couple. When he heard me move, he lifted his head.

I stared at him.

He stared back.

"You're awake," he finally said.

"Yeah," I croaked. I licked my parched lips. "Water?"

"Sure." Brian set down the magazine. It had a Kardashian on the front. I could never remember which was which. "We weren't sure you were going to make it."

Neither was I.

I hadn't even had a chance to tell the DEA that my cover was blown. They knew I was hurt, and more than likely, they had someone discreetly watching over me. Making sure I was safe. If they knew I was in danger, I'd be out of here. Now that I was conscious, I should probably tell them.

Maybe I could get relocated to Georgia, where Lucas was.

But then Tate popped into my mind, and I forgot all about that shit.

If I let the DEA reassign me, if I ran, Tate might go after Chris or Lucas. It would be my fault. If anyone was going to go down, it should be me. I was the one that got us into this mess.

Brian handed me the cup, and I struggled to sit up straight. "Thanks."

"Sure," Brian said, walking over to the window and looking outside. Snowflakes fell from the sky, drifting down slowly. "You've been out for a long time. Missed a lot of shit."

"Fill me in?"

"DEA raided Bitter Hill before we could kill them all.

Our guys managed to set the fire, and get a few shots off, but when the DEA swooped in, they scattered. The feds must have been watching Bitter Hill, they got there so fast."

"What happened after that?" I asked tensely.

"After our guys ran, every single Bitter Hill member there was arrested, since the DEA had grounds to enter their clubhouse and there was a shitload of drugs on hand. Street-level dealers were going to restock after the meeting. We'll see what happens after the DA gets through with them, but for now, we don't have to worry about Bitter Hill."

I collapsed against the pillow. "Thank God."

"Yeah." He turned back to me, his jaw hard. "Frankie and Tommy are missing, though. We haven't seen them since the shoot-out. We're not sure what that means."

Well, shit. "Think they ran for it when the shooting started, and are too scared to show their faces? Or that one or both of them are moles?"

"Maybe. Maybe not." Brian shrugged.

I looked out the window again. "What's Tate thinking?"

"He's as confused as the rest of us are. None of us are sure what to think right now. I can't imagine either of them running out of fear. But when shit gets real . . . who knows? Maybe they panicked."

I set my empty cup down and rubbed my jaw. I had a full-on beard going. "Shit."

"Yeah." He crossed his arms. "You talk a lot in your sleep."

I stiffened. "Oh yeah?"

"Yeah." He turned back to me. "You called for *her* a lot."

I forced my face to remain blank. "Who? My ma?"

"We both know who you called for, and it wasn't your ma." He locked gazes with me, flexing his jaw. "You better hope you didn't do that in front of Tate."

I stiffened. "He was here?"

"Of course he was. You saved his life out there." Brian came back to my side of the bed, sitting down again, and picked up his magazine. "He's not one to forget a debt owed."

"I was just doing my job."

Brian contemplated that. "You saved my life, too. Shielded me from the bullets when I was down."

I eyed his shoulder. "How's the arm?"

"Fine. Just a few stitches before I was sent on my way by Doc Hollins." He glanced down at my leg. "Nothing like you. You took a hit, man. I've killed people and I never saw so much blood in my life."

I grinned. "I'll take that as a compliment."

"You would."

I took another sip of water.

"She was here, too. Every day."

I stiffened. "She was?"

"Yeah. She'd sit and do her homework, or talk to you like you could hear her." He flipped open the magazine. After a little bit of silence on both our ends, he pointed to the page. "These people, they lead charmed lives. Great looks, lots of money, they're always smiling. Falling in love. Being normal. I wonder what that feels like."

I rubbed my jaw again. "Being normal?"

"Being *happy*."

I knew what happy felt like. I'd found it in Skylar's arms, and now I felt its absence every damn time I opened my eyes. "I don't know, man."

"Me either." He flipped the page. "Actually, I do. I was happy once. There was this girl. She had the prettiest blonde hair, and a laugh that sounded like a fucking song."

Blinking, I couldn't help but wonder if I was still sleeping.

Brian never opened up like this, and he never talked about his past. "What happened?"

"I joined the Sons, and I left her behind." He turned the page again. "Last I heard, she was married with two kids. Husband's a stockbroker or something."

"Sounds boring," I said.

"Sounds normal." He shut the magazine and tossed it on the table that was beside my bed. "After the shit we've been through, I could use a little bit of normal. Maybe that's why Frankie and Tommy are gone. Maybe they wanted some normal, too."

"Maybe."

Brian stood. "I gotta go. Got a few errands. Oh, and heads-up? Tate's calling a meeting as soon as you're out of here. Not sure what for."

"Okay," I said, keeping my tone even. "Keep me posted."

"I will." He shrugged into his leather jacket, watching me closely. "You know, Tate doesn't forget a favor, or a debt owed, but neither do I. Remember that."

I had the feeling he knew more than he was letting on. Exactly what that was? I didn't have a damn clue. But I had a feeling it was *something*. "Thanks, man."

"Sure thing."

He walked out, and I closed my eyes, taking a deep breath. I was alone for no more than thirty seconds before I heard footsteps. I opened my eyes. "What did you forget?"

"Nothing," Agent Warren said, walking in. He wore a hoodie and a pair of basketball shorts. "You're alive."

I sat up straighter, running my hands through my hair. "Yeah."

He came inside and sat down, resting his elbows on his knees. "We've had people with you, watching. Nurses, security officers, aides. We switched it up to avoid suspicion, but you've never been alone."

"I figured." I gestured to my leg. "Not that I'd have noticed anyway. This took me down pretty hard."

"I saw," he answered dryly. "Agent Torres was pleased with your work, despite the snafu at the clubhouse that held you guys back."

Snafu. It had been a full-on motherfucking ambush. "No one heard whispers of a leak? Because it seems pretty damn coincidental that Bitter Hill used the Sons' plan against them."

"I know." He rubbed his jaw, watching me over his fingers. "It's weird, isn't it?"

"Very." I cocked my head. "Almost like there was a mole."

We considered one another for a few beats, and then Warren said, "Yeah. That's one possibility, I suppose."

"Then again, Bitter Hill didn't know the DEA was going to raid the place. Otherwise, they'd have made sure there was nothing to find. They only knew enough to set up the counterattack."

Warren nodded slowly. "I noticed you referred to the Sons as 'them.' You no longer consider yourself a Son?"

"I never really was." I rubbed my temples. All this thinking, fresh out of my practically comatose state, hurt, but I realized that I'd stopped thinking of myself as a Son the day they killed Bobby, with me standing there silently, letting it happen. "I'm an undercover agent, not one of them."

"Yeah." Warren chuckled. "In this world, you never know where someone's loyalty lies. With undercover work like yours, it's even harder to sort out."

"Why are you here, instead of Torres?" I asked slowly.

"He's got a meeting with the interagency cooperation liaison all day. A new case came up." He shrugged. "So I came in his place. Now that you're awake, we can ask if your cover was compromised. We tried to lay low, to keep you clean, but your informant called us . . ." He shrugged. "We have plans in place if you need extraction. There's an opening in the Dallas office, and they'd be happy to have you."

For a second, I let myself picture it. A life away from here, where I could be normal. There was a lot of other non-undercover work in the DEA. And in this fantasy, I had a woman in my life. A woman who was, without doubt, Skylar Daniels.

That's where the daydream ended.

"No. My cover is good." I forced a smile. "I'll be fine."

Agent Warren looked less than convinced, and for the second time in as many visitors, I suspected he knew more than he let on. Everyone seemed to be hiding something from me. "Are you sure? Because if you're not, and they do some housecleaning, we might not be able to help you in time."

I thought of Lucas, and how happy he'd been when he and Heidi drove off.

Of Chris, when he rested his head on Molly's chest, clinging to her after she'd been hurt.

And Skylar, lying in my bed, her head on my chest as she slept.

I might not know who to trust, or what the hell to do next, but I knew one thing. Tate Daniels was a man of his word. If he swore to leave my family alone, he would, and I would give up anything to make sure they were safe . . . including my life. I'd already lost Sky. So, really, what was the threat of a little bit of torture and, ultimately, death when compared with that kind of sacrifice? If death was my fate, then so be it. I'd accept it. I'd be the hero one more time.

We all died eventually.

It was the only certain thing in life.

"I'm sure," I said, my tone final. "I'm in no danger at all."

CHAPTER 24

SKYLAR

I watched Tate as I sipped my coffee. It had been almost two weeks since he told me the truth. He'd been begging me to give him a chance to explain, and after lots of thought and a desire to let him wallow in his misery for a while, I finally answered the phone when he called at nine this morning, asking to meet me at one in the afternoon. I'd hoped it was Scotty finally returning my call, but nope.

He was back to pretending I didn't exist, apparently.

While he'd been in the hospital, I visited him every day. During those visits, he'd always wake up long enough to grab my hand and hold tight. But one day I showed up and I was denied entrance by a nurse who looked like she'd have no trouble taking me out. Scotty had taken me off the visitors' list. I'd gotten nothing but radio silence from him since.

Guess he stopped seeing superheroes, and, in turn, stopped wanting to see me.

Scotty originally pushed me away because of Tate's

threats, but his reluctance to hear me out was creating a lot of self-doubt. Maybe Tate had just given Scotty the excuse he needed to walk away. Just look at my track record with men.

"I know you're angry," Tate started, pulling me out of my mournful thoughts. "And you have every reason to be."

I set my mug down, clanking it on his dining room table. Opulence, wealth, and arrogance surrounded us, stifling me. I hated this house. It reminded me of his father. The bastard. "You think?"

"Yes," he said, even though my question hadn't really been a question. "I was trying to protect you."

"By breaking us up." I leaned back in the chair, crossing my arms. *"Riiight."*

He pressed his lips together. "He's a dangerous man. More dangerous than me."

I scoffed. I couldn't help it. "I think we both know that's not true."

"You're wrong. He's got secrets." He pointed a finger down at the table, emphasizing his point. "He's got so many damn secrets that his *secrets* have secrets."

His warning struck close to home despite my anger, because Chris had pretty much said the same exact thing. "And you don't?"

"Not like him." He flattened his palm on the mahogany table. "You have no idea what the hell you're getting into every time you walk up to his door."

"So you keep saying." I pursed my lips. "What secrets does he have that are so frigging dangerous to me? Huh?"

He tapped his fingers. "It's not my place to say."

"What?" I blinked. "Seriously?"

He reclined in his chair, crossing his arms. "Ask him if you want to know."

I'd been *trying*. I failed to mention this, though, because it was none of Tate's business. "Maybe I will."

"All right." He lifted a shoulder. "But I stand by my statement."

I narrowed my eyes at him. "Which one?"

"He's no good for you."

I picked up my coffee again, blowing on it. "If you still feel that way, why come clean at all? Why tell me the truth?"

"Because I owe it to him. He saved my life."

I swallowed hard. "He . . . did?"

"Yes." Tate avoided my gaze. "And as he was passing out, he thought he was going to die, and he used his last breath to say something about you."

"What did he say?" I asked breathlessly.

"Again, you'll have to ask him." A muscle in his jaw ticked. "I did the right thing. I came clean. I still don't want you with him, so that's all I'm going to say on the matter."

I frowned.

"I don't approve of him," Tate repeated.

"Unfortunately for you, I don't need your blessing or approval to love someone." I stood, and a hot rage rushed through my veins. "I choose who or who not to love."

He nodded. "I know."

"Do you?" I shot back. "Do you really?"

He frowned.

"I know that you truly believe you were acting in my best interests, but you *weren't*. None of this was for me—it was so you wouldn't feel bad for introducing us in the first place. Because you did, and I fell in love with him, and then I was connected to a part of your life you so desperately wanted me away from. So you fixed it."

"You're right. I didn't want you anywhere near the Sons."

He tightened his grip on his coffee mug, looking far too at home in the opulence that surrounded him. "I still don't."

"Well, too bad." I hugged myself. "We don't always get what we want. We should both know that by now. Dad taught us well."

I stared out the window at the rolling lawns, sprawling forth from an elegant garden enclosed by ivy walls. I'd only known Scotty for a few weeks. A short blip on the radar of my life. But the connection we had, the completeness I'd felt when he held me in his arms, it was something I knew, I just *knew*, I'd never feel again. Not in a million years.

No matter how many times I told myself that it was okay, that loving him for even a short time had been a wild roller-coaster ride, and that it had to end eventually as all rides did, it still *hurt*. How easy had it been for Scotty to send me away? To write me off? To never see me again?

Why wasn't *he* hurting, too?

Tate's chair scraped the hardwood floors. He walked to the bar on the side of the room, picking up a bottle of Irish whiskey and walking over to his untouched coffee. He poured in a healthy shot, and lifted the bottle to me, cocking a brow.

I shook my head.

After capping the whiskey, he picked up his mug and said, "Look. I'm sorry for my part in this. Can you ever forgive me?"

No matter what happened between us, no matter what he did, he was my brother. Nothing would change that. Not even this big, fancy house I hated almost as much as I hated the man who used to own it. And not even the fact that Tate was becoming more and more like him with each passing moment. "I just need time."

He nodded, his jaw tight. "Then I'll give you time. But . . ." He cut off immediately, staring over my shoulder at something. "Yes, Miles?"

The butler came in, clearing his throat. "You have a guest, sir. He says you're expecting him?"

He checked his watch, frowning. "He's early. Send him in."

"Work meeting?"

He nodded. "Yes, Brian—"

"Not Brian, sir," Scotty said. I froze, my heart shattering into shrapnel, all because I heard his voice. I dreamt of it every night, but it wasn't the same. "Sorry. I didn't know you had company."

Tate's entire body tensed as he stepped in front of me, as if I needed his protection from Scotty of all people. "This is . . . *unexpected*, Scotty," he said, his voice colder than ice. "To what do I owe this honor?"

Scotty took another step inside the room, carefully avoiding my eyes. In fact, he didn't even *look* at me. His long fingers were curled into fists, and his gray khakis bulged slightly where the bandages on his leg must be. A cobalt blue tie broke up the stark whiteness of his button-up shirt and made his green eyes seem impossibly bright. If it wasn't for the ever-present brown leather jacket, it would be easy to mistake him for the corporate intern he had claimed to be.

He looked so . . . so . . . different.

"Unorthodox, too, I know. We need to talk." Scotty flicked a quick glance my way, his eyes empty and . . . yeah. Empty. That was the only way to explain it. "Alone."

I knew a dismissal when I heard one. "I was just leaving, so . . ." Crossing the room, I grabbed my purse, slinging it over my shoulder. I walked right past Scotty, and his cologne teased my senses. "I'll call you later, Tate."

Scotty slowly counted down on his fingers, then grabbed my elbow. "Sky . . ."

I froze, heart pounding, and glared down at his hand. He immediately let go. "What?"

He shook his head. "Nothing."

"Why didn't you return my calls?" I whispered furiously. I could feel Tate watching us, eyes narrow.

He lifted his chin. "I've been busy."

"Too busy to answer the phone?"

He didn't say anything. Just stared straight ahead.

"Look at me," I snapped.

He did. And when he did, I almost wished he hadn't. There was nothing there. Just a bleakness that made me want to cry. It was like he wasn't fighting the good fight anymore, like he'd just given up. That hurt almost as much as his rejection had.

"Scotty . . ."

He opened his mouth, closed it, then pressed it into a tight line. "I've got to talk to your brother, Sky. I need to sort things out with him."

But not with *me*.

Me, he just blew off.

"Go to hell," I breathed, brushing past him. "You two deserve each other."

And then I walked out.

Leaving my mangled heart behind in his hands.

CHAPTER 25

SCOTTY

The second the door shut behind Sky, Tate spoke. "She knows the truth about why you broke up with her. I told her the morning she came to see you in the hospital."

"You knew about that?" I asked in surprise.

"Of course I did. She was at my place," Tate said.

"But you let her go?" I was still caught off guard, both by the unexpected run-in with Sky, and by Tate's almost-friendly tone as he spoke. "Why?"

"I think we both know that Skylar does what she wants." He shrugged. "And Bitter Hill has been neutralized for the moment, so there was no danger in her going to see you. Aside from the danger you pose anyway."

I stiffened. "I would never hurt her."

"Maybe not on purpose." He poured a glass of whiskey, and set it down in front of me. I didn't touch it. "But you will."

"Why would I?" I countered.

"You're in the DEA, for starters." He sat. I sat, too, slowly lowering myself into the chair so it didn't strain my stitches. "She knows all about me."

My chest tightened. "What?"

"She knows everything." He picked up his glass, spinning it in his fingers. "If you go after me, you'll be taking her down, too. You'll have to. She'll be culpable."

Well, shit. The last thing I wanted to do was put Skylar in jeopardy, and he knew it as well as I did. It also didn't leave me with many options—not good ones, anyway. Anger surged in my veins, choking me. "Did you tell her, just to fuck us up even more?"

"I would never do that to her," Tate snapped back angrily. "She figured it out years ago, on her own, and just recently admitted it to me."

So much went through my head. All those times I talked about the Sons, and what being in a gang meant, she'd known full well who my boss had been. And she'd never even *hinted* at it. She was better at this game than I'd thought. "Shit. That's that, then."

He frowned. "What?"

"Sky loves you." I tapped my fingers on my good thigh. "I won't take away her brother, and I won't risk her getting in trouble or having to testify against you." I sat up straight. "This game of metaphorical chess we've been playing is over."

Tate cocked a brow. "I didn't realize we were playing a game at all."

"Sure you did." I tapped harder. "But the terrain has changed. Bitter Hill is a nonissue for the moment and I upheld my end of the bargain with Sky, so it's time for you to do your part. I need your word you won't hurt Chris, Lucas, Molly, or Heidi."

Tate flexed his jaw, his eyes hard. "Does this mean you've decided to take me up on my offer?"

"No, not exactly." I shrugged my leather jacket off, laying it on the table between us. "You told me that the time would come where I had to make a choice between the Sons or the DEA. That time is now."

"Damn it, Donahue," he growled. "Don't do this."

"You've left me with no choice. I won't be dirty, so I guess I'm putting myself at the mercy of the Sons."

Tate shook his head, letting out another hard laugh, but his eyes told another story. He almost looked . . . upset. "You won't even *consider* playing both sides?"

"I can't," I replied.

"Can't?" He gritted his teeth. "Or won't?"

"Doesn't matter, does it?"

"You know what this means. You're asking me to put a death sentence on the man my sister loves," Tate pointed out. "Instead, why not continue on as we have been? I've always known what you are, you've always gotten intel, and then passed it along to your handler. Nothing has to change."

"I know the truth now." My nostrils flared. "I won't do it."

He made an angry sound. "I'll have to tell everyone what you are."

"Do what you have to do. I'll accept the consequences of my actions."

"What about Skylar?" he spat out. "What happens to her, if you're sentenced to death?"

I took a deep breath, my heart twisting at the thought of her in pain. "She'll be fine. She'll find another guy to fall in love with, one who's a hell of a lot better than me. Look, someone has to stand up for all the innocent people out there getting caught in the cross fire. No wife should lose a husband to pointless gang wars, no child should lose a father because of a shoot-out, and no mother should mourn her son because he couldn't run away fast enough."

Tate let out a harsh laugh. "And you're going to make all that happen? You're going to save them all?"

"Maybe. Maybe not." I shoved my hands in my pockets. "But I have to try."

Tate said nothing. Just stared at me.

"I've let loyalty to you and my brothers blind me for too long. I ignored the consequences of what the Sons do. I let myself believe that you weren't all bad." I shoved a hand through my hair. "But I see the whole picture now. Every move that the Sons make creates a ripple effect on Steel Row, and Boston, and I'm done being a part of that. Done being a Son."

"Then you're a fool." Tate leaned forward, placing a flat palm on the table. "And you must think I'm an idiot. The second I touch you, I'll have feds crawling all over me."

"No, you won't," I said quickly, dragging a hand through my hair. "You have my word."

"Your *word*," Tate said slowly.

"Yes." I cleared my throat. "Out of respect to you, and my brothers, I hand myself over to your judgment, as long as you, in turn, give me your word you won't hurt my friends and family."

"You're going to die. That'll hurt them," Tate replied.

"Maybe. Maybe not."

"Stop saying that," Tate growled.

Then he stared at me.

So I stared right the fuck back.

Tate stood, too. "You're not just a fool. You're a fool with a death wish."

"Do I have your word?" I held my hand out. "Or not?"

Tate hesitated, staring at my hand. After a few moments

of silence, he clasped my hand and shook it. "You have my word. They'll be safe."

We shook, and I let go. I pulled out the Glock Tate had given me last year when I was promoted. He watched me carefully as I laid it down next to the jacket. "And a word of advice if this ends with my death. I suggest you make it look like a mugging or a robbery. There will still be an investigation, but I trust you know how to keep your hands clean. The point is for Sky not to lose her brother."

I could feel his gaze on me with each step I took. I was almost out of the door before Brian walked in. I nodded at him, trying to pass.

He took one look at me, then the table where my jacket and gun were, and stepped in my path. "What the hell is going on?" he asked, his brow furrowed.

"Tate will fill you in, I'm sure." I glanced over my shoulder at the other man. He looked, oddly enough, pissed off. I wasn't sure why. What more did the man want from me? "It's been a pleasure working with you."

Brian frowned even deeper.

I walked out into the cool, afternoon autumn air, got in my Escalade, and drove. I cruised around the city aimlessly, no destination in mind, just not wanting to go home. I circled the same ten blocks three times, passing Saint Paul's and the Patriot, until I tired of that and swung out farther, to the West End. It wasn't until the sun turned the sky a pretty pink-and-orange hue that I realized where I'd wanted to go all along.

Skylar's apartment.

I slowed in front of her building, my grip on the wheel tightening when I saw her lights were off. I should be happy she wasn't home, or that she'd crashed early. The last thing she needed was me knocking on her door. I'd done enough damage to her life, to her heart.

But the thing was . . .

Her heart wasn't the only one breaking.

I could still feel her body underneath mine, her arms wrapped around me. And whenever I closed my eyes, I saw her. She was always smiling. Laughing. Kissing me. Looking happy. *Haunting* me. I had a feeling not even my death would stop her. Gritting my teeth, I swung a wide arc around her block, and then headed home. I had no way of knowing when Tate and the rest of the Sons would come for me, so I might as well make the most of the time I had and maybe send a letter off to Lucas, just in case.

Sky, too.

And Chris . . .

Damn it, what did I even say to the man who had become a brother to me?

I rubbed my forehead, focusing on the red light ahead. It blurred, shifting shapes, playing with reality. After a few more turns, I pulled up to my house, tightening my grip on the wheel when I saw a familiar Volvo parked in front of my house.

"Son of a bitch."

CHAPTER 26

SKYLAR

I held on to the wheel as I watched him slam his truck into park and jump down from the driver's side. Every limping step he took toward me radiated with anger. Good. I was angry, too.

Grinding my teeth together, I got out of my car. "Took you long enough," I snapped at him, itching for a fight. "You get lost?"

"What the hell are you doing here, sitting alone in your car?" he growled at me, ignoring my question. "You could have been robbed, or raped, or murdered."

I stiffened. "I used to live here. I assure you, I can take care of myself. But, hey, thanks for the concern. Glad to know you care."

"Shut up, Sky," he snapped. He dragged a hand through his hair, so it stood up. "Why are you here?"

"Because I've got some stuff to say to you, and you're going to let me say it." A curtain moved in the house across the way, but the streets were empty. Only people with a purpose went out in this neighborhood after dusk.

He rubbed his jaw, glaring at me. "The hell I am. Go home."

"No." Blinking, he reached for my wrist, trying to grab it, but I pulled back. "Don't touch me."

"Sky."

"I hate you, you know," I said, my vision blurring. "I hate you so much that I love you, and that only makes me hate you even more. I know that doesn't make sense, but to me it does."

He fisted his hands. "You need to get the hell out of here. It's not safe here."

"I told you, I can take care of myself."

"I know," he practically shouted, backing me against my car. "But that doesn't stop me from not wanting anything to happen to you, damn it."

"Is that why you pushed me away?" I asked, resting my hands on his chest.

He didn't say anything. Just stared at my hands on him.

"I know why you did it." I bit down on my lip, my heart surging when I saw panic light up his green eyes. "Tate made you do it. Tate made you say those things."

"No one *makes* me do anything I don't want to do," he said, his voice low. "I did what I had to do, and I did it for a good reason. Now go home."

"What did he threaten you with?" I pressed.

He hesitated. "It doesn't matter. Knowing won't change anything. It's over."

"If it doesn't change anything, then answer the question." I took a step closer to him. He tensed. "How did Tate convince you to break up with me?"

Something fell behind us, clattering on the pavement

down the road a bit, and he turned that way, reaching for something at his side, before letting his empty hand fall. After a few seconds of searching the deepening shadows, he grabbed my elbow. "Inside. Now."

Without arguing, I let him lead me up to his door. The second we were inside, I started in on him again. "What did he do to you?"

"He found one of my weaknesses and used it against me. It's what men like him do. I'd have done the same thing if I were in his shoes." He locked the door and leaned against it, watching me from underneath hooded eyelids. "He loves you. He'd do anything to protect you. And that's what he did."

Disbelief hit me hard in the stomach. "Are you *seriously* defending him, after what he did to you? To me?"

"Hell yeah, I am. He did the right thing, breaking us up." He lifted a shoulder casually. "You'll see it someday."

Rage, pure rage, crashed through me in a red tidal wave. I walked right up to him, shoving him. He didn't budge, because he was already backed up against the door, as far away from me as he could get without leaving. "I *hate* you."

The streetlight outside his door flickered on. "So you said."

"You don't even care about me at all, do you?" I pushed his shoulder again, and he grabbed my wrist, trapping it in his steely grip. Tears rolled down my cheeks unchecked. He'd done it. He'd finally made me cry. *"You never cared."*

"I *care*, damn it!" he shouted, a vein popping out on the side of his neck. "Why do you think I keep pushing you away? Why do you think I'm leaving you? It's because I fucking *care*. I care enough to make you get gone, because you *don't* want to be with me. Not really. So stop pushing me and just *go*."

"I can't," I rasped.

He made an angry sound. "Why not?"

"Because I *love* you."

"I love you, too, damn it!" he shouted.

Before either one of us could register what he'd literally just yelled at me, he spun me so my back was against the door and kissed me with so much pent-up passion, it was a miracle I didn't burst into flames. I wrapped my arms around his neck, and, God help me, I never wanted to let go.

His kiss held a desperation I'd never felt in him before. His hands roamed over me, touching every inch of skin he could, then slipping under my clothes to touch some more. He groaned, his tongue seeking and finding mine.

When his fingers slipped inside my panties, I broke off the kiss, breathing heavily. "*Scotty.* Did you mean it?"

Curling a hand behind my neck, he placed the heel of his palm against my jaw so his thumb rested on my cheek. When he locked eyes with me, there was something there, in those deep green depths, that I'd never seen before.

"Yes." Tenderly, he ran his thumb over my skin, making me shiver. "I love you, Sky. I love you so damn much."

Before I could reply, his mouth met mine again, but this time it was softer.

My heart quickened, and I urged him closer. I arched closer to him, needing every inch of his skin against mine. Needing . . . needing . . . *him.*

His mouth slanted over mine, and he picked me up.

I broke off the kiss, gasping. "Your leg."

"I don't give a damn about my leg."

He kissed me again, and I wrapped my legs around his waist and my arms around his neck. He walked up the stairs, stumbling a few times, with his hands on my butt, supporting me, his lips never leaving mine. When we got to his room, he lowered me to the mattress gently, his body covering me carefully as he slipped between my legs like he'd never left. I buried my hands in his hair and curled my tongue around his, arching against his hardness with a desperation I couldn't hide and didn't want to, but underneath it all was his words.

He loved me.

He actually loved me.

He broke the kiss off, grabbed my shirt, and hauled it over my head, then did the same to his. Sliding off the bed, he undid his pants and let them hit the floor, followed by his boxers. His leg still had a bandage over his gunshot wound, but it was clean and dry. I stared at it, swallowing hard, because I'd almost lost him. "Scotty . . ."

"I know." The second he was naked, he opened the nightstand and tossed a condom on the bed next to me. "I know, sugar."

When he gripped the top of my pants, I lifted my hips and he tugged my leggings down, tossing them over his shoulder to the floor. I fisted the comforter underneath me, lowering my lashes but not closing my eyes.

Instead, I watched him sit down on the bed and then slide up my leg, one soft kiss at a time. There was something about having him between my legs, staring at me like he couldn't live without me, that took my breath away. I moaned and shifted toward him, so he lowered his face between my thighs. His tongue flicked over me through my panties before he pushed my underwear to the side and ran a hard finger over me. My legs shook, and I moved against him, seeking more.

He pulled away, then came back with two fingers this time. When he thrust them inside me, I cried out and strained to get even closer to him. "*Scotty.* More. I need . . . need . . ."

"I know what you need, sugar."

He buried his face between my thighs, closing his mouth over me while moving his fingers deeper inside me. He quickened the strokes of his tongue, and I closed my eyes, letting pleasure creep over my body, pooling in my stomach and tightening until I came with a soft cry, my fingers buried in his hair, and my legs pressed against either side of his head. He flicked his tongue over me one more time, then crawled up my body, melding his mouth to mine as he reached for the condom.

There was a crinkle of a wrapper, and I felt his arms move as he rolled it on. The second he finished, he broke free of my mouth and kissed my jaw. My throat. The top of my breast.

He left hot, searing marks as he slid down my body. His hands slipped under my back, and he unclasped my bra. He moved the straps down my arms with gentle fingers, dropping it next to us. The second it was gone, his mouth closed over a hard, pink nipple and he sucked it in, his other hand closing over the opposite side. He played with me, squeezing and licking and dragging his teeth until I was once again lost in a haze of mindless lust.

When he finally stopped, he slid his hand between us, urging my panties down my thighs. Apparently, he wasn't done killing me, because he slipped his hands under my butt, lifted my hips, and blew on my heated flesh. I shivered, moaning. He wasn't going to . . .

Oh God.

He was.

Again.

He closed his mouth over my already sensitive flesh, dragging his tongue over me slowly, torturously, bringing me to the edge again. It was almost too much, the pleasure he brought out, but it was addicting, and oh-so-delicious, too. I rocked my hips against him wildly, every part of me straining to find that release I knew he could give me. My legs shook and went numb, as if every vein and muscle was focused only on him, and what he was doing to me.

When he thrust his finger again, a sob escaped me.

"Scotty . . . I . . ." I tugged his hair hard, and he dragged his teeth against me, then deepened the strokes of his tongue. "*Yes*. More . . . more . . . *Oh God*."

I came harder than I'd ever come before. It was magical, and mind-blowing, and I couldn't string a coherent thought together if my life depended on it. He rolled off me, onto his back, and shifted me on top so I straddled him, a leg on either side of his hips. I took a second to adjust to this new position, staring down at him with wide eyes. He gripped my hips, lifted me up in the air, and pressed his erection against me. "Hold on tight, sugar. You're going for a ride."

After a nervous glance at his bandaged wound, I rested my hands on his shoulders, right next to his older gunshot wound, and nodded once. "Do it."

He pulled me onto him with one stroke, burying himself deep inside. I half moaned, half cried out, and dug my nails into his skin as he lifted me and did it again. And again. And *again*. His hands roamed over my body, never stopping, and the way he touched me was almost . . . reverent.

Like he was memorizing every inch of my body.

Letting my eyes drift closed, I trailed my fingers down his chest, doing the same thing. Learning him, not just by sight, but by touch and smell, too. His hips under my thighs were solid, and muscles of his shoulders felt even harder. I grabbed the sides of his waist, right by that sexy V he had, brushing against my calves, latched securely on either side of him, and sucked in a quickened breath.

He groaned and moved me faster. His exploration of my body ceased, and his fingers buried in my hair. I took over the movements, catching the rhythm he'd established for me easily enough. When he felt me take control, he tugged my head down and fastened his mouth to mine, groaning my name as he pumped his hips up in perfect tandem with me. I cried out, coming again . . .

And this time, he was right there with me.

I arched my back when he thrust into me one more time, sending me over the edge. And I knew he'd be there to catch me.

"Jesus," he moaned out, long and slow. He pressed his forehead to mine, breathing heavily, and said raspily, "I have to tell you something. And you're not going to like it."

He hadn't even given me a second to come back down from the stars, and he was already ruining the high I'd been enjoying. "What's wrong?"

"You know what your brother is. What he does."

It wasn't a question, but I answered anyway. "I've known for a long time."

"So he said."

"He didn't want me to know, so I never said anything . . ." I lifted a shoulder. "But it wasn't all that hard to put the pieces together. Is this about you still being in the Sons? I don't care."

"I'm not a Son. Well, I am. Kind of." He lifted his head and locked eyes with me, still breathing heavily. "Not really. But even if I was a Son, I won't be one anymore."

I licked my lips, trying to make sense of his words. "I don't understand what you're saying."

"I'm not a Son." He took a deep breath. "I'm DEA."

For a second, I still didn't understand. But then . . . oh God, then I did. "You're . . . an agent?"

He nodded once.

"But you're a Son, too."

"Yes." He hesitated. "No." Pressing his lips together, he shook his head. "I was undercover."

I slid off him, sitting next to him on the bed, hugging my knees, naked and vulnerable. He was a DEA agent, which meant he was, what, spying on my brother while pretending to be a Son? Which meant . . . the man I loved might very well be the man who could kill my brother. Something told me Tate wouldn't go down without a fight when backed into a corner.

"You're undercover," I said slowly. "It was all fake."

He nodded once.

It didn't take long to put two and two together. He'd been running an op all this time, and if Tate found out . . . I didn't know who to worry about more. My brother or Scotty . . . or myself, because I was inevitably going to be caught in the middle. "He can never know. He'll kill you."

"He already knows. He's known all along."

I tensed, every muscle in my body aching. "What?"

"He knows." He sat up, too, then stood. As he worked his way unsteadily toward the trash can, he pressed a hand to his thigh. "In hindsight, it's probably why he sent me that night. Why he trusted me to watch over you. I should have figured it out then, that he knew."

I stared straight ahead. My mind was going a million miles a minute. Because he'd mentioned how Tate asked him to watch me, I had another horrible thought. "Did your boss at the DEA know we were together? Did I somehow become part of your cover?"

His shoulders bunched as he removed the condom. I knew the answer before he even opened his mouth. He hadn't been operating under orders from one boss, but *two*. God. "Sky . . ."

"Wow." I laughed and stood, wrapping my arms around myself. "Just . . . wow."

"What I said about you, the way you made me feel even from the beginning, that was real." When Scotty faced me, I saw it in his eyes. The truth behind his words. "I had two superiors telling me to keep my distance, to watch you but not touch you, but I still fell for you. It was real. It was all real."

I nodded once, swallowing past my aching throat.

He came a step closer to me. "And when Tate found out, he told me I had to break it off, or he'd hurt Chris." He hesitated. "And my brother. He threatened him, too."

"Your brother . . ." I cocked my head. "Your *dead* brother?"

"Lucas isn't dead," he admitted. "I helped him fake his death so he and his girl could get out. Live a normal life. Be happy. They're in Georgia, and Tate knows. That's the only reason I said those things in the hospital. To protect them. I love—"

"God." A small laugh escaped me, and I covered my face. "Was *anything* you told me real?"

He winced. "Sky—"

"Seriously. How could I believe anything you say now?"

"I love you," he said softly. "That's the goddamned truth."

I laughed. I couldn't help it. "Let's just recap here. First, you told me you were an intern—a lie. Next, you let me believe you were a former gang member—another lie. Then, you told me you couldn't stop thinking about me, and needed to be with me—not sure if that's a lie or not, but you certainly did your best to convince me it wasn't true. Then you told me you are still a gang member—an almost lie. Then, oh, wait, no, you're actually a DEA agent—which I assume is the truth, and, again, you were following orders." I fisted my hands, breathing rapidly. "And *now*, last but not least, your dead brother is miraculously alive and well, and living in Georgia."

He took another step. "I know how this sounds—"

"So, *please*," I interrupted, "tell me which part of any of those lies were real. I'm *dying* to know."

He crossed the room, resting his hands on my shoulders. "I didn't fake the way I feel about you. I knew you'd probably hate me after you found out the truth, so I never should have dragged you into this, but I did it anyway. That doesn't speak highly of me, but it's the truth."

I winced. His touch was softer than silk, but his words ran me through like a sword. I forced my mind to focus on what really mattered . . . Scotty's safety. "Tate knows about you being in the DEA?"

"Yes." His hands tightened on my shoulders. "It's why I told Tate I wanted out of the Sons. That's what I was doing at his house today."

I frowned, my heart picking up speed. "But you can't just leave . . . right? That's not how it works."

"I have no choice," he said slowly, running his thumbs over my skin almost absentmindedly. "He told me I had to go on the take or come clean to the rest of the men, and I can't be a dirty agent. It's not me."

Fear pierced me. "Oh God."

"It's done." He flexed his jaw. "By now, they all know."

"They'll kill you," I said, my voice cracking in tandem with my heart. "It's a gang, not a democracy."

"He won't do that. It's too risky." He stepped back, dragging his hands down his face. "They might jump me out, though."

"How does that work? Who decides? If it's Tate—"

"There will be a trial, and I'll be set in front of the lieutenants. Tate will present my case, and I'll answer any questions they might have. After it's all over, they vote on what should happen. Since I'm a federal agent, they'll probably decide to just jump me out, to avoid the attention. And then the DEA will probably relocate me, since my cover will be blown."

"What's getting jumped out include?"

He lifted a shoulder, not meeting my eyes. "A few punches here, a kick there. Nothing too bad. Nothing I can't handle."

"No." I shook my head. "You can't do this. It's too risky."

"It's too late, sugar." He gave me a sad smile, and let go. "I already did."

He was sugarcoating things for me. He kept saying he thought he was going to get out of this alive, but it was a lie. He was going to die, and it was going to be at the hands of my brother.

How had my life come to this?

I grabbed his biceps, shaking him, not letting him back off. "It's not too late. Leave. Run. Forget all about this place, and the people in it, and *go*."

"Sky . . ." He shook his head. "I can't run."

"Why not?" I said. "Your brother did, and it worked out great for him. You could just . . . just . . . get reassigned. Go to a different city. Never come back. Tate wouldn't chase after you if you gave him an out. I'd make sure of it."

"Yes," he said gently, cupping my cheek. "He would. He'd have to. It's a rule for a reason. He can't have people just leaving like that. Why do you think we faked Lucas's death in the first place?"

"But Tate didn't do anything to him!" I laughed in relief, because I'd found Scotty's way out—and he was *going* to take it, whether he liked it or not. "He'll let you go, too. Like you said, killing a federal agent will bring down a whole lot of unwanted attention on his head. So go. Run. Leave. Skip the whole jumping-out part. You're still recovering from surgery."

"Lucas and Heidi 'dying' gave Tate the pretext he needed to let Lucas go. It would be too coincidental if I also 'die' under suspicious circumstances." He shoved a hand through his hair. "I'd be endangering Lucas, since the gang might start looking closely at his 'death,' too, and Tate would be forced to reveal that he just 'discovered' Lucas was alive. For abandoning the gang like that, for plunging us into a war over a woman . . . Sky, they'd kill him."

I didn't say anything. Was my brother, the man who had thrown me a sweet sixteen birthday party, the man who sacrificed his future so I could thrive, really so ruthless? So cold? "Surely, if I asked, he'd let you go. He knows how I feel about you. Go, and I'll make sure he doesn't come after you or your brother. I swear it."

He shook his head. "I'm not leaving you."

"You'll leave me if you're *dead*," I snapped.

"I'd rather be dead than live the rest of my life without you," he said tenderly. "I'm not running away. I'm yours, and you're mine, and if there's even the slightest chance we can be together, I need to take it. I need to stay here, and fight for us."

"So fight by running." My heart twisted. "Take me with you."

He smiled sadly. "I'd never make you choose between me and your brother, Sky. You'd hate me for it. Maybe not right away. Maybe not until we were old and wrinkly. But at some point, it would happen. And I can't live with you hating me any more than I could live without you. I love you too damn much."

Tears filled my eyes and spilled down my cheeks, because I knew I was getting nowhere with him. He'd made his mind up, and nothing would change it. "But you might *die*. I can't live with *that*."

"They won't kill me," he said again, pressing his mouth to my temple. "After they jump me out, I'll be by your side when this is all over, and I'll get to continue doing my part to clean up the city. I can't run from that chance."

I swiped my hands across my cheeks, scanning the room for my phone. "Then I'll call Tate. I'll tell him if he touches one hair on your head, I'll never forgive him."

He caught my wrist, shaking his head. "First of all, it's not just him deciding, remember? And second of all, you can't interfere in this. You have to promise me you'll stay as far away from this mess as possible, for me. I made my decisions, and now I have to face the consequences. That's on me. Not you. Not Tate. *Me*."

A tear rolled down my cheek, and over my lip. "But if he hurts you—"

"Sh." He kissed the tear off my lips gently, his hands cradling my face, and I saw the truth of what might happen in the shadows of his eyes. The shadows he was trying his best to hide from me. "I love you, Sky. But you have to know that whatever happens to me, if I get hurt, that doesn't change the fact that Tate loves you. He's your brother."

I shook my head, straining against him. He kept telling me that Tate wouldn't kill him, but the thing was . . . I wasn't sure I *believed* him. And if he killed Scotty, there was no way I'd ever forgive him. "But I love you. I . . . I . . ."

"I know, sugar." He swept me in his arms. "I love you, too."

After lowering me to the bed, he rested his body on mine, sliding between my thighs easily. He ran his thumb over my wet cheek and kissed me gently, his mouth tenderly seducing me.

All the secrets were out in the open, and there was nothing left for us to hide behind.

I'd written the ending of our story a million times in my head, and it ended the same way every time. But now he was here, telling me he loved me, and that he might be hurt by my brother, and I wasn't ready to accept that.

He ran his hand down my thigh, lifting it up and sliding inside me easily. "I swear to you, Sky, if you let me, I'll never hurt you again. I'll never lie to you. Never pretend to be anything other than me. I'll love you forever, and I'll try my hardest to make you happy, if you'll let me."

I nodded, pulling him back down for another kiss. As he moved inside me, sending pleasure rolling through my veins, I didn't let go. Because I knew once I did, no matter what he said about Tate not hurting him, once he left for this "trial" of his . . .

He might never come back.

CHAPTER 27

SCOTTY

I slid a vanilla biscotti K-Cup—Sky's favorite—into my Keurig and hit the brew button. Last night, we'd alternated between holding each other, and making love with a desperation I couldn't deny. Around three in the morning we both passed out, and I'd held her tightly all night long, only letting go to come down and start some coffee for her. She didn't have class, but I wanted her out of here early in case the Sons came for me today like I suspected they would.

She didn't need to see that.

Didn't need to be put in the middle if Tate came.

I'd never really understood love before, but I got it now. It was putting someone first. It was always thinking of them before thinking of yourself. It was trusting them with the most vulnerable parts of yourself, the ones you hid from the rest of the world, and believing them when they swore they'd never use those things against you. It was a big-ass giant leap of faith you took if you wanted to be with them, and I wanted to be with her.

So I was taking that damn leap.

And hoping I came out of it alive.

I'd done my best to reassure her that Tate would never kill me, but I had no way of knowing if that was true or not. More likely than not, I was a dead man walking.

But she didn't need to *know* that.

When I was gone, she'd need her brother.

As the coffee finished brewing, I heard her come up behind me. I rubbed my jaw and pulled another mug out of the cabinet for myself.

"Good morning, sugar," I said without turning around.

"I prefer you call me Brian," a deep, un-Sky-like voice said from behind me. "But whatever floats your boat."

I stiffened. I wore nothing but a pair of boxers and felt way too damn vulnerable. "Brian. What a pleasant surprise. Want some coffee?"

"I think we both know what I want." He came up beside me, rested against the cabinet casually, and crossed his arms, looking anything but casual. His mouth was pinched tight, his eyes were cold, and his Glock stood out against the white of his shirt. "Where's the girl?"

"Upstairs in bed," I said slowly. "Let me wake her before you do anything. As you can see, I'm unarmed. Let me go up and—"

"No."

"I don't want her to see you. She doesn't understand," I said quietly, keeping my voice hushed. "I'm just trying to make it easier on her. She doesn't need to be here to see this."

"Then you should have kicked her out last night." He crossed his arms. "You can call her down, but you're not leaving my sight . . . Agent Donahue." He let out an angry breath. "What the hell, man?"

"Sky?" I called out, ignoring Brian's glare. There would be plenty of time for him to demand answers out of me. Now I needed to take care of her, and clearly I wouldn't be doing it my way. "Get dressed and come down. We have comp—"

"I'm already dressed," she said, coming into the kitchen, yawning. Her hair was a mess, but she'd thrown on her clothes from yesterday. "Is that coffee—?"

She broke off when she saw I wasn't alone.

Brian inclined his head. "Ms. Daniels."

"No." She rushed to my side, putting herself between me and Brian. *"No."*

"Sky . . ." I picked her up and set her aside, giving my back to the other man. She stared at him over my shoulder, her cheeks flushed. "We talked about this. I'll be fine. When this is all over, after they jump me out and let me go, I'll come to you, and you'll see you worried over nothing."

Brian snorted.

Sky shook her head. "But Tate—"

"Is only doing his job. If he hurts me, it's only because he has to. Not because he wants to." I forced a smile and cradled her chin in between my fingers. "Hey, I have a request. Can you go hang with my friend Molly? She's Chris's fiancée. She can keep you company." And if things went sour . . . Chris could help pick up the pieces. Sky would need that. He'd keep her safe, too, which I needed to know would happen. "Please?"

"I don't want to go," she said, her voice cracking as she grabbed my wrist and didn't let go. "Let me come with you."

"No way. It won't be a place for you. Go to Molly, and when this is over, I'll come back to you," I said.

Brian made a choking sound behind me. If he kept it up,

he'd see my fist, up close and personal, and I wouldn't give a damn that I was kicking the ass of one of the men responsible for deciding my fate. "We need to get moving."

"And if you don't?" she whispered, ignoring Brian. "If you don't come back to me?"

"Then you'll be okay. You have to be. For me." I kissed the tip of her nose. "But I'll be back. Okay?"

"You better be." She nodded, closing her eyes. "I love you."

Brian cleared his throat. "Scotty . . ."

"I love you, too," I said, ignoring him. "Let me write down Molly's address for you."

I handed her the address, kissed her one last time, poured her coffee into a to-go cup, and then I walked her to the door, holding her hand, Brian trailing after us. When I tried to pull free, she wouldn't let me go. I forced a laugh. "Sky . . . you have to let go."

"If he hurts you, I'll never forgive him," she said.

The sun was shining down on her strawberry blonde hair, and the tree overhead cast shadows over her eyes. A bird sang from behind her somewhere, and a bunny hopped into my backyard. Everything was calm, and quiet, and normal. Everything but us, anyway.

"You have to. He's your brother."

Brian stiffened. "You need to go, Ms. Daniels. Now."

"But—" she started, still holding on to my hand with a death grip.

"It'll only be worse for Scotty if we're late," Brian warned. "They're waiting for us."

I kissed her one last time, lingering over her tear-streaked lips. "See you soon, sugar."

Nodding, she turned and left without another word.

After her car pulled away, Brian cleared his throat. "You lied to her. You won't be coming back."

"I know." I smiled and waved until she turned the corner. "But at least she won't blame Tate for it. He can tell her I was reassigned, and couldn't come back."

Sighing, he shook his head and picked up a bag he'd set next to the door. "You know the drill. Shower time."

After I showered with the shower curtain open so Brian could watch and make sure I didn't pull any fast ones, like tucking away a hidden wire, I walked into my bedroom, running my hands through my damp hair. Brian tossed a set of clothing at me I'd never seen before. Another way to ensure I wasn't wired. They were being smart.

If I planned to have any tricks up my sleeve, I'd be screwed right now.

After I dressed, Brian frowned at me. "Why did you do it?"

"Why did I do *what*? You'll have to be more specific."

"Become a fed." He rested his hand on his Glock. "Why'd you do it?"

I eyed the hand on his weapon. Maybe I'd be dying here, in my house, in the same room my mother breathed her last breath. It was almost poetic. A cold calmness washed over me. "I wanted to clean up Steel Row. Make it a place tourists came to see, instead of being number one on the list of areas for them to avoid."

Brian's frown deepened. "Were you going to turn us in?"

"I'm DEA, not ATF." I shrugged a shoulder. "It wouldn't have come to that."

"But if it had?" Brian persisted.

"Then I would have done my damn job, and slapped the cuffs on you myself."

Brian's face flushed with anger. "Start walking."

I walked down the stairs and out the door. When I passed two other Sons waiting for me, I didn't even acknowledge them. We must've taken too long, and Tate had sent reinforcements. Once outside, I walked right up to Brian's truck and slid into the passenger seat. The two recruits got in a Ford Focus. They'd follow us to the docks, then leave.

Brian started the engine.

We drove in silence. Apparently I didn't have much to say on the way to my death. No wise words. Nothing that would live on after they put a bullet in my brain. Instead, I would meet my end with a silent dignity. If they chose to kill me, I'd hold my head high and accept it. When we passed the clubhouse, I glanced at it in confusion, because we went right by it without stopping.

That meant—*shit*.

It was clear how they thought this was going to end. If we were doing this in the warehouse as opposed to the clubhouse . . . I was definitely a dead man walking.

No way I was getting out of this alive.

I'm sorry, Sky.

I tapped my fingers on the window, watching as we pulled off the exit for the docks in Steel Row. He pulled into an area I'd never seen before. The Sons owned a small section of the waterfront, with an empty warehouse that we used for deals. It would have been the perfect place for murder. I would know. I'd seen it used once or twice, on traitorous members such as myself. Instead of that warehouse, though, we pulled up next to a small, dilapidated building that was practically a shed.

"New property?" I asked.

Brian parked. "We needed somewhere the feds didn't already know about."

I said nothing to that.

"Why didn't you run when you had the chance?" he asked as he took his keys out of the ignition, white-knuckling them.

I wasn't going to tell him about Tate threatening my family, because as far as they knew, I didn't have any family left . . . besides Chris, who wasn't *actually* blood. If I was going to die, I'd do it while keeping my brother's secret safe. "Because I didn't want to. I'm exactly where I need to be."

"Under trial?" he asked incredulously.

Shrugging, I undid my seat belt.

"You're protecting someone. Or something." Brian studied me, and I could practically *hear* him thinking, trying to figure out why I hadn't run for my life like any sane man would have. "But what could it be?"

I opened the door, not answering him.

Soon enough, I'd be gone, and he'd stop worrying about why. Walking right up to the entrance, I tugged the handle, but it was locked. I turned around, half expecting Brian to be pointing a gun at my head. Was this where it was going to end?

He held up a pair of cuffs. "Hands behind your back, Agent."

I stiffened, but did as told. The scent of the salt water from the ocean mixed with the smell of decaying fish parts and old, musty wood. Shivering slightly against the brisk fall air coming off the water, I stood completely still as Brian cuffed me. As soon as he finished he checked my pockets, and once he confirmed I was still clean of anything suspicious, he opened the door for me.

We walked in to *exactly* what I suspected to see.

Since Tommy was still missing, along with Frankie . . . that left the rest of the living lieutenants as my judge and jury:

Tate, Brian, Roger, and Jamie. Chris was nowhere in sight. While I was secretly happy he wouldn't be around to do something stupid, his absence wasn't necessarily a good thing.

When they all continued to stare at me, frowning, I forced a grin. I hated tense silences more than I hated that I'd let myself get in so deep that the only way out was a body bag. "Hi, guys. How's it going? It's chilly outside today, huh? At least it's not snowing again. I'm sick of that shit."

Brian shook his head and locked the door. "You've got a real pair, Donahue."

"So I've been told," I said dryly, fixing my eyes on the oldest member in the room. He had the hottest temper and would be the first to pull the trigger. He already had a hand on his gun, like he couldn't wait for the order to shoot. "How's it going, Roger?"

Roger stepped forward, glowering, face flushing red. "You won't think this is so damn funny when a bullet is lodged in your—"

"Go ahead," I snarled, stepping forward to go at him, even though my hands were cuffed behind my back. If I was going to die, might as well get it over with quickly. No point putting it off, or pretending to have a trial. At this location, it was clear how this was going to end. If Tate thought I'd be walking away from this, we'd be at the clubhouse. *"Do it."*

Brian grabbed my arm and hauled me back. "Easy."

"No." I struggled to free myself. "Enough bullshit. If you're gonna do it, just fucking do it already. I'm done waiting. You wanna shoot me? Shoot me. I don't give a damn."

Roger lifted his gun, his wrinkled hand holding it securely. "Gladly, you dirty—"

"Enough," Tate interjected, stepping between us.

We both fell silent.

"Put the gun down. *Now*."

Roger didn't lower his gun.

"We all know why we're here." Tate stepped forward, tugging on his tie, and forcibly pushed Roger's hand down. "Scotty Donahue is a fed. A DEA agent, to be exact. He's been living among us, pretending to be one of ours. He's been lying to us. Endangering us."

I squared my jaw when they all eyed me like I was a snake. "I never endangered you."

"You never told the DEA about us?" Tate cocked his head. "Never, I don't know, maybe . . . told them our plan to take down Bitter Hill once and for all?"

He knew damn well I had.

But what happened to them in that parking lot wasn't on me.

"They were working *with* you in that op, not against you. They saved the first wave of Sons' asses, because they were worried I might be in that group, and swooped in to stop that attack before you lost more men."

Brian rocked back on his heels. "And if they'd known you weren't?"

"They would have waited until shots were fired and then arrested everyone, and you know it," I snapped.

Tate nodded. "I do. I think we all do."

I didn't say anything as they nodded.

There was nothing to say.

"Were you operating alone? Is there another undercover agent?" Tate rubbed his jaw, looking like he was thinking, but I knew better. He'd rehearsed this speech long before today. He always did. A good leader was always prepared. "Or an informant?"

I gritted my teeth. If this was heading where I thought it was . . . "No, sir. I worked alone."

"I see." He paced in front of me, still rubbing his jaw. "You pretended to be one of us. You turned on your brothers and sold us out for a badge."

A murmur of assent filled the big room, echoing off the cement walls and floors.

"I was both, an agent and a Son, but the time for leading a double life is over."

"You can't be both," Tate agreed. "When I found out your secret, I told you you'd have to choose, and you chose them, not us. Your loyalty is to them, not us."

I lifted my chin. "Yes."

Brian's face flushed, and he fisted his hands.

Roger cursed under his breath and kicked a metal machine of some sort.

Jamie just stared.

"So you knew, when you came to me and asked for a chance to be one of my men, that you would be betraying us the whole time," Tate said slowly.

It wasn't a question, but I nodded anyway.

Roger lifted his gun again, pointing it at me.

I smirked at him.

Jamie ran his hand down his face, looking upset.

It was so quiet in the room that I swore I could hear a clock ticking. It was counting down to my last breath, and it was starting to go faster, cutting my time down even more.

"So it was always them," Tate finally said.

I tore my gaze off Roger and nodded again. "Yes. I tried to do right by the Sons, too, tried to balance on the line, but no more."

"Why?" Jamie asked.

"I don't want to see another dead kid bleeding out at my feet. I want to clean up the city, and the DEA knew that the best way to make a difference was from the inside. Steel Row could become a safe place again."

Brian shook his head. "That's impossible."

"Maybe." I locked eyes with him. "But look at what happened with Bitter Hill. They won't be recruiting from the high schools any time soon."

Roger laughed.

"I respect that." Tate nodded. "Or I would have . . . if your path to cleaning up the city wasn't running directly through us."

I shrugged.

"You say you were alone in this," Tate added.

I narrowed my eyes on him. I thought we'd moved past this topic. "Yes. I was absolutely alone."

"No one helped you from the inside."

I tugged against my cuffs. "No one."

"Bring him out," Tate said, tipping his head toward the office.

I stiffened as Roger went to the door, opened it, and entered the room. "Bring *who* out?"

All too quickly, Roger came out . . .

And so did Chris.

Son of a bitch.

He had his hands cuffed behind him, like me. When he was led out, his mouth bleeding, more than likely from someone's fist crashing into it, we locked gazes. The resignation he felt was there, loud and clear, for all to see. It mirrored my own.

My gut tightened, and my heart sped up, and I saw red. Motherfucking red.

I growled, lurching forward, gaze locked on Tate. *"You promised me."*

Brian grabbed me from behind, stopping me. "Easy, Agent Donahue," he said, low, his voice almost nonexistent. His grip, however, was very clear. "Don't be stupid."

"Chris, tell Agent Donahue what you told me," Tate said, ignoring me, his jaw tight.

Chris shot me an apologetic look, and I knew what he was going to do before he opened his mouth. I could *see* it. "It was me. I'm the agent, not him."

Damn it. And damn him. He'd promised not to sacrifice himself for me. He should have kept his mouth shut and let me handle this on my own. "He's lying."

Tate held his hands out. "And he told me *you'd* say that. You're both insisting the other is innocent, so I did a little digging myself. Turns out, Chris is affiliated on the DEA's payroll, just like you. It makes me wonder about your brother, and his death, the timing of it all."

I growled, lurching toward him again. Brian hadn't let me go yet, so he easily yanked me back. "You gave me your *word*, you son of a bitch!"

Chris cursed and pushed forward. Roger held on to him, but he wasn't as strong as he used to be, and Chris had survived an abusive father and a childhood from hell, so he wasn't easy to hold back.

Roger hit the floor, and he the second he was free, Chris launched himself toward Tate.

At the last second, Jamie stepped forward, shoving him back. Since Chris's hands were clasped behind his back, he went down—and he went down *hard*.

The sound of his skull crashing against cement was deafeningly loud.

"Chris!" I shouted, straining against Brian's hold.

It didn't budge.

Chris let out a strangled groan, and tried to rise. Jamie

slammed his fist into his stomach and kicked Chris's ribs. Then he climbed on top of him, grabbed Chris's head, and slammed it into the ground again.

"Stop!" I shouted, my voice strangled.

Jamie paused.

Chris rolled to his side, taking a loud, raspy breath, spitting out more blood. "Asshole," he managed to get out between gasps. "Uncuff me and then we'll see how this goes."

When Jamie growled and lifted his bloody fist again, Tate called out, "*Enough*. Get off him."

"Sir?" Jamie asked, his fist still in the air. "But—"

"I said enough," he said, his voice low but deadly calm.

Jamie glanced at me over his shoulder, then hauled Chris to his feet.

Chris spat out more blood on the floor, avoiding my eyes. "There's no need for this shit. I'm guilty. Let him go."

I stiffened even more. "Chris, I swear to God I'll fucking—"

"Hey." Brian tightened his grip on me and whispered, "Easy."

Tate ignored all of us, continuing on. "It's clear we have, at the very least, one DEA agent in our midst. And we have a bigger problem than we thought. It's dangerous enough to get rid of one fed without detection, but now there's two federal employees . . . and don't even get me started on Tommy and Frankie. Who knows where the hell they went, or if they're involved in this mess somehow. Maybe they're feds, too."

Chris flexed his already bruising jaw. "Let him go, and keep me. Problem solved."

"You know we can't do that," Tate said, crossing his arms. "You're both trying to shoulder the blame, and the bottom line is, you're *both* on the payroll. So you have to stand trial under a jury of your peers."

Chris growled and jerked free of Jamie, making the other man stumble back, but Roger was there, waiting, gun pointed at his head. Chris froze, breathing heavily. "Assholes," he growled.

"Roger, put the gun away." Tate sighed. "And both of you, hold him, please. Don't let go this time."

"Yes, sir," Jamie said, his cheeks red.

"There are two courses open to us," Tate continued, once both men had a hold on Chris. "We could do what we would usually do for this type of betrayal, and rip them to pieces. Dump an arm here, a leg there, a head in the ocean . . ."

Brian's hands tightened on my arms.

Jamie avoided my eyes.

Roger spit out a wad of tobacco.

Chris locked gazes with me.

"Or . . ." Tate rubbed his chin. "We ruin their cover. Jump them out of the gang, and announce their betrayal to everyone we know. Let everyone know they're feds, and to never deal with them again."

I stiffened. "If you tell everyone, they'll kill us anyway."

"Only if you come back to Steel Row." Tate looked at Chris, then me. "If you do, yes, you can guarantee you'll be shot on sight."

Jamie grinned.

Roger grunted.

Brian was silent.

I looked at Chris. He was pale, minus the blood that was smeared all over his chin.

"I live here," I finally said.

"Not anymore." Tate shrugged. "Your home won't be

yours anymore. It's a small price to pay to continue breathing."

Losing my ma's home wasn't small.

It was all I had left of her.

"I know which option *I'm* leaning toward, but this isn't a dictatorship." Tate looked at the other men in the room. "You are my only remaining lieutenants, and you have a say. We'll vote. If there's a tie, then Jamie's vote is forfeited, since he's the newest lieutenant here."

Brian nodded. "If we vote to kill them, do you think it's too risky?"

"Well, I . . ." Tate paused, rubbing his chin. "I think it could bring unwarranted attention to us, and have the DEA breathing down our backs with the ATF at their side. It could be the thing that sets them after us, even though our crimes aren't in their jurisdiction. At the very least, I think the DEA would share their intel with the ATF, and send them our way with a vengeance."

Jamie frowned.

Roger rested a hand on his gun.

"With that in mind . . ." Tate said, clearing his throat. He looked at me, then turned to Chris. "Are we ready to take a vote?"

Chris grinned, showing no fear even though we were dead men. There was no way they'd *all* decide to let us live. It was too risky. Sons didn't like loose ends, and we were dangling through the air like ripcords. "Can't wait to hear the results. I feel like I'm on *America's Got Talent*."

Tate walked behind me. "All in favor of killing them, raise your hand."

Two hands went up.

I stiffened, because I couldn't see the other two.

"Those in favor of jumping them out?" Tate added from behind me.

Chris paled, sagging against Roger and Jamie.

Shit. What had Tate and Brian voted?

"Well, then, I guess we know what comes next, don't we?" Tate pulled his gun out, and approached me. "I'll do the honors."

I tensed when Tate stopped in front of me, gripping his Glock with white knuckles. After I took what would probably be my last breath, I said, "Don't let her know it was you. She's going to need you. Take care of her for me, okay?"

Tate tensed, his jaw flexing. Chris screamed curses and struggled to break free, but it was useless. He raised the gun and then pain burst through me. I sagged toward the floor, but Brian hauled me up as Tate raised the gun a second time.

Once again, all I could think of was Skylar.

I love you, Sky, so much. I'm sorry.

CHAPTER 28

SKYLAR

"How much longer are we going to have to wait?" I asked, pacing in front of Molly's fireplace. Her bodyguard watched me, his arms crossed, looking less than impressed with my nonstop pacing. It was probably annoying, but there was no stopping it. "It's been *hours*."

She bit her lip and pet her orange cat's head. The bags under her eyes were deep and dark. Mine were probably the same. We'd been worrying ourselves to death ever since I'd knocked on her door and introduced myself. At first, she'd been standoffish when she heard my last name, but once we spoke a little bit, we bonded over our bone-deep terror and soul-shattering worry. "I don't know."

"Have you ever done this before?" I asked, stopping in front of her.

Molly sat on the couch, under a blanket. She was pale, possibly paler than me, and she'd been staring off into the distance, fear etched on her features. I'd been beside her until a minute ago, when I'd gotten up because I couldn't handle just sitting here anymore, doing nothing, when Chris and Scotty were in danger. "No. Not like this. He's left a lot, and I've been scared he wouldn't come home, but this . . . this is different."

I sat next to her, staring at the fireplace and the happily crackling fire her bodyguard had set up for us. "I'm going to kill him."

"Scotty?" Molly asked.

"Tate." I pulled my phone out, checking it for the millionth time. I'd texted him this morning, and told him if he killed Scotty, I'd never forgive him. Because I wouldn't. He hadn't read it or replied. "This is wrong. What he's doing is wrong."

Molly said nothing.

Really, there was nothing to say.

"They'll be okay." I shoved my hair behind my ears. "They have to be okay."

Molly nodded. "Yeah."

She sounded less than convinced.

"What kind of world do we live in where we have to sit and wait to see if our men will be killed, and we can't do anything about it?" I turned the phone in my hand. "Should I call his handler? The DEA has to have some kind of contingency plan for situations like this."

"Do you know the number?" Molly asked slowly. "Did he give it to you?"

I frowned. "No . . ."

"Could you find it?" she asked, petting the cat under his chin. He purred and flopped over onto his back. "Do you know where to look?"

"No." I covered my face. "I can't *do* this."

Molly rubbed my back. "I know. It—"

Knock, knock, knock.

"Open up!" Tate called out.

Relief punched me in the chest, and I ran toward the door, Molly's bodyguard two steps behind me. Tate wouldn't be showing up here if he'd killed Scotty and Chris . . . right?

This had to be a good sign.

I unlocked the door and swung it inward. "Where are—? *Oh my God.*"

Behind him, two men supported Scotty, every inch of visible skin looking bloodied or bruised. Farther back, another group of men held Chris upright, and he looked just as dead on his feet as Scotty.

Molly peered around her bodyguard and gasped, letting out a strangled cry. She tried to rush past me, but the bodyguard pulled her to a stop. *"Chris!"*

He roused, grinned, and said, "Hey, Princess."

And then he promptly passed out again.

Tate stared at me throughout all this, his face pale, and whispered. "What are you doing here? You're not supposed to be here."

Swallowing bile, I glanced at Scotty again, ignoring my brother as I tried to assess his injuries. I could barely see his eyes through the swelling on his face, and his ragged breathing indicated at least one broken rib. I tore my horrified gaze off the man I was in love with, and focused on the other man I loved.

My *brother.*

The man who'd *done* this to him.

I backed up slowly, my stomach rebelling.

"You . . . You . . ." I looked at Tate. He wouldn't meet my eyes. "How could you do this to him when you know—?"

"You're Scotty's girl, right?" he interrupted loudly.

I blinked at him, confused. "What?"

"Scotty Donahue. This asshole?" He tipped his head toward Scotty, his mouth pressed in a tight line. "You the woman he's been shacking up with?"

It was then that I realized what he was doing.

He was pretending he didn't know me, so no one would put two and two together.

He was still "protecting" me.

I recognized one of the guys holding Scotty as the one who came into my apartment last time, so he knew very well who I was. But the other guys . . .

"Yes," I managed to say, though it came out more of a croak than anything. "He's mine."

"Good." Tate gently pushed me backward, into the house. "Let us in, before someone sees and calls the cops. The last thing your man needs right now is that kind of attention on him."

I stood there, watching them carry Scotty's body in. I gripped the doorknob so tightly it should have branded my skin. "Is he . . . ?"

"He's alive," Tate said, loud enough for the other men to hear him. "Bring Chris in, too."

Molly was frozen, watching in horror, a hand pressed to her belly.

I tried to go to her, but Tate pushed me back against the wall, holding me there. "Stay. We'll be out of here in a minute."

The bodyguard finally let Molly go to Chris, keeping himself between the couple and the gang members, palm resting on his gun.

I tried to push Tate's hand off. "Let go of—"

"Just stay still." Then, leaning down, he whispered. "They're out of the Sons now. This was the only way I could save them."

My mouth dropped. "Save them? You almost *killed* them."

"Almost," Tate growled. "It had to be done."

He glanced toward the men.

One was tapping Scotty's cheek.

He moaned, but didn't open his eyes.

Chris was conscious, and cursing the men out as he struggled to get up.

The bodyguard hovered, keeping close to Molly.

"Who . . . what . . . *are* you?" I asked, shaking my head. Not only had my brother sentenced them to this hell, but *he'd* helped send them there. "*You* did this to them?"

"I had to." Tate continued on as if nothing had changed between us, while *everything* had. This level of brutality was shocking. "It was either this or death, Skylar. This is actually the best-case scenario."

My stomach rolled, because this wasn't my brother.

This wasn't the Tate I knew.

"They'll live." He didn't seem to notice my recoiling. "I'm sorry you're upset, but this was the only way you could be together. It was in your best interests—"

I pulled free, anger and . . . and . . . *fear* rushing through my veins. This man, this version of Tate, wasn't the same man I'd grown up beside. As a kid, he'd refused to kill a spider or an ant, and would set them free outside instead. But now . . . "Get out."

He opened his mouth, closed it, and opened it again, and for a second, he let that ice-cold mask slip long enough to show me what he really felt. It wasn't enough. "Skylar . . ."

"Out." I raised my voice. "All of you. *Get out.*"

The other two men looked at Tate.

Molly nodded, picking up the phone with trembling hands. She still had wet cheeks, but she was standing on her own now. The bodyguard stepped forward, looking more than ready for a fight. "I'm calling 911. You better get out of here if you don't want them asking you questions."

"You heard her," I said to Tate, my voice hollow.

He leaned back as if I'd hit him, shock etching lines into his face. *"Skylar."*

"I love you, and you're my brother, but it's going to take a long time for me to forgive you for this." I lifted my chin. "You and your men leave Molly's house. Now."

"Clear out," Molly's guard called out. "I have more men coming, and you won't want to be here when they arrive. There will be questions. Lots of questions."

Tate hesitated, but then walked out, gesturing for his men to follow him.

The last one out closed the door, and I rushed toward it to lock it.

Molly was on the phone with 911, so I fell to my knees at Scotty's side, my breathing coming hard and fast. A bruise was starting to spread across his cheekbone and I lifted his shirt to see a fist-sized blotch of purple bruising his torso. He was likely bleeding internally. I counted his breaths. They were shallow, but steady. I grabbed his wrist, closed my eyes, and counted his pulse.

Not good . . .

But not horrible either.

Molly hung up, grabbed a massive first-aid kit from under the kitchen sink, and knelt beside Chris, talking quietly. I heard the low murmur of Chris's reply, and then Molly latched fingers with him, nodding. I hurried to his side and knelt, giving him the same check I'd given Scotty. Chris's pulse was faster, and a little less steady, but it was still strong enough not to raise alarm.

Jesus.

Swallowing past my swollen throat, I hurried back to Scotty's side. I touched Scotty's cheeks with the backs of my knuckles, examining him for more injuries now that I knew he was breathing and help was on the way. "Scotty? Can you hear me?"

He didn't make a sound.

I pressed my fingers to his throat, feeling for a pulse again. It was there. Weak, but there. Fumbling with the kit, I pulled out alcohol wipes, determined to clean him up a bit so I could see if he was bleeding anywhere else. Softly, I swept his hair off his sweaty forehead. "Hey. Answer me. *Please?*"

He moaned and shifted, his eyes opening slightly. When he saw me, he smiled. The new scab on his lip opened, blood seeping out. But still . . . his eyes shone with happiness.

All because he'd seen *me*.

"Sky?" he whispered.

"Yeah." I forced a smile. "It's me."

He shifted, moaning, and I began to gently dab at the dried blood on his face with the wipe. He looked at me again, blinking. "Am I in heaven? I thought for sure I'd go to hell, but if I'm seeing you . . ."

There were small nicks marring his skin, where whatever object they'd beaten him with had broken the skin. Pain radiated out of my chest because seeing me made him think of heaven, but if we'd never met, this wouldn't have happened. "Sh."

He grabbed my wrist, his gaze locked on me. "Why are you here, too? Are you . . . ?"

"I'm not dead, Scotty, and neither are you." I touched his cheek. It was rough and cold. "You're at Molly and Chris's house. Tate brought you here, after he . . . after he . . ."

I couldn't say it out loud.

"They jumped me out?" he asked, his brow wrinkling. "Oh God. Chris."

He tried to sit up, but I pushed his shoulders back down. "Where do you think you're going?"

"Chris. I need to see—"

"I'm alive, man," Chris called out from the other couch. "I'm here."

Scotty collapsed in relief. "Thank God."

"Glad to know you care," Chris said.

"When I feel better I'm going to kill you for that stunt you pulled."

Molly stiffened. "What stunt?"

"Nothing, Princess," Chris cut in. "Nothing."

Their voices lowered, Molly's sounding pretty darn angry, and I turned my attention back to Scotty. He was silent, letting me clean him up, and then he took a breath, holding it in for a while, cringing when he let it out. "I thought they were going to kill us."

Where were the paramedics?

"They still might, if you don't get medical care soon. This isn't Steel Row, they should be here by now."

"I have you," he said, smiling slightly. "That's enough."

"No, it's not." I had a small pile of used and filthy alcohol wipes, but Scotty needed actual medical intervention. I got up and retrieved a bag of frozen vegetables from the freezer, and wrapped it in a kitchen dish towel. When I returned to Scotty, I held it gently to his bruised cheekbone. "I thought they were going to kill you, too. This is the worst day of my life."

"It's pretty high up there on my list of shitty days, too," he said, smiling again.

The smile made him wince, and I frowned.

"How can you smile about this?" I kept the ice pack on his face as I caught his hand, holding on tightly. "My brother almost killed you."

"Because I'm alive, and so is Chris. We're out, and we're

not dead, and you and I can be together now. We can be happy, sugar," he said, his voice fading out at the end.

I smiled, even though tears blurred my vision, turning my view of him into a messy watercolor painting. "You're right. That's something to smile about."

Sirens sounded in the distance, getting closer, and I exchanged glances with Molly. She offered me a reassuring nod, kissed Chris's forehead, and stood.

As she made her way to the door, I turned back to Scotty. "So it's over?"

"It's over. No more gang wars, no more death. No more bloody surprises." He reached out, cupping my cheek. "Just you and me, sugar."

Thank *God.*

"I love you," I said, leaning down to gently kiss his lips as the paramedics rushed in. After I pulled back, I stood and moved out of the way. "So much."

"I love you, too, sugar."

My phone buzzed with a text message.

I ignored it.

"That's probably your brother."

I shrugged.

"You should answer him," Scotty said, frowning as the paramedic poked at his arm. "He did the best he could, considering the circumstances. He voted in our favor."

Biting down on my tongue, I shook my head. "I don't care. I'm still mad at him."

"So be mad. But he loves you." The paramedic wrapped a splint around Scotty's finger, and he cursed under his breath. "And you love him," he finally gritted out.

Wrapping my arms around myself, I said nothing on that matter. In my opinion, this discussion was over. "Do I need to call anyone for you?"

"Nah." The paramedics lifted him slightly. "They'll find me," he gritted out. "Shit. I'm going to the hospital for the third time since you met me."

"You know what they say," I murmured. "Third time's the charm."

He laughed, but it ended on a groan.

Molly came up to me. Her guard followed behind her, a cell phone pressed to his ear as he spoke quietly. "Want to ride to the hospital with me? I'm going to follow the ambulance."

"Sure." I pushed my hair behind my ears, watching as they loaded Scotty onto a stretcher. Chris was already being wheeled out. "Thanks."

She smiled and headed for her purse, her bodyguard trailing her.

As the paramedics pushed the stretcher past me, Scotty grabbed my hand. "Wait."

They stopped, one guy shooting me a *hurry up and let us do our jobs* look.

"What's wrong?" I asked.

"Nothing. I just wanted to kiss you."

A smile lifted my lips, despite the fear that still coursed through my veins that he might not be okay. "Silly man."

"Over you, I'll always be a little bit silly." He reached out and caught the back of my neck, pulling me down. "Kiss me, woman."

I did.

He whispered something deliciously naughty in my ear, then nipped it. I laughed, covering my mouth, and stood straight, my cheeks heating. *"Scotty."*

"Later?" he asked, his voice thick and full of promise.

Cheeks heating, I nodded. "Oh yeah. Definitely later."

He finally let me go, and the EMTs rushed him out of

the house. Despite everything that had happened in the past twenty-four hours, my heart expanded with hope, happiness, *love*. Because, despite all the odds racked up against us, we'd *won*.

We'd gotten our happy ending.

EPILOGUE

SCOTTY

One year later

The restaurant around us was packed tight, filled with conversations, laughter, and wine. The tables were covered in fine white linen, and tall pink and green candles gave the room a romantic glow, which provided a soft ambience that was perfect for what I wanted. And it was symbolic, too, me bringing her here. It was the restaurant we'd gone to for our first date, when I'd tried to scare her off and failed.

Thank God.

A life without Sky in it wouldn't be a life at all.

I'd learned that the hard way, and it was a lesson I'd never forget.

We'd been dating for a year now, and we'd never spent more than two nights apart, and those two nights were always the worst nights I'd had in a long damn time— including all the nights when I almost died. I couldn't sleep without her by my side, snuggled up against me, all softness where I was hard. She was my heart. My world. My life. And if I was lucky enough . . .

Soon she'd be my wife.

Absentmindedly, I rubbed my thigh where I'd been shot in that parking lot over a year ago. I still had residual pain from the injuries I'd sustained in those first few weeks we were together, but I'd miraculously managed to avoid going back to the hospital since.

Life had been calm. Quiet. Perfect—because of Sky.

She sat down across from me, smiling. I forced my mind back to her, focusing on her words. ". . . said he might stop by on his way home. He wanted to say congrats to me for having the best GPA."

That's why we were here celebrating. She was immersed in school right now, but it had paid off, and now she was number one in her class, which was huge. She studied every night, and I usually went over files, or read, or just enjoyed being with her as she scribbled notes, her forehead furrowed with concentration as she—

"Scotty?" she asked, frowning.

"What?" I snapped out of it. "Huh?"

"Is something wrong?" She leaned in and nibbled on her lip. "Are you upset because Tate's coming? Because I can tell him not to—"

"No, of course not." I forced a smile, but my heart was pounding because at any second, the waitress was going to bring the champagne. "You know I don't mind that."

It had taken her a while to start to forgive Tate. They'd gone months without speaking, but eventually, I'd put my foot down. Life was too short to hold on to grudges, and she loved Tate as much as he loved her, so I finally interfered, something I'd sworn not to do. When she came home and found him sitting there, drinking a beer with me, they argued for a good ten minutes, and then everything was fine.

Tate and I had come to an understanding of sorts, too. He did his thing in Steel Row, and never talked about it, and I did mine with the DEA on the opposite side of the city, and stayed equally silent. I wasn't undercover anymore, and I hadn't gone back to Steel Row since the day I almost died. I might have lost my home and my cover, but I'd gotten a promotion, and Skylar.

I didn't miss my old life in the slightest.

I was done with secrets. Done lying.

Now, I was just me, and I liked myself again.

Agent Torres hadn't been happy I was dating Tate's sister, but after a thorough background check on her, I'd gotten the green light. And life had been pretty much perfect since then.

I'd gotten everything I wanted, and I was still fighting for Steel Row . . .

Just from the outside.

"Then what's wrong?" she asked slowly.

"Nothing." I rested an elbow on the table, eyeing the kitchen door. "Remember the first time we came here?"

She glanced around us. "How could I not? You were a jerk to me the whole time."

"Yeah . . ." I winced. "But even so, that night, I knew we had something. And when you were talking and yelling at me because you thought I was different, I remember watching you and thinking, 'Holy shit, this girl is right. She feels the same things I do, and she's not afraid to admit it.' That scared the shit out of me, knowing you saw me, the *real* me, within an hour or two of meeting me. I wasn't sure what to do, but I knew that I couldn't walk away after you said all those things. I had to stick around to see what came next. I had to *know*."

She laughed nervously. "Well, that, and your bosses kind of made you, so . . ."

"Doesn't matter. I would have stayed anyway, because I *needed* to. And I still feel like that, every single day I spend with you." I took a deep breath, dragging a hand through my hair. "Usually, I let you take the lead, because you're so much damn better at this shit than I am. When you rolled over, kissed me, and asked me to move in with you, I knew that it was the right thing, just like I knew staying with you that first night was the smartest thing I'd ever done at the time. And that falling in love with you was the best thing. And now . . ." I glanced over her shoulder. The waitress approached, two glasses of Sky's favorite champagne in her hands. "Now I know what comes next."

She gripped the edge of the table, her cheeks flushed. "And that is . . . ?"

The champagne was set down in front of us, and she glanced at the ring tied to the stem of the glass with a small blue ribbon that matched her eyes perfectly. I slid out of my seat, down to one knee, and the room around us hushed.

She covered her face, her eyes wide. *"Scotty."*

"Skylar Marie Daniels, I love you with all my heart, soul, and mind. Before you came into my life, I was lost on a crusade, and my life was empty. Everything was gray. Nothing was bright, or shiny, or colorful. But now . . . everything is filled with vibrant colors, and shades, and life, and that's because of *you*. Because you love me, and I love you, too. Now I'm ready for the next step, and I'm hoping you are, too. Will you marry me and make me the luckiest man alive?"

She nodded frantically "Yes, God, yes." She fell to the floor on her knees and threw her arms around me, pressing her mouth to mine. She tasted like champagne, tears, and Sky. It was a combination I'd never forget. Pulling back, she laughed nervously and buried her hands in my hair. "So much frigging yes."

Grinning, I helped her to her feet, and the room clapped. I bowed and Sky curtsied. I untied the ring and she watched, biting down hard on her plump lower lip. As I slid it onto her finger, a shadow fell on us. "I assume double congratulations are in order?"

"Tate!" Laughing, Sky flung herself at him. "Did you know?"

He caught her easily, meeting my eyes and nodding once. "Of course I did. Scotty asked for your hand, and I said yes. Let me see the ring."

She stepped out of his arms, still smiling, and held her hand out. It was a simple round diamond in a halo setting, platinum. It fit her perfectly. Tate had helped me get her measurements, and Chris went with me to pick it out, even though he'd been getting little to no sleep lately. Newborns weren't on the best schedule, after all.

"It's gorgeous, Skylar," Tate said, holding her hand steady so he could admire it. "Congrats." He glanced at me, nodding once. "To both of you."

She beamed at me. "Thanks."

"I have an early wedding present for you. I'm going to walk you down that aisle," Tate said, looking at me briefly. "And before I do . . . the Sons of Steel Row will be no more."

I stiffened. "What?"

"I'm going straight. I'm going to have little nieces and

nephews soon, I'm assuming, and I don't want to be the uncle that's in jail. I don't want to miss out on their lives because someone finally caught up to me. I'm done. I never wanted this life in the first place, and it's time to let it go." He stuffed his hands in his pockets. "I'm going to see it done."

Sky smiled even bigger. "Thank God."

Tate and I locked eyes, and he gave one shake of his head. Sky might be happy that her brother was going clean, but *we* both knew he couldn't just walk away. If he was disbanding the gang, then it was going to be dangerous, and ugly, and . . .

Shit.

I was going to have to save his ass.

Again.

A woman came up to Tate, and he stiffened. She had olive skin, brown hair, and even browner eyes. Her lips were red, and she was beautiful—almost as beautiful as Skylar. Tate stared down at the woman, his face paling as he stepped back, his jaw tight. "Lucille? What—?"

She smiled, flung her brown hair over her shoulder, and slapped him across the face. Tate staggered back, shock written all over his face, and she stormed off, not looking back.

Both my and Sky's jaws dropped.

Tate tightened his mouth and stared after the woman, his eyes narrow. I cleared my throat, putting an arm around Sky, and asked, "Is she a friend of yours?"

"Yeah." Tate touched his cheek. "Something like that."

He turned and walked away without another word, following the woman with long strides.

Sky tried to go after him, but I tugged her back. "Let him go."

"But—"

I kissed her, effectively silencing her. She curled her hands into my shirt, holding on tight, and moaned into my mouth. By the time she pulled back, we were both breathing quickly. "Let your brother handle his own battles. He's perfectly capable. Are you ready to order some snails?"

She laughed, her lips plump from my kisses. "You hate snails."

We sat again, taking our time throughout our meal, but Tate never came back. When we walked out a few hours later, hand in hand, there was still no sign of Tate or the mystery woman, and the night air was pleasantly cool. Sky shivered, so I shrugged off my black suit jacket, slinging it over her shoulders. She cuddled into it, and the moonlight played with her strawberry blonde hair, making her even more beautiful than ever before. I couldn't look away. She caught me staring, and smiled. "Like what you see?"

"Love it." I wrapped my arm over her shoulder, urging her against my side. "What do you think of Hawaii?"

"I think it's warm and sunny." She side-eyed me. "Why?"

"Our honeymoon."

"Hmm . . ." She smiled and rested her head on my shoulder as we walked side by side. "I think that sounds perfect. You. Me. A tiny bikini."

My cock hardened, and I caressed her shoulder. "Or no bikini at all . . ."

She laughed, and the sound washed over me like music. Her soft floral scent tickled my senses, and her hair teased my fingers. We walked down the dark streets of West Boston, where there were no leather jackets and no badges. Just us. Now that Tate was also working toward ending the Sons, my dream of making Steel Row a safe place might come true yet. Then Lucas could come home, and meet Sky. Steel Row, and Boston, could be different. Better. And I would have made that mark on the world I ached to make for me, Lucas, and Ma.

I could be that man, the man my father had never been.

There were more battles to fight, but I knew I'd win.

With Sky by my side, how could I possibly lose?